THE BLACK LOTUS

A MESSAGE FROM CHICKEN HOUSE

Why hat would your special power be? Kieran Fanning's astonishing young team have amazing abilities to cope with awesome threats from a truly mighty foe, but it's friendship that turns out to be the most unbeatable power of all! Still, I'd choose something practical but cool – walking on the ceiling, I think. You?

BARRY CUNNINGHAM
Publisher
Chicken House

THE BLACK LOTUS

KIERAN FANNING

2 PALMER STREET, FROME, SOMERSET BA11 1DS

Text © Kieran Fanning 2015

First published in Great Britain in 2015
Chicken House
2 Palmer Street
Frome, Somerset BA11 1DS
United Kingdom
www.doublecluck.com

Cover and interior design by Steve Wells
Typeset by Dorchester Typesetting Group Ltd
Printed and bound in Great Britain by CPI Group (UK) Ltd, Croydon CR0 4YY

The paper used in this Chicken House book is made from wood
grown in sustainable forests.

1 3 5 7 9 10 8 6 4 2

British Library Cataloguing in Publication data available.

PB ISBN 978-1-909489-92-9
eISBN 978-1-909489-93-6

For Carol

IN MEDIEVAL JAPAN, THREE MAGICAL SWORDS –
BEARING THE EMBLEMS OF A BUTTERFLY, SNAKE-
EYE AND MOON – ARE FORGED FOR POWERFUL
SHŌGUN, LORD GODA. CREATED FROM A CURIOUS
SKY-METAL, EACH KATANA HAS THE POWER
TO CUT THROUGH TIME AND SPACE; UNITED,
THEIR POWERS ARE UNIMAGINABLE. THE SWORDS
OF SARUMARA ARE NOT LONG MADE WHEN THE
MOON SWORD IS STOLEN. IN ITS PLACE, THE THIEF
LEAVES A SMALL FLOWER THE COLOUR OF INK:
A BLACK LOTUS. THE SYMBOL OF A SHADOWY
RESISTANCE GROUP.

BUT WITH THE TWO REMAINING SWORDS LORD GODA
CAN STILL BECOME A FORMIDABLE FORCE. WITH HIS
WIFE, LADY KIKO, HE BEGINS TO CARVE OUT A MIGHTY
SAMURAI EMPIRE, AND BY THE TWENTY-FIRST CENTURY
IT STRETCHES FROM JAPAN TO SOUTH AMERICA.

BUT THE MOON SWORD ELUDES HIM STILL.

THE BLACK LOTUS PROTECTS IT WITH ALL ITS STRENGTH,
AND WITHOUT IT GODA WILL NEVER CONQUER THE
GREATEST PRIZE OF ALL.

PART ONE:

TWENTY-FIRST CENTURY.
THE SAMURAI EMPIRE IS AT
THE HEIGHT OF ITS POWER ...

RIO DE JANEIRO, BRAZIL

Ghost winced with every step. He *hated* wearing shoes! This was his first pair and, according to his friend Squint, they were handmade and had cost a fortune. If all shoes were this uncomfortable, maybe that was why Empire people always looked so snooty when they walked! Mostly they were sons and daughters of the first samurai settlers who'd arrived decades ago, but they walked as if they'd always owned the place. The only people who disgusted Ghost more were the rich Brazilians who'd started dressing, eating and, indeed, walking like them.

But this morning *he* was supposed to look like one of the Empire people too, and not like some poor Brazilian teenager wearing shoes for the first time.

The plastic bag in his hand didn't exactly go with his new look, he realized, so he knelt and shoved it under a parked car. Hopefully he wouldn't need what was inside. Standing up, he caught a glimpse of himself in the glass and admired the whiteness of his shirt against his dark skin, and his Shiroma suit, all provided by Squint. He stuck his nose in the air and clicked his heels as he made his way out of the side street, trying to ignore his throbbing feet.

Unlike his mates back in the favela, Ghost only did jobs here in downtown Rio. Squint thought he was mad, risking being caught by Kyatapira police – or Kats, as they were known – when there were plenty of gas stations and stores close by. But though the risks were high for doing a job downtown, the rewards were even higher.

Avenida Atlântica was something else, he thought as he walked painfully on – high-rise luxury apartments and hotels with two roads running in opposite directions, divided by palm trees. You could smell the money. Beyond them lay the white sands of Praia de Copacabana. Of course, the Samurai Empire had replaced all signs with Japanese ones, but Ghost and his mates still spoke Portuguese, and Copacabana would always be called Copacabana, whatever President Goda said.

The beach was quiet, but in a few hours the wealthy Empire people would be out sipping cocktails under paper umbrellas. In the Brazilian section, boys would play footvolley to a stereo's samba beat, super-vised by the Kats, who made sure the music wasn't too loud, that players were wearing enough clothes and that all games adhered strictly to the rules and were part of a registered competition. Playing 'just for fun' was a sure way to become acquainted with the fists and boots of Kyatapira.

It was only a matter of time, thought Ghost, before samba and footvolley disappeared altogether, like the giant statue of Jesus that had once looked out over the city. Old people talked about the Rio Carnival that had once been so famous but, like the statue, Ghost had never seen it.

A thunderous roar filled the sky, and Ghost stopped and looked up. Six aircraft screamed overhead, two swords crossed in an X on the underside of each wing clearly identifying them as Empire fighter jets. All week, aircraft had been flying over the city, heading north to the US border. The news reports were filled with the imminent war between the Empire and America, one of the few unoccupied countries left.

But today Ghost had more important things to worry about. He had a job to do. Taking up his position on his favourite bench, he trained his eyes on the electric gates of the Nikkou apartments. He didn't have long to wait. As soon as the gates began to open, he started walking.

As Ghost reached step number thirty-one, the sleek nose of a Lexus LFA eased out of the gate. Just as it did every morning at 9.20 a.m. The driver of the car – and owner of apartment 729 – glanced over the top of his designer sunglasses and then accelerated into the passing traffic. From his weeks of watching, Ghost knew the man wouldn't return until evening. And Ghost had a key to his apartment.

Twenty-one more paces should take him to the gates just as they closed – he'd practised it enough times. The bit he hadn't practised was what happened when he stepped inside.

Just as the gates closed, he slipped in and casually continued walking on to the apartments – he was a resident after all, he told himself.

If that didn't work, plan B was to say he was lost.

Plan C involved the plastic bag under the car. But he hoped it wouldn't come to that.

As on all the other mornings, the security guard was asleep in his bulletproof booth after a long night. Ghost hurried past, catching a glimpse of a semi-automatic pistol in the guard's holster. Private security guards were worse than Kats. Bored and underpaid, they shot first and asked questions later.

Ghost pushed open the doors to the apartment building and stepped on to plush green carpet. He hit the lift button and watched the Japanese numbers count down. The lift doors pinged open, and he stepped inside. He pressed button number seven and straightened his tie in the mirror. It was all about attention to detail – that's what had got him this far.

A few seconds later the lift doors pinged open again, and Ghost peered out on to the seventh floor. From the safety of the lift, he figured out which way the door numbers ran. He needed to look like he knew where he was going. Just before the doors closed, he stepped out into the corridor and turned left.

Bosta! An Empire woman with narrow eyes, bright lipstick and a floral kimono was walking towards him. He continued on, hoping his surprise and panic hadn't shown on his face. He smiled and nodded at her as he passed, but he could have sworn he caught a glimpse of suspicion in her eyes. He also thought her footsteps had suddenly stopped behind him. Was she watching him? Every instinct screamed at him to turn around and check.

Stay calm and look like you know where you're going.

In his panic he had walked past two doors. If one of them was number 729, he was in trouble. Without moving his head he quickly looked left and right until he found the correct door. He took out his key and pushed it into the lock, praying that Squint's preparations had been as meticulous as always. From the corner of his eye he could see the woman standing at the lift. Whether she was watching him or not, he couldn't tell. He twisted the key and hoped there wouldn't be an alarm or room-mate inside.

There wasn't. He stepped inside and closed the door, holding his breath as he waited for a knock. None came, and relief hissed out of him like air from a balloon.

Stupid woman! If he hadn't met her, he could have stayed in the apartment for a while: enjoyed it, eaten some posh food, had a soda from the fridge, watched TV. But there was no time for that now. He needed to grab what he could and run.

The apartment was classy, like something he'd seen on TV, with white leather sofas and a view of the ocean. He peeped down over the balcony and saw the Empire woman talking to the security guard, who was now awake and reaching for the phone. *Bosta!*

Ghost raced through the place, rifling through drawers, searching cupboards and upturning mattresses. He found some cash, the owner's passport, a designer watch and some gold jewellery. He was stuffing these into his pockets when there was a loud rap on the door, followed by a shout in Japanese: 'Keibiin da. Akero!'

Security! Ghost's heart stopped. Plan B was definitely not going to work – no one would believe he was lost in someone's apartment. He was trapped. The only other way out was the balcony, but that was seven floors above ground.

Time for plan C.

He took off his jacket and spread it out on the floor, then ripped off his tie and shirt and placed these on top. Next, he added his shoes, socks and trousers. He looked down at his briefs, then at the apartment door. He whipped them off and added them to the pile. Using the sleeves of the jacket, he tied up the bundle and stepped out on to the balcony.

His first thought was to throw the bundle down to the ground and collect it later. He cursed when he saw the flashing lights of a Kyatapira squad car coming through the electric gates. In a few minutes, the door of the apartment would come crashing down and they'd be upon him, guns blazing. He had to get rid of the bundle a different way. Another balcony lay directly beneath his.

He leant over the stainless-steel rail and swung the bundle on to the balcony below, just as the squad car pulled up at the front door of the block. Two armed Kats with padded shoulders and wide trousers jumped out and ran, swishing into the building in a blur of black.

Ghost stepped back into the apartment, trying not to panic. He only had minutes left. He closed his eyes and took a deep breath.

If ever he had needed the Bleaching to work fast, it was now.

Shutting out the noises around him, he allowed his mind to relax, become blank. His heartbeat slowed, and he released the connection to his body. He breathed out until he had no breath left. He fought the impulse to inhale and, just as the reflex kicked in, he pushed. He pushed into the imaginary wall in front of him and felt the chill that signalled the Bleaching was working. It was like passing through an ice-cold liquid curtain.

Sucking in a badly-needed breath, he opened his eyes. Arms stretched out in front of him, he studied his dark skin. It was paling slightly, but too slowly. *Come on!*

'Kyatapira da!' came a shout from the other side of the door. 'Akero!'

Through his skin, his bones appeared, and through them, the carpet. He looked down at his legs, which were also fading.

He moved, but froze halfway across the room when he heard a key rattle in the lock. They were coming in. Ghost looked back at his arms. A faint outline remained. He looked at the door. The handle moved.

The two Kats entered, guns drawn, fingers on triggers. Japanese swords hung from their belts. They were as much for show as anything else, but Ghost had seen enough favela raids to know the Kats weren't afraid to use them. They scanned the room and nodded towards the open bedroom door.

Ghost stood between them and the bedroom, but he didn't move as they approached. The impressions his feet would make on the carpet, a cracking ankle bone, or any other sound from a moving body might arouse suspicion, enough to cause one of them to swing around wildly and crash into him, or – worse – shoot. So he stayed still and watched them creep closer.

Even without their uniforms and weapons, the men could easily be identified as Kyatapira. Their inner wrists were tattooed with President Goda's crossed swords, the crowns of their heads were shaved and their remaining long hair was oiled and tied in a knot on top.

Ghost carefully turned sideways to allow them to pass on either side of him. One of them wrinkled his nose as if he'd got a whiff of Ghost's sweat.

Kyatapira scum!

When the Kats had passed, he crept towards the door. In the hall, the Brazilian security guard stood on high alert with his weapon drawn. He reeked of cigarettes and Cachaça.

Ghost walked past, unnoticed, and headed for the stairs at the end of the corridor. The lift would be too risky – somebody could easily bump into him. He checked the coast was clear before opening the stair-well door, then quickly padded down the steps, making sure at each corner that the way ahead was clear.

He reached the ground floor without incident and eased the outside door open a crack. Using doors when he was in this state was always dodgy. People tended to get a bit suspicious when doors opened on their own. He stepped out into the sun, but felt no heat. Cold ran through his veins like liquid ice. It was just one downside of going invisible; another was the pure exhaustion afterwards.

The next problem was getting past the electric gates. He stepped through the open door of the security guard's empty booth and pressed a red button. Slowly the gates parted, offering Ghost a reassuring view of the sea and his escape route.

He walked back out on to Avenida Atlântica, aware of the danger of being in a public place. You never knew when some dumb cyclist or jogger was going to go straight into you. Even kicking an empty soda can by mistake could alert somebody's atten-tion. Worst of all were dogs. They always seemed to sense his presence and their confusion often turned to aggression.

He was about to take off when he noticed an

Empire man sitting on 'his' bench across the road. He wore a pale linen suit, and a black eye-patch covered one eye. The other eye seemed to be staring straight at Ghost. Frantically he checked his body, but he was still invisible. Ghost didn't know what the guy was looking at, and he didn't care. He started walking. The man on the bench followed his movements with his single eye.

Ghost quickened his pace and turned down the side street where he'd hidden the plastic bag. When he reached it, he looked back over his shoulder. The street was empty. Had anyone been present, they would have witnessed a plastic bag float out from under a car and off into a narrow alley.

In the shadows of the alley, Ghost dropped the bag and leant against a wall. Shivering with cold, even though it was around thirty degrees, he closed his eyes and relaxed. It always helped if he tried to go to sleep, emptying his mind with slow breathing, drifting into a deep . . . And that's when he felt it: the first traces of warmth entering his body, like sunshine coursing through his veins. He watched the gradual filling-in of his outline with bones, flesh and hair. Not waiting for the scar on his chest to appear, he opened the plastic bag and pulled out a vest, shorts and a pair of sandals, and quickly dressed.

'We need to talk,' said a voice behind him.

Ghost spun around and found himself face to face with the one-eyed man.

'I know what you can do,' said the man, in English. Ghost understood English because that's what most tourists spoke, and if you wanted to pick their pockets you needed to be able to speak their language. But it was strange to hear an Empire man speak English – they usually only spoke Japanese. The man's single eye sparkled like broken glass.

He knows about the Bleaching!

Ghost turned and ran.

'Wait!' the man called after him. 'I'm here to help you.'

But Ghost didn't stop.

He zigzagged his way through the streets to the bus stop, continually looking over his shoulder. On the ride home he paced the bus, examining the faces of the other passengers and staring out of the back window to see if he was being followed.

When he got off the bus, he ran as fast as he could – his sandals slapping on the cracked mud – until his favela appeared ahead of him, a ramshackle pile of houses and lives stacked on top of each other. Even if the one-eyed man had somehow followed him this far, he'd never follow him into it. An Empire man in a favela? He'd be eaten alive.

In a recent TV address, Goda, President of the Samurai Empire, had said the favelas were a cancerous growth on Rio, and plans were afoot to rid the city of these 'dens of danger'. But the favelas were home to thousands of Brazilians and, to Ghost, there was nowhere safer. Strangers were spotted from a mile away and Kats only came in when there was trouble. Sure, the place was full of criminals, but they looked after their own.

Just to be on the safe side, Ghost took a round-about route through the tangle of alleys. Soon he was lost in the sights and sounds of home: dogs poking about in rubbish bins, kids selling bread and ice lollies, gangsters playing pool, women singing sambas and old men drinking caipirinhas. The smell of fried chicken gizzards and cow heel soup wafted from windows along the way.

Ghost's hut crouched at the base of a teetering tower block. Cobbled together with reclaimed breeze blocks and broken bricks, it had a rusted iron roof which kept him dry in the rain – also hot in the summer and cold in the winter. But since his brother, Miguel, had died, it was his home. And the sight of it made him relax.

Until he reached his door. It was ajar.

He always locked the door. Always.

Tentatively, he pushed it open.

The man with one eye sat in Ghost's wicker chair. He smiled. 'My name is Makoto,' he said.

Ghost glanced behind, ready to run again. 'How did you get here so fast?'

'I've been here ever since you left.'

Ghost pulled the door closed. 'You have to leave. If I'm seen with an Empire man in my house . . .'

'I hate Goda and his Empire as much as you do,' said the man, standing.

Ghost crossed his arms. 'What do you want?'

The man stepped closer. His black hair was streaked with grey and tied in a tight ponytail. From his long, angular face, the single eye shone like a beacon. 'I want the same thing as you: to see the Empire burn.'

Ghost laughed. 'Impossible!' But the thought of the Empire going up in flames piqued his interest enough to keep him listening.

The man shook his head. 'Nothing is impossible.'

He held out his hand. In his palm was a small black flower.

BALLYHOOK, IRELAND

Rain came down in driving sheets, cold and grey. Cormac wiped the drops from his face and splashed through another puddle. He could hear them running after him.

'Keep running, Hinin Boy!' they mocked. 'Go tell your mammy!'

They erupted into laughter, but Cormac wasn't really worried about being caught. He'd escaped from them before – he'd do it again. He rounded the corner into Spiller Terrace. Like the rest of the town, the street seemed long ago to have given up caring what it looked like. Grass grew from clogged roof gutters, paint peeled from doors and weeds poked up between the cracks in the pavement. A dripping

Empire banner sagged from a flagpole, corkscrewing its crossed swords out of shape. When President Goda made one of his rare TV appearances, it was always preceded by images of the jewels in the Empire's crown: Tokyo, Paris, London. They never showed places like this – the neglected villages and towns whose factories and workers fuelled the Empire's economy.

Spiller Terrace was where Cormac usually lost them. But this time it was different. At the end of the street, three more boys were waiting.

'We forgot!' the one called Frog shouted. 'You don't have a mammy!'

'Or a daddy!' added one of the other boys.

Their taunts were becoming a bit annoying. It was the same thing every day – teasing him because he was from the Hinin House. The ironic thing was that some of his persecutors were also Hinin. Or used to be, before they became Kittens.

Cormac slowed to a trot, his tormentors' laughter churning his stomach. The boys at both ends of the road started walking towards him. Their sleeves were rolled up to their elbows, the single samurai sword tattooed on their inner wrists clearly displaying who they were: Kyatapira Youth. Also known as Kittens, these boys would have a second sword tattooed across the first in an X when they graduated as fully trained Kats.

But not Cormac. Even if it was a way to escape the misery of the Hinin House, he'd never betray his father by becoming Kyatapira.

'No escape this time, Hinin Boy!' shouted Frog.

Cormac knew he could outrun any one of them, but he wasn't a fighter, and there was no way he could take on six boys. He could try knocking on a door for help, but nobody wanted to get on the wrong side of Kyatapira, or even their Kittens. And then he spotted the alley between two houses. It was worth a shot.

As soon as he began to run, the mob took off too. Cormac swerved around a dustbin and realized his mistake. The alley was a dead end. Even worse, instead of a low wall he could jump over and escape through someone's back garden, it ended in the wall of a two-storey house.

Behind him, six silhouettes filled the entrance to the alley, cutting off what little light came from Spiller Terrace. Towering buildings surrounded him, blocking out the gloomy sky. Frog's words echoed in his ears, 'No escape this time, Hinin Boy!'

Cormac knew he shouldn't do it, but what other option did he have?

He ran straight for the wall at the end of the alley, picking up speed as he went. Behind him, the laughter stopped and he heard someone gasp. A six-metre wall blocked his path. The same flanked him on both sides. There was nowhere to go, but still he ran, now sprinting, the red bricks fast approaching.

When he reached the wall, he leapt, right foot first, on to the vertical surface, then kept running up the house. Looking up at the distant chimney stacked against the grey sky, Cormac sprinted two, four, six metres up the wall.

Suddenly, the soot-caked cowls of the chimney pots loomed over the rooftop, and he launched himself upwards, fingers splayed, aiming for the capping stone on the chimney. His two feet left the wall just as his hands made contact with the stone. His fingers fumbled to find a hold on the wet surface and then gravity took over, slamming his body into the wall and willing him downwards. His arms jerked into a painful stretch, and his entire body dangled from the protruding capping stone.

He swung a leg up on to the greasy tiles and reached over to grab one of the chimney's cowls. It lurched unsteadily, but held firm, allowing him to pull himself up on to the slanting roof.

He looked down into the alley, where six drenched upturned faces wore looks of absolute shock.

'I don't play with Kittens,' he shouted down through the rain. 'Come back when you're Kats!'

As he turned to set off across the rooftop, something caught his eye. At the alley's entrance, behind the six boys, stood a lone figure. He wore long yellow robes and a shiny black cap. *A priest?*

Even more unusual was that this Shintō priest only had one eye. A black eye-patch covered the other. But it was obvious where his good eye was looking: at Cormac.

What does he want?

Cormac didn't wait to find out. He ran across the rooftops, swinging around chimneys and skipping over loose ridge tiles, wanting to put as much distance as possible between himself and the alley, but also aware that the longer he spent up here, the greater his chances were of being seen by someone else.

He spotted a flat roof below and skittered down the inclining tiles, leaping as he reached the edge. Like a cat, he landed on the flat roof on feet and hands, immediately rolling forwards to break his fall. Crouching on the lip of the felt roof, he surveyed his surroundings: overgrown back garden, house windows boarded up. Safe enough. He jumped down to the ground.

'Hello, Cormac.'

He spun around. The priest with the eye-patch stood under a white umbrella. The sharp cheekbones, the long face, the robe – they were all bone dry, as if he hadn't been standing out in the rain moments ago.

He knows my name! Cormac took a step back. 'But I saw you . . . How did you do that?'

'I could ask you the same thing.' His single eye sparkled.

He speaks English? Cormac remembered he hadn't bowed. 'Sorry.' He bowed low, feeling his crucifix move beneath his shirt. He wore it because it was all he had left of his mother. He wasn't one of those 'Christians' that practised the old religion in secret. But that wouldn't matter if he was caught wearing it.

The man smiled. 'You don't have to bow to me.'

'But you're . . .' his eyes drifted to the priest's headgear, '. . . a shinshoku.'

The man laughed. 'This?' He pulled off the hat, but instead of revealing a priest's shaved head, long black-and-grey hair tumbled out from underneath. 'My name is Makoto.'

Cormac's fear intensified. Even if this guy wasn't a priest, he was still Empire, and that meant trouble. Cormac glanced behind him, looking for an escape route.

The man held up his index finger. 'Hold on. Let me show you.'

He closed his one eye, his brow wrinkling in concentration. Then he opened his eye and said, 'Look behind you.'

Cormac turned around. At the bottom of the overgrown garden stood a man wearing an eye-patch and a yellow priest's robe – a mirror image.

'Impressed?'

Cormac looked back to the man with the umbrella. 'But how can you be in two places at the same time?'

'I can't. That's just a projection. Though I can see through my projection's eyes.'

Cormac glanced behind again. The 'projection' was gone. 'So that wasn't really you, back in the alley?'

'No. I've been here the whole time.'

Cormac swallowed. 'But you saw what I . . . what happened?'

'You mean, did I see you defy gravity by running up a wall on to the roof of a house?'

Uh-oh. Cormac nodded.

'And did I see those "Kittens" mocking you for being an orphan, calling you a Hinin Boy?'

Cormac nodded again.

'Those Kittens epitomize everything that is wrong with the Samurai Empire. The bushidō ideals of the real samurai – loyalty, honour, wisdom – have long since been forgotten in President Goda's quest for power. You've seen the news. As we speak, Empire forces gather at the borders of America, one of the last free nations on Earth.'

'And what's this got to do with me?'

'You can help us stop them. You can help us protect what's left of the world's freedom – and perhaps fight back.' The man held out his palm – a small black flower rested in its centre.

'What is this?' asked Cormac, watching the rain gather inside the dark petals.

'This is what you can become.'

Cormac blinked the rain from his eyelashes. 'A flower?'

'A Black Lotus,' said the man, handing him an envelope. 'Part of the resistance. And in here is every-thing you will need to join us: ID papers, passport and a one-way ticket to Japan.'

'Resistance? Japan?' It seemed all he could do was ask questions.

'Inside are instructions which tell you everything you need to know. Memorize them – then destroy them.'

Cormac looked at the envelope, now speckled with rain. Not knowing what else to do, he put it inside his jacket. When he looked up, the man was gone.

NEW YORK CITY, AMERICA

Kate looked around to make sure no one was watching, then slipped into the trees surrounding the zoo. She opened her backpack and took out her good sneakers and the neatly folded jeans and sweater. One of the hardest things about being homeless was keeping clean clothes. But they were essential to blend in with the crowd. She removed her grubby clothes, the ones which always drew the attention of security guards, and dressed in the clean gear.

Next, she took out a piece of broken mirror, a hairbrush and a bottle of water. Positioning the mirror on her bag so that she could see herself, she brushed the knots from her blonde hair. Then she poured water into her cupped hand and splashed it on to her face.

Using both hands, she scrubbed her face and neck before checking the mirror again.

Good enough.

And if security weren't convinced, that would change once they heard her speak. Kate didn't have the accent of a girl living on the streets. Instead, she spoke in the refined tones of a middle-class, educated girl. Which is what she was. Her accent was her secret weapon, allowing her to go places other homeless people couldn't.

As she began to repack her belongings, she frowned at a piece of paper at the bottom of her bag and pulled it out.

MISSING
Kate Douglas

Last Seen
Elmsford Children's Home,
Elmsford, New York . . .

Kate stuffed it back to the bottom, eyes stinging, annoyed she'd kept it so long. She'd got a fright when the flyers had started appearing around the Bronx. No way was she going back into care. She'd spent a whole week taking the flyers down. But she'd kept one – she wasn't sure why. She looked at herself in the mirror. The girl in the mirror looked different from the one in the photo – older, smarter, tougher.

Lonelier.

Memories of shooting hoops with her dad, and

cuddling up in front of the TV with her mom and Jamie were like pieces of glass in the soles of her feet. Every time she moved, she was reminded of them.

People had said her mom and dad were crazy to volunteer as aid workers in war-torn Norway, but Kate had been proud of her humanitarian parents. Until they were captured and imprisoned by Empire forces for being revolutionaries. Then she was angry with them. Angry with them for having abandoned her and her little brother to America's social services.

Jamie had been placed with a foster family who turned out to be really nice, so that was one weight off Kate's mind. But she'd ended up in Elmsford Children's Home, where rule number sixteen was 'No animals'. She could live with the other fifteen rules, but animals were her life. She'd climbed out of the window on her first night, and had been on the run ever since.

Living on the streets was no picnic, but at least it meant Kate could be herself. She gathered up the rest of her stuff and stepped out of the trees. Again, she checked that nobody had seen her, before continuing down the footpath.

She passed two billboards: 'Be prepared – learn Japanese in three weeks' and '20% off all Prefabricated Fallout Shelters'. At a news-stand, she glimpsed the headlines on the *New York Times*: 'Empire Troops Gather in Guatemala'. Everyone was obsessed with this impending war. She wondered what it would be like to be occupied by the Empire. She'd heard they didn't tolerate homeless people, that they were forced into workhouses. There was a word for them, but she couldn't remember it.

She finally reached the perimeter fence. No matter how many times she saw the red-and-black sign, it never failed to make her smile.

WARNING! Dangerous animals live behind this fence. If you climb it, they could eat you, and that might make them sick. Thank you. The Bronx Zoo.

She followed the chain-link fence around a corner to where it was hidden from the street by trees. With the skill that came from practice, she scaled the fence. At the top, she threw her leg over a small section that didn't have barbed wire, and climbed down to the other side.

'I thought you'd never get here.'

She turned around. 'Hey, Gol. What's the matter?'

'We have to do something about that bully, Eddie.'

'But he's tiny,' said Kate. 'And you're enormous.'

'He's been calling me names.'

'What names?'

'Big Ears.'

Kate suppressed a smile. 'But you *have* big ears.'

'And he's been calling me Long Nose.'

'Tell him it's a trunk, not a nose,' said Kate, glaring across at the chimpanzee enclosure where Eddie, the 'bully', watched from the top of a pole. She wagged her finger at him, and he immediately buried his head in his armpit.

She patted Goliath, the large African elephant, on the head. 'If he says anything else to you, let me know.'

Goliath nuzzled her with his trunk. 'Thank you, Kate.'

'I'd better go,' she said. 'I'm not supposed to be in here.'

The elephant nodded his large wrinkled head.

She dashed across the elephant enclosure, glanced around to check the coast was clear and then climbed over the fence to the path on the other side.

It was early, so the zoo was quiet, but already visitors were starting to arrive. First stop was the penguin pond, and luckily there were no people gathered around it. As soon as Percy, the eldest male, saw her, he dived off the rocks and swam across the pool. Kate leant over the fence and waited for him to emerge. He torpedoed out of the water and shook himself dry on the concrete bank.

'Hi, Percy,' said Kate.

'Hi, Kate!' he brayed in his funny honking voice. Kate always thought he sounded more like a donkey than a penguin.

She scanned the floor of the pool. 'Much down there today?'

'A few bits,' said the penguin, diving back into the water.

Kate watched him scrabble about on the tiled floor of the pool, where coins had been thrown by visitors. People were funny. They obeyed the 'Do not feed the animals' sign but couldn't resist throwing money into pools of water to make a wish. Still, she wasn't complaining. Percy's head broke the water with two quarters in his mouth. He stretched upwards, offering them to Kate. She looked around before plucking the coins from his bill. He immediately dived in again to fetch more.

As she waited for Percy to return, she looked across at Zula, the lioness, who was standing up on her hind legs against the bars of her compound. Something was wrong. Zula only ever got excited at feeding time.

Percy slid from the pond and Kate took more coins. 'Thanks, Percy,' she said. 'I'll be back in a moment.'

He nodded and dived back in.

Kate made her way over to Zula. 'What do you need?'

The lioness dropped down on to all fours and snarled. 'That's a nice waaaay to greet your frieeeend.'

'Sorry,' said Kate, 'but you normally only move if you want something.'

'Chaaaarming,' replied the lioness. 'And I was just about to give *yoooou* something.'

'What?'

Zula licked her paw and looked away.

Kate crouched down to the cat's eye-level. 'I'm sorry.'

Zula peered out at her, the sun glinting in her amber eyes. 'Apology aaaaccepted.'

Kate smiled. 'So what were you going to give me?'

'Informaaaation.'

She frowned. 'What sort of information?'

'Somebody has been following yoooou.'

Kate glanced around. 'What did you say?'

'A maaaan with a patch over his eye has been following yoooou.'

'Are you kidding?'

Zula was about to reply when the wailing sound of a siren filled the air. Kate stood up and looked around. A group of tourists raced by, towards the exit. At the far side of the pond, more visitors ran with strollers and screaming toddlers towards the gate.

'What's going oooon?'

'I don't know,' replied Kate. 'I'd better go and find out.'

She joined the stream of people rushing towards the exit. At the gift shop, a crowd gathered around a large TV screen mounted on the wall. Kate pushed closer to get a better look.

The words 'Emergency Alert' flashed on the screen. Text scrolled across the bottom on a red ribbon.

A CIVIL EMERGENCY HAS BEEN DECLARED FOR
MAINLAND UNITED STATES, EFFECTIVE UNTIL
FURTHER NOTICE. TODAY AT 08:00, FORCES OF
THE SAMURAI EMPIRE INVADED MEXICO.
PRESIDENT GODA HAS THREATENED TO ADVANCE
THE INVASION ON TO AMERICAN SOIL UNLESS THIS
MESSAGE IS PLAYED.

A collective gasp rippled around the crowd

before the instantly recognizable face of President Goda appeared on screen. He wore a white suit, and his long black hair was tied into the traditional Empire topknot. His broad shoulders and strong, handsome jawline gave him the look of a Marvel superhero. Behind him, mounted on the wall, two ornate swords crossed each other in the shape of an X – one engraved with a butterfly, the other the eye of a snake.

The camera zoomed in on his face to eyes full of strength and power. The corners of his mouth twitched ever so slightly upwards as if he was about to smile. He wore the look of a chess master who had just checkmated his opponent.

Boiling anger hissed through Kate's veins. *You murdering dictator! My parents are rotting in one of your jails!*

When he began to speak, the crowd fell silent, though most probably couldn't understand his Japanese. The scrolling ribbon of text, however, translated his address.

GREETINGS, PEOPLE OF AMERICA. BY THE TIME YOU SEE THIS, YOUR ALLY, MEXICO, WILL HAVE FALLEN UNDER EMPIRE RULE. I HAVE INVITED YOUR LEADERS TO TALK, BUT THEY HAVE REFUSED. SO NOW, I EXTEND MY INVITATION DIRECTLY TO YOU, THE PEOPLE. YOUR COUNTRY HAS LOST ITS WAY, BUT IF YOU JOIN THE SAMURAI EMPIRE, I PROMISE A RETURN TO TRADITIONAL VALUES. JOIN PEACEFULLY, AND YOU WILL FIND THERE IS A PLACE THERE FOR EVERYBODY.

Not everybody. Kate suddenly remembered the word she'd been trying to think of earlier. Hinin. In Empire states, so-called 'undesirables' – like the homeless, disabled, addicts and orphans – were rounded up and put to work in Hinin Houses, *Hinin* meaning 'non-human' or 'outcast'. And she would be one of them.

President Goda smiled and bowed, before the screen went blank. Then the text began to scroll again.

ALL CITIZENS OF THE UNITED STATES ARE ASKED
TO STAY ALERT FOR A POSSIBLE ATTACK AND
STAY TUNED TO ALL MEDIA OUTLETS FOR
FURTHER DETAILS. THIS CONCLUDES THIS
EMERGENCY ALERT MESSAGE.

A woman beside Kate waved her fist at the screen and shouted profanities about the Empire. The crowd, full of anxious faces and nervous chatter, quickly dispersed, rushing for the exit. But one man remained. He wore a baseball cap, jeans and a denim jacket. When he turned to face her, Kate saw the eye-patch.

The fight-or-flight instinct that she had honed since leaving the home kicked in immediately.

She bolted for the exit, pushing past a gang of students in navy blazers. After leaping over the turn-stile, she sprinted across the road to the safety of the trees where she'd dressed earlier. She peered out from behind a tree trunk, but there was no sign of the man. Deciding to stay put until the coast was clear, she turned to go deeper into the woods.

The man stood in front of her. He was Asian, with a black-and-grey ponytail hanging from his baseball cap. 'Kate, I need to talk to you.'

She turned and raced through the trees. *How did he do that? And he knows my name!*

Ahead of her, the man stepped out from behind a tree.

What the . . .?

She swerved to the left, only to find the man standing before her again.

Fight or flight.

She jabbed a fist at the man's face, only to find that her hand went straight through his head. It connected with nothing. The guy was just air.

'If you stand still, I'll tell you what's going on,' he said.

Kate kicked hard between the man's legs, but again, her foot didn't connect and continued up through the man's ghostly body, throwing her off balance. She crashed on to her back and looked up helplessly at the man. He shimmered and then disappeared.

Heart racing, and gasping for breath, she sat up.

'I don't know what that lioness said about me, but I mean you no harm.'

Behind her, the one-eyed man leant against a tree.

He knows my secret!

'Yes, I know you can talk to animals. And now you know what *I* can do.'

Kate stood up. 'You can disappear?'

'No. That person you attacked wasn't me but an optical illusion. I can project my body into different locations.' His eye glittered as he spoke.

'You mean that wasn't you in the zoo either?'

The man shook his head. 'I've been here, waiting for you. My name is Makoto.'

'But how can you do that?'

'What I do is no more amazing than what you can do, Kate. In fact there are many others like us. We call ourselves the Black Lotus.'

'Is that, like, some kind of freak club?'

'You've seen the newsflash. The Empire is about to go to war with your country, one of the last free nations on the planet. The Black Lotus are the only ones who can stop them from winning. The street doesn't need you, Kate. We do.'

And he handed her an envelope and a black flower.

Ghost shuffled towards the security checkpoint at Goda International Airport. Shoes no longer hurt his feet. Twenty-four hours on a flight from Rio to Tokyo had given him plenty of time to get used to them.

He smiled at the boys around him, who looked nervous. They were probably homesick already and missing their parents. But really, what had they to worry about? They weren't pretending to be a trainee Kat on his compulsory pilgrimage to Japan. They weren't from favelas. They hadn't just taken their first flight on an aeroplane. They weren't carrying a fake passport and ID papers. They weren't anti-Empire rebels travelling into the heart of the enemy's territory to join some secret resistance group.

It was Ghost who should be worrying.

But he wasn't. Instead, he was repeating in his

head the information he had memorized from Makoto's envelope before burning it in the little stove in his hut.

My name is Cardosa Takehiko. My father's name is Cardosa Leonardo, occupation: Kyatapira officer, Shizunai Division, Registration Number: 234976. My mother's name is Cardosa Gabriela, occupation . . .

The Kat in the security booth beckoned him forward. Copying the boys who'd gone before him, Ghost handed the Kat his passport and papers, before turning his palms up to show the sword tattooed on each of his wrists. The Kat glanced at the passport, then at Ghost's face and then at his wrists. He grunted, handed the passport back and nodded for Ghost to proceed.

He followed the other Kittens out into the airport arrivals area where a line of Kyatapira officers waited with cardboard signs displaying the names of the boys who would be in their charge while in Japan. But it wasn't the sign displaying the name 'Cardosa Takehiko' which caught his eye, but the Kat who was holding it. He had a long, sharp face, and from behind his sunglasses the cord of a black eye-patch was visible.

Again copying the other Kittens, Ghost bowed. Makoto took his bag and indicated that he should follow.

They walked out of the airport to a black SUV with tinted windows. Makoto glanced around before opening the rear passenger door for Ghost. Inside, he saw a boy and a girl who looked about thirteen, the same age as him. They smiled nervously. Having stowed Ghost's luggage in the trunk, Makoto sat in the passenger seat. Their driver, a tall, thin Asian man, said something in Japanese. Makoto shook his head, took off his sunglasses, closed his single eye and appeared to fall into a state of deep concentration. A vein pulsed in his neck.

Ghost remembered the way Makoto could project himself to other locations. Perhaps he was checking that the route ahead was safe.

The driver seemed to be awaiting instructions.

Makoto's eye opened wide. 'Go!' he ordered.

The SUV took off with a jolt, flinging Ghost back into the seat. He turned to the others, but they wouldn't meet his eyes. Everyone seemed too nervous to speak. Their driver continually checked his rear-view mirror. Ghost looked out of the back window, but there was nothing behind them except traffic. Makoto too was quiet, the lines etched into his forehead making it obvious that something was on his mind.

As they left behind the bright lights of Tokyo and made their way along a highway into the country-side, Makoto seemed to relax. He turned to face his passengers. 'Ghost, this is Cormac and Kate.'

The boy, Cormac, nodded. He had pale skin with tousled brown hair and a freckled face. He didn't have the same soft pampered eyes as most of the other boys Ghost had seen on the flight. His were the eyes of a favela kid: tough, strong and full of secrets.

'Are you from the Empire too?' asked Kate, leaning forward to see past Cormac. She was pretty – blonde with long eyelashes and nice teeth.

Ghost nodded. 'You?'

'Nope, well not yet anyway. I'm American.'

Cormac shoved his tattooed wrists towards Makoto. 'Can we get rid of these now?'

'Best keep them on you till we get there.'

'Which is where, exactly?' asked Kate, her tone fearless and her blue eyes twinkling.

These are my type of people, thought Ghost.

'Guess I should tell you guys what's going on, eh?' said Makoto.

All three back-seat passengers nodded.

'As you will know, through the ages, each Lord or President Goda has been famous for his two swords – the butterfly and the snake-eye – together the symbol of the Samurai Empire. And they're more than just a symbol – they're powerful in their own right. But there is a third sword.'

'Huh?' History wasn't Ghost's strong point, but everybody knew about the Empire's two swords. Their image was everywhere. A *third* sword? Cormac and Kate seemed equally confused.

'The three swords were forged at the same time, five centuries ago. The Black Lotus also formed at this time, with the sole intention of stopping Goda. And our first act was to steal the third sword. We've been protecting it ever since.'

Ghost's head spun as he tried to process the information. *What's so special about the third sword?*

'No offence,' said Kate. 'But you haven't exactly

been successful in preventing the rise of the Empire.'

Makoto snapped his head towards her, his eye narrowing ever so slightly. 'Your country is still free, isn't it?'

'Yeah, but maybe not for long.'

'If it hadn't been for us, America would have been under Empire rule long ago. We may not have stopped the Empire, but we've hampered its progress.' Makoto inhaled deeply, then glanced out of the window, as if checking for something. 'Combined, the three swords are capable of catastrophic damage. That's why the Empire has spent hundreds of years searching for its missing sword – and why the Black Lotus has spent all that time hiding it. We've also been building an army of talented soldiers to continue our work.'

'Guarding the sword?' asked Kate.

'More than that: spying, reconnaissance, war preparation. Anything we can do to help bring down the Empire. And you,' said Makoto, looking from Kate to Cormac to Ghost, 'are our newest recruits.'

Ahead of them, backed-up traffic caused the SUV to stop. Makoto spoke to the driver. Though Ghost couldn't understand the words, he sensed their urgency.

Makoto closed his eye again, and his brow puckered with concentration.

'Get out of the vehicle,' he snapped suddenly, his eye opening.

Ghost looked blankly at Cormac and Kate.

'Get out. Now!' shouted Makoto.

Ghost opened the door and the three of them scrambled out. Four lanes of traffic had ground to a standstill. Ahead, a long truck had jackknifed across the road.

Makoto pulled an earpiece out from under his collar and attached it to his ear. He then tapped his chest twice and spoke in a commanding voice. 'All agents, this is Makoto. They're about to attack. I'm taking my charges to the wooded valley north-east of our position. Send backup.'

Ghost looked around. *About to atta—?*

Gunshots rang out, and the windows of the SUV cracked. Makoto pulled his new recruits behind the vehicle.

'What's going on?' yelled Kate, as gunfire rained on to the motorway, smashing glass, ricocheting off metal and puncturing tyres.

Makoto shouted, 'Lie down!'

Ghost dropped on to his belly as a bullet hit the car door exactly where he'd been kneeling a second earlier. Their driver left the relative safety of the SUV and grabbed the bumper of an empty van whose occupants had fled. With one hand, he dragged the vehicle over to their SUV and flipped it on to its side to form a shield against the incoming gunfire.

'Jeez,' said Kate to Ghost. 'Did you see what that guy just did?'

Ghost was dumbstruck. All around him, people ran from their vehicles, screaming, ducking for cover. Some fell to the tarmac, bleeding.

But some drivers were obviously Black Lotus. A

bald man leapt from his car and levelled a high-powered rifle across the hood. The gun's sight swept back and forth over the distant trees. A woman in a floral dress did a forward roll between two cars and came up firing a machine gun at the unseen enemy on the hillside.

'Run!' called Makoto.

Their driver ran to another car and tossed it beside the van, creating a shield of vehicles leading to the edge of the motorway. Ghost, Cormac and Kate dashed behind the upturned cars.

Crouching down, Makoto removed two small spheres from his pocket. He pulled a pin out from each of them and rolled the balls across the motorway. They emitted a white smoke, covering the area around them in dense cloud.

'Go!' said the driver, pulling out a gun. 'I'll cover you!'

Makoto turned to his new recruits. 'Head for the trees,' he said, pointing to the side of the motorway. 'Quickly!'

They took off. Bullets peppered the upturned cars, but they reached the edge of the road unharmed.

There was no time to catch their breath. They heard a whistling noise as something flew across the sky, then a gigantic explosion. Kate was thrown to the ground. Behind her, a car burst into flames, sending debris in all directions and spewing thick black smoke into the sky.

'Come on!' yelled Makoto, pulling Kate to her

feet. Bits of smouldering metal and rubber showered down around them.

Ghost accelerated, leaping over the motorway barrier on to a grassy incline on the other side. He ran faster than he'd ever run before, his eyes firmly fixed on the clump of trees ahead. Behind him, he heard gunshots, explosions and screams.

Somebody overtook him. All he saw was a blur of colour streaking away from him at supersonic speed. It was only when he reached the woods that he realized who the mystery sprinter was: Cormac. And he wasn't even sweating. They dashed behind a tree trunk.

Ghost's breath was coming in gasps. 'How did you do that?'

Beside them, Kate fell to her knees, also panting heavily. Peering back around the tree, Ghost saw Makoto following in his black Kat uniform.

As Makoto approached the trees, something hit him on the shoulder and sent him spinning to the ground. Ghost saw it as if in slow motion. The older man's face crumpled in pain, and he fell.

'No!' Ghost ran out towards the body, his heart racing. Without Makoto, he felt sure the Kats would catch them. Was this the end of his new life, before it had even begun? But, as suddenly as he had fallen, Makoto sprang to his feet.

'Get back!' he cried, pushing Ghost away towards the trees.

As soon as they were under the canopy, Makoto began undoing his shirt.

'Have you been shot?' asked Ghost.

Makoto opened his shirt. Underneath, he wore a curious vest, which seemed to be made from mirrored sequins that reflected the colours of the surrounding forest. He dug his fingers into a small indentation in the sequins and plucked out a bullet.

Ghost leant closer. 'A bulletproof vest?'

Makoto didn't answer, but tapped his chest and spoke into his hidden communication device. 'All three charges have safely reached the rendezvous point.' He began buttoning up his shirt. 'Keep enemy engaged. Prepare for attack from the air. Keep me updated.'

A massive explosion diverted Ghost's attention, and through the trees he watched a fireball engulf the motorway. It was immediately followed by the sound of choppers. They appeared in the sky like black wasps, each bearing the crossed-swords insignia of the Empire.

'Quick, follow me,' said Makoto. He ran uphill, through the trees.

Ghost helped Kate up off the ground. She looked terrified.

'Elvis has left the building,' he said, pointing in the direction Makoto had gone.

Kate attempted to smile before stumbling ahead. Ghost and Cormac followed.

'Scary, huh?' said Cormac.

Ghost raised his eyebrows. 'I guess.'

Cormac looked at him as if he had two heads. But Ghost wasn't scared. Yes, he'd had a fright, but he wouldn't say he was scared. He rubbed his chest, feeling the scar beneath his shirt. Since his brother had died, nothing frightened him. In the favelas, fear was a weakness, and the weak didn't survive.

Cormac followed the others out of the woods and upwards through long grass. He'd always considered himself tough, but the shoot-out had really shaken him up. Although the attack had been meant for the Black Lotus, the motorway was full of innocent people too. What had he got himself into?

Kate also seemed petrified. But not Ghost. He looked like he'd seen it all before.

Although he could still hear the battle behind him, Cormac became aware of a new sound: a mechanical whooshing, like a giant turbine.

Cresting the hill, he spotted a sleek black helicopter on the ground. He saw the Empire flag on its side, the pilot in a Kat uniform, and his belly flipped with fear.

'That's a Kyatapira chopper!' he shouted, ducking down in the grass. Kate and Ghost instinctively copied.

Makoto shook his head. 'This is one of ours.' He smiled, and offered Cormac his hand. 'Come on.'

Still recovering from his embarrassment, he followed the others under the whirring blades, their powerful beat almost taking his breath away. The wind whipped around him and the engines seemed to scream with impatience.

Makoto strapped the three teenagers into seats in the back, handed them headphones to block out the noise and then sat in the front with the pilot. It was only then that Cormac realized the pilot was actually a boy his own age! Short and stocky, with a thick neck, the pilot never once glanced back at his new passengers, but operated the cockpit equipment as if he'd been doing it his whole life.

Cormac's stomach lurched as they took off, rising rapidly into the sky. He stared out of the window at the swarm of black helicopters hovering over the motorway, which was now littered with the smoking remains of burning vehicles. He'd always known Kyatapira were ruthless, but he was gobsmacked that they'd attack a busy road full of innocent people. They must really hate the Black Lotus. He'd known so little about the organization when he agreed to join – he couldn't have imagined how dangerous it would be. He wondered whether he'd made the right choice in accepting the little black flower. But then again, he'd had nothing to lose.

As they left the scene, Cormac looked behind

him to see if they were being followed. They weren't. *I suppose the last thing the Kats would suspect is for us to escape in one of their own choppers.* You had to hand it to these Black Lotus guys. Whoever they were, they knew what they were doing!

Through his headphones, he heard Kate speak. 'Those other drivers on the highway, they were Black Lotus too?'

'Some of them,' said Makoto.

Across from him, Kate glanced at Ghost and then Cormac. 'What will happen to them?'

'I don't know.'

She hesitated. 'They'll die?'

'We just have to hope they get away.' He turned to Kate. 'They were doing their job: protecting you.'

Her eyes widened. 'Were we the targets?'

'We don't know, exactly,' replied Makoto. 'It could've been opportunistic. They might've followed one of you, and taken the chance to strike.'

Cormac pulled the headphone mic down. 'Why is your headquarters in the middle of the Empire? Why not somewhere else, like America?'

'We have a saying: sometimes the best place to hide is perched on your enemy's eyelashes. We've survived here for hundreds of years. But all the time, the Kyatapira net closes in.'

'So those guys could've died for us?' asked Kate.

'For the Black Lotus,' replied Makoto. 'You are our future.'

Suddenly the enormity of the situation hit Cormac with a force that made him want to throw up.

People were willing to die to get him here. There was no going back now.

The conversation stopped as they flew over tree-covered hillsides, mountaintops studded with sharp outcroppings of rock, meandering rivers and gushing waterfalls. Cormac wondered where exactly they were going, and what would be expected of them once they got there.

After about an hour, the helicopter banked sharply to the right and descended towards a forested mountainside. A clearing opened up beneath them. They had no sooner landed than Makoto opened their door, beckoning them out. When everybody had disembarked, the machine took to the sky again.

'Where are we?' asked Kate.

'This is the safe zone,' Makoto replied. 'We call it Niwa.'

Cormac knew that word. 'Garden?'

Makoto smiled, clearly impressed. 'So you have been listening at school.'

He shrugged. 'Reluctantly.'

Makoto looked at Kate and Ghost. 'We have quite a bit of ground to cover. So we had best get going.'

He headed into the forest and up the mountain. The others followed. The air was spiced with the scent of pine, the ground soft underfoot. There was no path, and yet Makoto seemed to know exactly where he was going. The teenagers walked three abreast, with Ghost in the middle.

'Can you believe this?' asked Kate.

Ghost smiled. 'Maybe we chewed off more than we bite.' His thick accent suggested English wasn't his native language.

Kate laughed. 'I think you mean "bit off more than we can chew".'

'Yes,' said Ghost. 'My English isn't so good.'

'It's very good,' said Cormac. 'Did you learn it in school?'

Ghost shook his head. 'I teach myself. I have a book.'

'You're a dark horse, Ghost,' said Kate.

Ghost looked at her blankly.

'I mean, you're full of surprises,' said Kate. 'Like back on the highway – you didn't even look scared.'

Ghost shrugged. 'I don't have a life like you. I have no family. I live alone. My life is scary. *This* is exciting.'

A seedling of hope sprouted in Cormac. 'You're Hinin too?'

'No.' Ghost shook his head. 'I'd die before I go to one of those places.'

His reply crushed the seedling like a heavy boot.

'I know that word,' said Kate. 'It's like an orphan-age, right?'

Cormac nodded.

'You live in a Hinin House?' asked Ghost.

Cormac swallowed and looked away. What could he say? He was embarrassed.

Kate touched his arm. 'Nothing to be ashamed of, Cormac. I live on the streets.'

'What?' asked Ghost, clearly as surprised as

Cormac, who presumed a smartly dressed, well-spoken American girl like Kate came from a nice family and had a pet dog and a pretty house with a back garden.

'I guess we all have something in common,' said Kate. 'Which makes sense. I mean, what parent in their right mind would let their kid come here?'

Ghost put a hand on Cormac and Kate's shoulders. 'We're like beans in the pod.'

'Peas!' chorused Kate and Cormac together.

The three laughed, causing Makoto to turn around and scowl. 'Just because it's safer here, that doesn't mean you should draw attention to yourselves,' he said sharply.

Cormac raised his palms in apology. Makoto continued walking. But Cormac stared into the trees.

'What is it?' asked Kate.

'I thought I saw something.'

'Where?'

He pointed into the undergrowth, to where he was sure he'd seen movement – a furtive shift of light and shade. 'Probably just an animal.'

'Let me check,' said Kate. She closed her eyes and tilted her head sideways, as if she was listening for something.

'What are you doing?' asked Ghost.

Kate kept her eyes closed, but held up her hand. 'Shh!'

Confused, Cormac glanced at Ghost, who shrugged.

When Kate finally opened her eyes, she said,

'That's weird. There's not an animal within three hundred metres of us, not even a bird.'

Cormac frowned. 'How can you tell?'

'It's my thing.'

'Your thing?'

'Yeah, you know, my special ability. I can communicate with animals.'

'No way!'

'Yes way. Like you can run abnormally fast.'

Cormac blushed.

'Sorry, but we all saw you sprint away from that highway.'

Cormac bowed his head. He was normally good at hiding his talent, but when bullets and missiles are being fired at you, instinct kicks in. It felt weird to hear people discussing his skill openly.

His mother had told him that even as a baby he'd been 'different'. He'd sat up at two weeks and walked at two months. She had ended up lying about his age so he'd seem normal. By the time he started school he was an expert at keeping his abilities secret. Life was easier when you were the same as everyone else.

Again, Kate seemed to sense his discomfort and changed the subject. 'So what about you, *Ghost*? Do you scare people or something?'

He didn't reply, but was staring at the place where Cormac thought he'd seen something move.

Cormac followed his line of sight. 'What is it, Ghost?'

'I think I see something move too.'

'He's kidding,' said Kate. 'He just doesn't want to

answer my question.'

Ghost started walking in the direction of the movement. 'No, I see something.'

Cormac looked up the hill, but there was no sign of Makoto. Ghost was pushing aside plants and stepping over branches, heading towards a group of trees. Cormac and Kate glanced at each other, then followed Ghost.

When they reached him, he raised his finger, signalling for them to be quiet. He stepped closer to the gnarled trunk of an old tree, his eyes squinting into the murky shadows. He crept closer and closer, until it looked like he was going to walk right into the tree. Looking puzzled, he raised a hand to touch the bark . . .

The tree suddenly came alive, taking human form, grabbing Ghost's extended hand and twisting it sharply. With a cry of pain, he fell to the ground.

Cormac was about to shout when a hand clamped firmly over his mouth, stifling his cry. A searing pain shot through his bicep as his arm was forced up behind his back. A kick to the back of the legs brought him to his knees, before his face was shoved into the dirt. A foot pinned his neck to the ground.

Then he heard a distant shout, and the pressure lifted. He sat up, spitting out dirt and leaves. Nearby, Kate and Ghost struggled to their feet. Four figures wearing weird bodysuits surrounded them, watching through slits in their face masks. Their boots, suits and masks were all made from the same strange material. It changed colour as they moved, reflecting the forest around them. When they weren't moving, they seemed to disappear into their immediate environment.

Makoto burst through the trees. 'What are you doing?'

Kate's eyes narrowed. 'You said this was the safe zone!'

'It is,' replied Makoto. 'But that doesn't mean you can wander off on your own.'

He raised his arm and called out.

More masked figures dressed in the same reflective suits stepped from behind tree trunks, rolled out from under bushes and dropped silently from overhead branches. Cormac gasped. There were twenty, at least, but he hadn't spotted a single one until they chose to reveal themselves.

'They are what makes this the safe zone,' explained Makoto. 'They are the Black Lotus shinobi.'

'Shinobi?' Even Kate knew that word. 'Ninjas?'

Makoto smiled. 'Ninjas have always been highly respected saboteurs, deadly martial artists, trained assassins and expert spies. Many fought injustice, but others became mercenaries, hired by the Empire to do their dirty work. Those who wouldn't do the Empire's bidding were hunted down and many were killed. A small group continued to fight against the Empire. They were called the Black Lotus.'

Makoto raised his hand, and with a flick of his wrist the shinobi melted back into the trees, as if they'd been nothing but a mirage.

'It's like magic,' breathed Kate.

'Not magic. Skill.' Makoto gestured to their invisible watchers. 'And one day, you will join their ranks.'

Cormac frowned. *We're going to be ninjas?*

'Now, we must go,' said Makoto, turning to leave. 'Our master is waiting.'

Cormac stared into the trees, but could see no trace of the hidden people.

'Come on,' said Kate, pulling his arm.

He followed, unsure how he felt about becoming a ninja. His natural instinct was to immediately reject all things Japanese. But it seemed Japanese wasn't always the same as Empire.

'And there I was,' said Kate, 'thinking I'd be heading up a team of scientists to breed an army of mutant penguins to fight the Empire.'

Cormac laughed, suddenly banishing whatever doubts he'd had. Although the shoot-out had shaken him, something felt right about what was happening: wherever he was going, or whatever he was to become, it couldn't be any worse than his life in Ireland. He didn't know why, but this felt like his destiny.

Eventually they crested the mountain and came to a grassy clearing. The sky stretched out above them, an uninterrupted blanket of blue, and all around were forested slopes in varying shades of green. Distant snow-topped mountains traced a jagged horizon across the sky.

'Wow!' Cormac gasped.

Kate picked a purple flower off a tree. The twisted vines of wisteria hung from the branches, filling the air with sugary sweetness. She held the delicate petals to her nose and inhaled deeply.

'You can see why we call this place Niwa,' said Makoto.

Ghost spun around slowly, taking in the breathtaking panorama. 'I've never seen anything like this.'

'If you are having second thoughts about joining us,' said Makoto, 'speak now, before we step inside.' His gaze moved from face to face, but nobody spoke.

Inside where? Cormac looked around.

Makoto tapped the communication device on his chest and spoke into it. Something clicked nearby, followed by an electric whirring noise.

Four hydraulic rams pushed a square section of the ground into the air. It stopped at head height, making it look like a weird pagoda with a grass roof and four steel legs. A black hole yawned beneath it with steps leading down into the darkness.

PART TWO: RENKONDO

'Welcome to Renkondo,' said Makoto. 'Renkon means "lotus root".'

'Root? The Garden? Black Lotus?' said Kate. 'What's with all the gardening terms?'

Makoto smiled, the sun sparkling in his single brown eye. 'The lotus flower only grows in muddy water. It shows that beauty and hope can blossom in the darkest of places.'

Kate nodded.

'Black is the colour of night, the colour of shadows. It doesn't call attention to itself – it goes unseen. A black flower is a paradox, a contradiction. It cannot grow naturally, but can be cultivated.' He pointed down the steps into the darkness.

'Renkondo,' said Kate, finally understanding. 'The root grows underground.'

'And eventually lives in the garden,' said Makoto, gesturing at the curtains of purple wisteria hanging from branches all around them. He bowed to her and disappeared down the steps.

Kate looked at Cormac and Ghost, who were both smirking. 'What?'

'The root,' imitated Cormac in a dreamy voice, 'grows underground and blossoms in the garden of life.'

Ghost burst out laughing.

'Get lost!' Kate said, following Makoto down into the darkness. But if they could have seen her face they'd have known she was smiling.

Cormac and Ghost followed Kate to the bottom of the steps, where she saw a chamber constructed of giant stone slabs which wouldn't have looked out of place in an Egyptian pyramid. A heavy steel door was set into one of the slabs. It had no handles, locks or hinges, just a picture of a flower embossed into the metal: a lotus. An electronic panel beside the door reminded her of *Star Trek*.

Makoto stood in front of the panel and placed his hand on a pad. A green light glowed beneath it. At the same time, an infrared beam scanned his single eye. Finally, there was a beep, and the door slid to one side.

They followed Makoto down more steps lit by feeble bulbs overhead. The roughly-hewn rock walls dripped with moisture. Kate shivered, her breath clouding in the dank air. At the bottom of the steps Makoto used a keypad to open another door and they were immediately hit by a blast of warmth.

Beyond was another ancient-looking tunnel, but unlike the stairs it was bright and dry. As they walked, Kate felt fresh air being pumped into the tunnel through ventilation shafts in the ceiling. Long fluorescent lights lit the passageway. At one point they passed a doorway which led into a vast cavern, but they were walking too quickly for her to see what was inside.

They finally arrived in a large circular room with a high rock ceiling from which more tunnels led off in different directions. Kate counted them – eight in total, each marked with a letter or letters. 'Compass points!' she exclaimed.

'That's right,' said Makoto. 'Renkondo is laid out like a wheel, each tunnel being a spoke, and this is its centre.'

He pointed towards the tunnel they'd just come down. 'The South Tunnel leads back out, but you must never leave Renkondo without permission.' He turned around to look at them, his face deadly serious. 'Understand?'

Kate and the boys nodded.

Makoto continued. 'You'll soon get used to the layout. All tunnels lead back here so it's impossible to get lost. Let me show you around.'

The teenagers followed Makoto into the North-West Tunnel, where they heard distant voices echoing. The further they walked, the louder the voices became. And the tunnel became more modern too, with tiled floors and concrete walls.

'Renkondo has grown over the centuries,'

explained Makoto. 'This is one of the more recent extensions.'

A sign hung on the wall, pointing towards the dining room. There were also noticeboards, lists of rules, trash cans and a fire extinguisher.

'This is just like a school,' said Kate.

'Because it is,' said Makoto. 'A school for shinobi.'

He stopped outside a door with a small glass window in it. He motioned for them to look through.

Inside was a classroom with a dozen students sitting at desks. Some of them looked to be the same age as Kate, but others looked older, and they all wore the same bodysuits that the shinobi in the forest had worn, except without the face masks. A Japanese lady with bobbed hair and wearing a yellow dress wrote English verbs on a whiteboard at the front of the classroom.

'Cool,' said Ghost, looking confused.

Kate rolled her eyes. 'It's a classroom, Ghost.'

He stared through the window. 'I've never been in a classroom before.'

Cormac raised his eyebrows. 'We'll see how cool you think it is after spending a few hours in one.'

Makoto led them down the corridor past more classrooms. Through the glass windows, Kate saw kids in bodysuits reading, writing, doing science experiments, meditating and practising first aid. Ghost beamed from ear to ear.

At the next junction, Makoto pointed to the left. 'Dining room is that way,' he said, before turning right.

They passed more doors, including a metal one

with a keypad and a 'No Entry' sign.

'What's in there?' asked Kate.

'Nothing,' said Makoto, clearly not wanting to discuss it.

Cormac and Ghost exchanged mischievous grins.

'What?' whispered Kate as Makoto walked ahead.

'Obviously *something* is in there,' replied Cormac.

'Something important?' added Ghost.

Kate sighed. 'It's just a door. Are you guys gonna get excited about every door and classroom you see?' She pointed ahead to where Makoto was waiting for them at another junction. 'Come on.'

They ran to catch up as Makoto turned right into a long corridor with numbered wooden doors on either side.

'We're now in the North Tunnel,' said Makoto. He stopped outside a door marked 23 and opened it. 'Cormac and Ghost, this is your room.'

The boys entered and Kate peered in from the doorway. It was bright, clean and sparsely furnished with bunk beds, a desk, two chairs and some metal lockers. An open door at the far side of the room revealed a white tiled bathroom.

'Normally I'd let you unpack,' said Makoto, 'but your bags have probably been blown into a million pieces, so we can skip that part.'

'My favourite underpants were in my bag,' sighed Ghost.

Kate laughed, but Cormac looked upset.

'Did you lose something valuable?' asked Makoto.

'Just a necklace.' Cormac put his hand up to his

chest. 'It's no big deal.'

Makoto led Kate on to room 17. Cormac and Ghost followed. The door was opened by a small girl with short brown hair pulled into two pigtails. She was wearing a tracksuit and had an open book in her hand. She closed the book and bowed.

'Chloe, I have a room-mate for you.' Makoto put his hand on Kate's shoulder. 'Meet Kate.'

'Finally!' said Chloe in an Australian accent. Her wide smile pushed the freckles on her cheeks up towards two big brown eyes. 'Good to meet you, Roomie!'

Kate shook her hand, then turned to the two boys. 'This is Cormac and Ghost.'

'Awesome! More newbies!' Chloe waved at the boys. Then she looked Kate up and down. 'Where's your stuff?'

'Long story,' replied Makoto.

'Oh,' said Chloe. 'Have you been initiated yet?' she asked Kate.

Kate looked at Makoto. 'Erm, I don't think so.'

'We're going to do it now,' said Makoto. 'They've had a tough day. Chloe, why don't you come along – help them settle in?'

Chloe's eyes widened. 'To the actual ceremony? You bet!' She flung her book on to the bunk bed.

They followed Makoto, past many more wooden doors and a security camera, until they finally returned to the circular room – the centre of the wheel.

'We've gone around in a loop!' said Cormac.

The group headed down the East Tunnel past

doors and corridors, all guarded by security cameras with red blinking lights. They passed a glass room full of people working on computers. At one point, they met a group of teenagers wearing the shimmering bodysuits. The boys and girls of various nationalities chatted and laughed together, until they saw Makoto approach. Then they fell into a reverent silence, stood to one side and bowed as he passed.

Makoto led them down a steep flight of steps into a more disused-looking tunnel. Kate shuddered to think how deep inside the mountain they must be. As they walked, she could feel the air grow cold and damp again.

'Where are we going?' she whispered to Chloe.

'To the sword room,' replied Chloe, her large eyes twinkling in the gloom.

'You seem excited.'

'I am. Most people only get to go in here once – on their first day. Thanks to you, I get to go again.'

'How long have you been here?'

'Just a few months.'

'What's it like?'

Chloe put her finger to her lips. They had reached a gigantic steel door. Like the entrance to Renkondo, it didn't have hinges, a handle or a lock. Makoto tapped his chest and spoke under his breath.

The sound of large bolts clicking open could be heard, before the door slid to one side with a hydraulic hiss. When they stepped inside, it closed behind them with a robust thud, the locking mechanisms moving back into place behind the steel plate.

They followed Makoto down a concrete tunnel, the walls of which were lined with stainless steel devices.

'Motion, sound and temperature sensors,' explained Chloe in a whisper. 'If they weren't deactivated they'd release a VX nerve agent from the overhead sprinklers. It kills upon contact. If that didn't get you, the high-energy impulse noise of over 200 decibels would shatter your eardrums and you'd be dead in seconds. Survive that and you'd be facing a series of lethal assaults from automated laser and machine guns.'

'Cool!' said Ghost, looking up at the ceiling.

'You'll learn all about it in Security Class.'

Rounding a bend in the tunnel, they arrived at a large concrete chamber, in the centre of which stood three guards wearing helmets with dark visors, full body armour and stun guns and swords on their belts. They also carried assault rifles.

'Fuyu,' whispered Chloe. 'Elite ninja guards.'

The three sentries bowed to Makoto and stepped aside to reveal a glass case on a pedestal. Inside on a wooden stand lay a sword. The deeply lacquered black scabbard reflected the overhead lights, its smooth surface inlaid with an intricately designed moon in gold and silver. *So this is the famous third sword*. Kate shivered as she thought of Goda's two crossed swords, and what it would mean for him to have all three.

Makoto removed the glass case and placed it on the ground. He then separated the hilt of the sword from the scabbard, revealing some of the polished steel engraved with flames and a moon. From behind the pedestal he produced a sheet of parchment, a pen, a small pile of cloth and a ceramic bottle and bowl. He arranged each of these carefully next to the sword, before summoning the four teenagers forward.

'Kneel,' he said.

Chloe knelt. Kate, Cormac and Ghost copied.

The room fell silent. Kate's eyes were drawn to the sword. She leant forwards to see the grain, a tempered line running down the middle of the blade. It might have been her imagination, but the metal seemed to hum and glow with a kind of energy. She looked up at Makoto, expecting something to happen. But nothing did. And then she heard the tramp of feet. Many feet.

She turned as a dozen shinobi in rippling body-suits escorted an old man into the chamber. He wore a white kimono and long silver hair hung to his shoulders. He stood in front of the four teenagers, beside Makoto and the sword, his bodyguards kneeling in a protective ring around them.

The old man's eyes were vibrant, youthful and blue. And there was something else strange about him, something about his skin, but Kate couldn't quite figure out what it was.

'This is our Jōnin,' said Makoto. 'Our leader.'

The silver-haired man bowed, examining his new recruits in silence.

'He welcomes you to the Black Lotus,' said Makoto. 'Some of you already know what it's like to live under the oppressive rule of the Empire. Some of you fear what is coming. This is why you are here. In front of you is the third Sword of Sarumara – the secret blade. It is called the Moon Sword. Were our enemies to get their hands on it, they would be unstoppable. But as long as we hold it, there is hope. The Black Lotus's sole purpose for five hundred years has been to protect this sword and work against the Samurai Empire. This is now your purpose too.'

As she watched the Jōnin, Kate realized what was strange about him: his skin glowed as if light burnt within him. He seemed lit with luminous white light. *Why doesn't he speak for himself?* She was unnerved by his silence.

'In medieval Japan,' continued Makoto, 'all teenagers were given a sword in a coming-of-age cere-mony called genpuku. This is your genpuku. Joining the Black Lotus binds you to the Moon Sword. You are its guardian – as is every member of the Black Lotus.'

Makoto called Kate forward. He pointed to a spot on the paper and told her to write the date and her signature. Half the page was covered in years and names, and after each signature there was a rust-coloured smudge. The last name on the list was Chloe Jones. Kate signed her name underneath.

Flashes of colour moved along the blade as Makoto placed a cloth beneath it. The tang of alcohol tingled in Kate's nostrils when he poured a clear liquid from the bottle into the bowl and then dribbled it over the exposed blade. It ran down over the moon-and-flames engraving and dripped on to the cloth.

Makoto turned to Kate. 'The sword is extremely

sharp so place your thumb very carefully on it until it draws blood.'

Blood! She glanced at Chloe, who nodded that it was OK.

Moving towards the sword, she gently placed her thumb on the razor edge. As soon as she felt her skin touch the metal she drew her hand away. A thin red line of blood scored her thumb.

'Now place your thumb on the page after your name,' said Makoto.

She did, leaving a scarlet thumbprint.

Makoto carefully wiped the blade with a new cloth before handing it to Kate. She wrapped it around her bleeding thumb and took her place on the floor beside Chloe.

The same ritual was repeated with Cormac and Ghost. When they were finished, Makoto said, 'Your blood binds you to the Moon Sword until the day you die.'

As he spoke, Kate never took her eyes off the Jōnin. His very presence was commanding, and beneath his silence she sensed something powerful. The man's bright blue eyes moved in a steady glare from one teenager to the next. When his gaze fell on Kate, it felt as if he was looking into her soul.

The Jōnin bowed, and left the chamber inside his protective ring of shinobi bodyguards. Makoto resheathed the blade and removed the other items, placing them inside the pedestal. He then returned the sword to its glass case and stood aside as the armed guard took up their defensive stance around it.

He motioned for them to stand. 'Let's go.'

Kate took one last look at the sword before following Makoto.

'Pretty cool, huh?' said Chloe as they approached the steel door.

'Apart from the blood.' Kate unwrapped the cloth from around her thumb. The wound had stopped bleeding, but it still stung.

'Why can't that Jōnin guy speak?' Cormac asked Chloe.

'Rumour has it that he was tortured by Kyatapira and bit off his own tongue rather than give away secrets.'

'Cool!' said Ghost.

'What's cool about that?' said Kate. 'It's disgusting.'

Makoto was waiting for them at the open steel door. 'You guys hungry?'

'Yeah!' chorused the two boys.

Kate hadn't thought about it until now, but she hadn't eaten since breakfast on the aeroplane. She was starving.

Makoto marched ahead. Kate and Chloe followed and, behind them, Ghost and Cormac talked and laughed like they'd been friends for ever.

In the dining room, around fifty other students were chatting and laughing at long wooden tables laden with food. Chloe found them spaces, and Cormac and Ghost were soon stuffing their faces with rice, sushi and other Japanese delicacies.

Kate looked across at Chloe. *All my life I thought I was a freak, that I was the only one like this. And here I am in a school—*

'I was the same,' said Chloe. 'I hid my talent until I came here.'

Kate stared at her.

'Sorry,' said Chloe, holding her hands up. 'Force of habit. I didn't mean to listen.'

'But I didn't say anything. Unless . . .'

Chloe smiled.

'No!'

Chloe laughed. 'Yes.'

'You can hear thoughts?'

Chloe smiled. 'I prefer "read minds".'

'Wow!'

Kate helped herself to some noodles and steamed vegetables. They smelt delicious.

'So what's your special power, Kate?' asked Chloe.

'You're the mind reader.'

'OK, say it in your thoughts.'

I can talk to animals.

'Awesome!' said Chloe. 'Can you understand them too?'

Kate nodded.

'I inherited my ability from my grandmother,' said Chloe. 'She was a famous fortune teller in Australia. Madame Mist was her name. Well, her stage name. Maybe you've heard of her?'

Kate shook her head.

'Has someone in your family got the same gift as

you?' Chloe asked.

'Nope.'

'I bet if you searched hard enough, you'd find someone like you – a horse whisperer, or a lion tamer, or something like that.'

'Listen, you're talking to Kate Douglas of the Douglas Family dating back to . . .'

Talking about her family hurt. So did thinking about them. Chloe probably didn't have to be a mind reader to know the conversation was over.

'Sorry,' said Chloe, shifting her attention to Ghost and Cormac instead.

'Makoto is important?' asked Ghost, nodding towards another table, where a group of adults were listening intently to Makoto. He was still wearing his black Kat uniform.

'Yes,' said Chloe. 'The Jōnin is the boss. But Makoto runs the show.'

'Who are the other guys?' asked Ghost.

'More teachers,' said Chloe. 'The small bald guy with the braided goatee is Sensei Iwamoto. He teaches martial arts, weapons and stuff. The big guy with the buzz cut is the Bear. He's an ass.'

'What does he teach?' asked Cormac.

'Physical training.'

'Important question,' said Ghost. 'Who is the lady?'

Kate looked at the only female teacher. Her skin was white and flawless, like porcelain. In contrast, her sleek hair was so black it looked almost purple.

Chloe laughed. 'Why am I not surprised? All the

guys love Ami. She's in charge of equipment, technology and gadgets. She's nice.'

From across the room, Ami glanced over at them and smiled, but quickly returned to her conversation.

'I agree,' said Ghost.

Chloe shook her head. 'I meant, she's a nice person.'

When they'd finished their meal, the teachers left the room and the students stood as they did so.

Makoto stopped at their table. 'You look like you're settling in,' he said approvingly. 'Does anyone have any questions?'

'*Please* can we get rid of these tattoos now?' asked Cormac, holding up his wrists.

Makoto nodded.

Cormac immediately began rubbing his wrist, the temporary sword tattoo flaking on to the table like ashes. Kate and Ghost copied. Kate's sense of relief when the ink was gone surprised her. It felt like she'd just removed handcuffs.

Ghost raised his hand. 'Why do you speak English, not Japanese?'

'The Japanese language is still our mother tongue, but when the Black Lotus first formed in medieval Japan, they used English as a means to communicate secretly. When we began to recruit people from around the world, it made sense to continue using this "international" language.'

A bell rang overhead.

'What's that?' asked Kate.

'That's the lights-out bell. We're quite strict here about bedtimes. Once the bell goes, you are not permitted to leave your room. You guys should be in bed – we've an early start in the morning.'

Makoto seemed to be waiting for a reply so they all nodded.

'Then I'll say goodnight.' He bowed. 'I'll see you in the morning.'

It's me.

Ghost's eyes snapped open. *Miguel!* His heart was beating like crazy. He looked around, but could see nothing in the pitch dark. Trembling, he leapt from the bed and switched on the light. Nothing. He was sure he'd heard it.

His brother's voice.

'What the . . .?' grumbled Cormac from the bottom bunk.

Ghost threw open the bathroom door and flicked the switch. His reflection stared back at him from the mirror. He was plastered in sweat.

'What's wrong?' asked Cormac.

'Nothing – just a dream.' He switched off the lights and climbed back into bed. It hadn't felt like a dream. It had felt like his little brother was really speaking to him. But it couldn't be true. Miguel was dead. He had died in the fire two years ago.

The scar on his chest burnt as the day replayed in his mind like a video clip.

As two orphans living alone in the favela, Ghost was solely responsible for Miguel's care. Normally, he didn't mind, but that day his friends had organized a big football match in the street, so he'd left Miguel in front of the TV.

Miguel hated being left alone, and he'd pleaded with Ghost not to go, but Ghost didn't listen.

His team was a goal down with only five minutes left. When the ball landed at his feet, he took off down the left wing, skipping over a sliding tackle. As he approached the goal, someone shouted 'Kats!' Everyone ran.

Gunshots exploded nearby, followed by three young men sprinting across the street and into Ghost's block of shacks. In the brief moment of silence that followed, a faint blare of TV cartoons drifted down from Ghost's open window.

From behind the burnt-out shell of a car, Ghost watched in horror as the Kats launched a firebomb at his house. The mish mash of wood, cardboard and plastic immediately burst into flames. People poured out of the building, shouting, pushing and carrying small children. He battled through them and was almost to the stairs when his friends stopped him. He screamed and kicked, and tried to run into the crumbling bonfire just as another explosion blasted him into unconsciousness.

Cormac grumbled something in his sleep, snapping Ghost out of his flashback. He rubbed his chest, and blinked away the tears.

For the remainder of the night, Ghost slept restlessly. He was awake when the bedroom door flew open and the lights came on.

'Rise and shine, ladies!' shouted a man in an American accent. 'You got four minutes to get your butts dressed and outside.'

Ghost recognized the guy. What had Chloe said his name was? Wolf or Bear or something? He was built like a mountain, hardened muscle bulging beneath his army fatigues. Even his head seemed to be carved from a cube of granite, his blond buzz cut formed into four sharp corners on top.

The door slammed shut.

Ghost climbed down out of the bunk and poked Cormac, who was shielding his eyes under the blanket.

'What time is it?' he groaned.

Ghost put on the T-shirt and tracksuit bottoms he'd been wearing yesterday. 'Time to get up.'

This was so weird. Living alone, he would get up whenever he felt like it. Every morning, he'd open the door of his hut and see how high the sun was in the sky before deciding what to do. Now, here he was in a school, deep inside the middle of a mountain, being told when to get up.

Bleary-eyed, the boys dressed and together they stepped out into the hallway. A line of kids stood waiting, hands by their sides. They were all – except Cormac and Ghost and a little further down the line, Kate – wearing the same shimmering bodysuits.

'Good morning, fresh meat!' shouted the army guy, clearly addressing Ghost and Cormac. 'My name is the Bear. When I say four minutes, I mean four minutes, not . . .' He looked at his stopwatch. 'Six minutes and five seconds.' He grinned. 'You've just used two of tomorrow's minutes, so tomorrow morning, everyone has *two* minutes to be outside their door, *standing to attention*.'

The boys straightened up, squaring their shoulders.

'Now follow me!' shouted the Bear, marching down the corridor.

A small, stocky boy beside Ghost turned to him with narrowed eyes. 'Thank you!' he spat in a heavy accent. Ghost recognized him – the helicopter pilot. He had a shaved head and hard, cold eyes.

But Ghost had met worse than him in the favela. 'No problem, my friend.'

The boy seemed confused for a second before turning and marching down the corridor with the rest of the recruits. From the circular room, they took the South Tunnel, leading towards the exit. This lifted Ghost's spirits, because although for the most part Renkondo was bright, warm and fresh, it felt unnatural to be deprived of sun and sky.

But instead of continuing straight ahead towards the exit, they turned right into a gigantic cavern carved out of the rock. Ghost remembered passing it the previous day. It was easily the size of a small football stadium. The centre of the cavern was filled with all sorts of wooden equipment, like soldiers might use on an assault course. Pillars of sunlight streamed in at different angles through holes in the ceiling, lighting the place up like spotlights.

A gravel path ran around the edge of the cavern, and on it stood the Bear, hands on hips, waiting.

'The first part of your training is fitness,' he barked, 'and you'll do that every morning with me. Do at least three laps, and as many as you can after that.'

From a rucksack at his feet, he removed a clipboard and pen. 'Well, what are you waiting for?' he bellowed.

The group took off running. Concentrating on not tripping over in the tight bunch of runners, Ghost moved closer to the inside of the track because that meant shorter laps.

Cormac joined him. 'You OK?'

'Yes.'

'You didn't sleep very well.'

'Nightdream.'

'Nightmare?'

'Yes.' *I hope that's all it was.* That voice, Miguel's voice, had seemed so real.

A boy pushed between them, sending Ghost stumbling. The stocky boy who'd spoken to Ghost outside their bedroom looked back and smirked.

'What's his problem?' asked Cormac.

'Ice Man got into bed on the wrong side.'

Cormac laughed. 'Where did you get all these sayings?'

'I have a book,' replied Ghost. '*1001 English Phrases*.'

They completed their first lap, the Bear marking his clipboard as they ran past. By the second lap, the group of runners had started to spread out, some beginning to lag behind, others joining the Ice Man up at the front. Instead of running, one girl bounced past them like a kangaroo. Her muscular legs propelled her forwards in five-metre bounds. The boys stared in amazement.

After completing the third lap, most of the group pulled out, falling on to the ground with exhaustion.

'Pathetic!' barked the Bear.

Of the runners remaining on the track, Bouncy Girl and Ice Man were in the lead, but Kate wasn't far behind them. Ghost wasn't a great runner, and was starting to get a stitch. By the end of the fourth lap, though, his side was killing him.

'I'm out,' he panted as Cormac hesitated beside him. 'You go on.'

Cormac nodded, not a bead of sweat on his face.

Ghost left the track and collapsed on the ground as Cormac shot off towards the front of the group. Those seated around Ghost gasped at Cormac's speed as he overtook Kate, Bouncy Girl and Ice Man. By the fifth lap he had passed the other runners so many times that they all dropped out in frustration, until he was the only runner left. He sped around the track like a racing car until the Bear finally called him in.

'Beginner's luck, I'd say,' said the Bear. 'Let's see how you do tomorrow.'

Cormac sat on the ground between Ghost and a red-faced Kate.

'Show off,' she said. But Ghost could see she was as impressed as everyone else.

The Bear led them back to the dining room for breakfast. Cormac, Kate and Ghost sat together at a table laden with pickles and fish.

Kate's nose wrinkled. 'Don't suppose they have Cheerios?'

'What are Cheerios?' asked Ghost, filling his plate.

'Never mind,' she replied, reaching for some fish. 'I'm so hungry I could eat a horse.'

'But it's fish,' added Ghost.

Kate laughed before shaking her head and biting into the fish. Her facial expression changed from caution to pleasure. 'Actually, it's not bad.' She poured herself a glass of water. 'So, guys, what do you think of the place?'

'I think it's cool,' said Cormac.

Ghost didn't answer.

'Don't you think it's all a bit weird?' said Kate. 'As if there's something they're not telling us?'

'Yes!' Cormac put down his cup. 'I was thinking the same thing!'

'Explain,' said Ghost.

'Well,' said Kate. 'They say the purpose of the Black Lotus is to keep this sword from the Empire, right?'

The boys agreed.

'But you saw it. It's just a sword. What could be so special about it that they need an army of ninjas with superpowers to guard it?' Kate paused. 'There's more to this than meets the eye.'

As Ghost was trying to make sense of this new phrase, the Bear and the other teachers entered the dining room. He called out names from his clipboard and escorted a group of students out. One by one, the other teachers did the same, until there was just Cormac, Ghost, Kate and the technology teacher, Ami, left.

This morning, Ami wore a figure-hugging body-suit which rippled with a thousand colours as she walked. When she stepped closer, Ghost smelt her perfume – a rich vanilla fragrance.

He bowed low. 'I'm Ghost.'

'Pleased to meet you. From Rio de Janeiro, right?'

Ghost nodded eagerly.

Ami turned to Cormac. 'And you must be Cormac, from Ireland?'

'Yes,' said Cormac.

Kate bowed her head. 'I'm Kate from New York City.'

'Ah,' said Ami. 'Times Square is my favourite place in all of America.'

Kate smiled.

'Anyway,' said Ami. 'Your next class is with me.'

She led them out of the dining room and down the corridor past the metal door with the keypad and

'No Entry' sign.

She stopped outside a wooden louvred door, and looked at them with eyes as dark as her hair. 'When I call, come in and find me.' She opened the door, disappeared inside and closed it again.

Eyebrows arched, Kate glanced at Cormac and Ghost. It seemed like she was about to say something when Ami called out from the room.

Ghost pushed open the door and entered a grey room with a black-tiled floor. Five changing cubicles, like those in a department store, lined the far wall. Their curtains were open, revealing a coat hook and wooden stool in each. Apart from a large mirror on another wall and a red suitcase in one corner, the room was empty – no Ami, no other exits and nowhere to hide.

Ghost's first thought was that Ami must be like him – she could turn invisible. And he wasn't sure how he felt about that. Glad to have a kindred spirit? Or envious that someone else in the world had the Bleaching too?

Cormac stood in the middle of the room looking around, dumbfounded. Kate nodded towards the suitcase.

'I'm not in the suitcase.'

The three kids spun around in the direction of Ami's voice, but she was nowhere to be seen.

'I'm in the middle cubicle.'

Ghost walked closer, scanning the cubicle for some sign of a hidden doorway. As he reached the cubicle, the interior undulated, and Ami emerged from the wall. He could only see her because she was moving, but her suit had taken on the exact colour of the wall. To the unsuspecting eye, she was invisible.

She pulled down her balaclava-like hood and shook her dark hair free. Now that she'd stopped moving, her head seemed to float in mid-air.

Ghost remembered the way the suits had made the shinobi in the forest disappear. He didn't think they would have worked so well indoors.

'Please tell me we get to wear one of these suits,' said Kate, her blue eyes big and bright.

It was only when Ami moved, stepping out of the cubicle, that they could see her body again. 'The suit is called a shinobi shōzoku. It is made from millions of tiny mirrored beads. Each bead is weighted and reacts to the earth's gravitational pull. Regardless of the wearer's position, the mirrored surface of each bead faces sideways or downwards, but never upwards. Therefore, the suit always reflects the environment around it, never the sky. It will camouflage you anywhere. But it only works if you stay still. As soon as you move, you become visible again.'

She walked over to the red suitcase, unzipped it and removed another beaded suit. It changed from red to grey as she pulled it out. Kate let out a squeal of delight.

Ami checked the label inside before handing it to Kate. 'Your shōzoku has been custom-made to fit you perfectly.' She handed one to Cormac. 'Each is lined with ballistic fibres, which makes it highly resistant to bullets and blades.' She handed one to Ghost.

He examined the beaded suit. Cormac and Kate were clearly more excited about their new clothes than he was. Because Ghost didn't need a special suit to turn invisible. That was his skill, the thing that made him different from all the other kids here. But if they could all now turn invisible too, how was Ghost going to shine like Cormac had done earlier?

Ami handed them each a pair of boots made from the same beaded material, and pointed towards the cubicles. 'Now, get changed.'

In the cubicle, Ghost pulled the curtain. This suit couldn't really make someone invisible. It was just a trick. Ami had said it only worked when you stayed still. Ghost was the only one who could truly disappear. Perhaps he'd just have to work harder to outshine the others.

He undressed and changed into his new gear. He marvelled at how well the suit fitted him. Normally, Ghost hated new clothes, but these felt different, more like a second skin. He put his arm on the seat of the wooden stool and watched the tiny mirrored beads change colour from grey to pine.

Pulling back his curtain, he found Cormac and Kate looking at themselves in the mirror. They looked good, especially Kate, the tight-fitting suit accentuating her trim, athletic figure.

Ami showed them how to remove the hood from the back of the suit and fit it over the face so that only their eyes showed.

'The cowls have integrated earpieces and microphones to allow you to communicate with any shinobi in a two-mile radius. To activate the comm, you must tap the small disc on your chest twice. Remember, whatever you say into the comm will be heard by *every* shinobi. Comms can also be detached and used without the shōzoku.'

She unclipped the comm from the cowl and held up the earpiece and microphone, which were connected by a wire.

'Detached, it is activated by a tiny button on the microphone.'

They each practised removing and replacing their comms.

Ami then pulled a transparent mask up from the neck of her shōzoku and sealed it around her face like a ziplock bag.

'Once the mask is sealed, it supplies oxygen from chambers in the suit. When not in use, these chambers automatically replenish. It is very effective under water or in smoke or gas, but the oxygen supply is limited to five minutes, so be careful. You will hear a beep in your comm when you have one minute left.'

Ghost pulled his mask up and mimed walking on the moon. He tapped the disc on his chest, and said, 'One small step for man.' He made a crackling noise like static, and pointed at Kate. 'One big step for woman.'

Everybody laughed, even Ami.

'There are hidden storage compartments all over your shōzoku, designed to hold specific pieces of equipment which you will receive during training. Whenever you can, practise using your cowl, comm and mask so that when you need to use them, they'll be second nature to you.'

'I thought ninjas dressed in black?' said Cormac.

'They dressed to fit in with their surroundings,' replied Ami. 'In the snow they wore white, in the forest they wore green, but mostly they dressed like the people around them. For night missions, however, they did wear black.'

She held up her wrist and turned down the sleeve of her shōzoku, revealing a small button inside. 'In night mode, the magnetized beads turn their reflective surface inwards.'

When she pressed the button, the mirrored balls shifted and the shōzoku morphed to black.

Everybody 'oohed.'

'For now, get used to the suits. They are your uniform. You must wear them every day. And don't worry about washing them – they're self-cleaning.'

They brought their old clothes back to their bedrooms, and then separated. Kate, because she wasn't from the Empire, joined a Japanese class for beginners. Cormac took an intermediate Japanese class, and Ghost joined an intermediate English class with four other teenagers. One of his classmates was Ice Man, whose real name turned out to be Kristjan.

Ghost had seen kids in Rio heading to and from school and he'd always wondered what it would be like. He couldn't believe he was now actually going to school – though he suspected most schools weren't like this one.

It turned out that learning English in a classroom

wasn't nearly as much fun as practising it on English-speaking tourists in Rio, while secretly removing their wallets and purses. Cormac had been right – after an hour of grammar exercises, Ghost never wanted to see a classroom again.

When class was over, he met his friends for lunch in the dining room.

'So, Ghost,' said Kate, 'how was your first lesson in a classroom?'

'Boring,' said Ghost, plonking his tray of food down.

Cormac and Kate laughed. Over lunch they chatted about the teachers they'd had, the other students and the bizarre school where they were now pupils.

'I'd love to get a proper look around,' said Cormac.

Ghost agreed. 'Lots of tunnels we haven't been in yet.'

'Maybe we can explore later,' said Kate.

But their afternoon was so busy they didn't get a chance. They had a history lesson with Makoto, followed by a Japanese culture lesson with Miss Taneka, and the day finished with more physical training with the Bear.

By the time Ghost sat down to dinner that night, he was too exhausted to even think about exploring. It seemed the others were too.

'We'll do it tomorrow,' said Cormac. 'All I'm fit for is bed.'

'Me too,' said Ghost, nodding. 'I'm cat tired.'

Kate laughed.

'What?' asked Ghost.

Kate shook her head and smiled. 'Nothing. I'm cat tired too.'

The days were jam-packed full of activities – physical training, mainly, but plenty of classes too: botany, security, meditation and first aid. Cormac hated the Japanese classes because they reminded him of his school back in Ireland. Ghost was moved up to the advanced English class and he was becoming more fluent by the day, though he still mixed up a lot of the phrases from his book. Kate loved the history classes. In school she'd only learnt American history, so the history of the Empire was new and exciting to her. And, now, relevant.

But even so, at the end of the fourth day they still weren't ready to give up on the idea of exploring the school.

'We haven't a spare minute in the day,' said Kate.

'True,' said Cormac. 'But there's always the night.'

Kate frowned at him. 'We're not allowed out of our rooms.'

Cormac shrugged and looked at Ghost. 'Are you up for it?'

Ghost nodded.

'But what about the cameras?' asked Kate.

'We'll avoid them. They're not in every tunnel.'

Kate hesitated. 'I don't know. I'd hate to see what the punishment is in this place.'

'It's fine,' said Cormac. 'Myself and Ghost will go.'

'Jeez!' said Kate. 'I can't let you two go alone. God knows what trouble you'd get into.'

Cormac smiled. 'So we're all in?'

'I guess so,' said Kate.

Cormac and Ghost lay in the dark, fully dressed, waiting for Kate. Voices quieted, doors closed and silence descended on Renkondo as everyone went to sleep. It reminded Cormac of nights in the Hinin House when he'd done the same – waited until all lights were out and the place had fallen silent, before stealing out of the window. Those nights running up walls and skipping across the rooftops while Ballyhook slept were the only things he missed from his old life.

He reached for his mother's crucifix before remembering it was gone. He'd never forget the day she gave it to him.

He was about seven years old. His father was gazing out of the window of their small cottage by the sea when suddenly he pulled the curtains closed.

'What is it?' asked his mother, rushing into the kitchen.

'Kats,' said his father. He knelt down in front of him. 'I love you, son,' he said, kissing Cormac on the forehead. He hugged his wife and dashed out of the back door.

His mother held Cormac's hand and together they watched the front door. There was a loud knock and a gruff voice shouted, 'Kyatapira!'

His mother opened the door to three men in black uniforms. 'Where is he?' one of them barked.

'He's not here,' she replied.

They pushed past her and began searching the house. While they were alone, his mother removed the cross from underneath her blouse and put it around Cormac's neck, under his shirt. 'Always keep it hidden.'

When they couldn't find his father, they took Cormac instead. Took him from his mother's arms, as the tears ran down her face. Took him to a town many miles away. Took him to a Hinin House.

He'd always wondered why Kyatapira wanted his father, but now a thought occurred to him for the first time. *What if my father was a Black Lotus agent and that's why the Kats were after him? Perhaps I inherited my gift from my father?*

There was a gentle knock on the door and then it opened, the room brightening as light spilt in from the corridor. Cormac sat up. Kate closed the door gently.

'You guys ready?' she asked, her face lit by the

thin crack of light coming through the bathroom door.

Ghost climbed down from his bunk.

Cormac moved to the door. 'Is the coast clear?'

Kate pushed a strand of blonde hair off her face and nodded. 'Where are we going, exactly?'

'That circular room – the hub – is probably a good place to start. There're four tunnels we haven't been in yet.'

'But there's a camera at the end of this corridor.'

'So we go the other way, around by the class-rooms.'

Kate shrugged, and Cormac eased the door open and poked his head out, looking left and right, before leaving the room.

They crept down the corridor, past rooms full of sleeping students. At the end of the hallway they turned left and saw the metal door with the keypad and 'No Entry' sign.

Ghost turned to Cormac, eyebrows raised.

Cormac nodded, and together they pushed and pulled at the door, but it wouldn't budge.

Kate put her fingers to her lips, her eyes wide with alarm.

'What is it?'

She pointed to her ear and then down the corridor towards the bedrooms.

Cormac heard it too – the unmistakable sound of footsteps. Getting closer. 'Hide!'

They ran ahead and turned left towards the classrooms. Cormac tried a door, but it was locked. He tried another narrower wooden door. It swung open and all three of them bundled into a small, dark room full of buckets, mops and detergents. Cormac pulled the door, but didn't fully close it. They heard the footsteps stop, then beeps, a click and the bang of a metal door shutting.

Cormac whispered to Kate and Ghost. 'We can't get into that room without a code.'

'Yes, we can,' said Ghost.

'What do you mean?' Kate asked.

'I can become invisible.'

'You mean, with your shōzoku?'

'No, properly invisible. I can really disappear.'

'Are you serious?' Kate turned to Cormac. He shrugged, speechless.

'I can become invisible and wait at the door until whoever's in there comes out. Then I can sneak in before the door shuts.'

'Awesome,' said Cormac.

'I must go naked first,' Ghost said.

Kate held up both hands. 'Hold on. What do you mean by "go naked"?'

Ghost grinned, his eyes and teeth glowing white in the darkness. 'Close your eyes.'

He fumbled for the zip on his shōzoku, but Kate stopped him. 'Can't you turn invisible first? And *then* take off your clothes?'

'Yes, but it is not so much fun.'

'Tough! That's the way you're gonna do it.'

Ghost looked at her and then Cormac. 'In private, please?'

Cormac and Kate turned their backs.

Ghost breathed heavily behind them – long, deep breaths, followed by a period of silence, and then a sharp hissing inhalation.

'You can turn around now,' he said.

Cormac gulped. The light coming through the gap in the door revealed a figure dressed in a shōzoku and boots, but with no head or hands.

Kate leant forwards. 'That's so weird.'

'And talking to the animals is so normal,' said Ghost.

They heard the shōzoku unzip.

Kate turned her back again. 'You could have warned us.'

Cormac laughed. 'But you can't see anything.'

'It's still weird.'

The sleeves of the shōzoku wiggled and became limp as Ghost undressed. The boots were kicked off next, followed by two white socks. The suit rolled the rest of the way down to the floor, uncovering a pair of white underpants.

'Well, there's something you don't see every day,' said Cormac, but Kate refused to turn around.

The underpants hovered in mid-air, wiggling from side to side. Cormac tried to smother his laughter.

Then the underpants dropped to the floor, floated back upwards and flew towards Cormac, hitting him in the face.

'Yuck!' He peeled them off, and flung them to the ground. Ghost sniggered.

'Are you guys done messing around?' asked Kate.

Cormac leant towards her. 'You can look now.'

Slowly, she turned around. Her eyes darted to the pile of clothes on the floor. 'This is so weird.' She put her hand out in front of her, feeling for Ghost. 'I don't even know where you— Ah!'

She recoiled instantly, stepping back into an empty bucket.

'Shh!' said Ghost.

'What did I touch?'

'My belly.'

'It felt like a butt.'

Ghost's voice sounded serious all of a sudden. 'I should hurry. You wait here.'

The door opened, and they heard Ghost leave.

Cormac pulled the door closed, plunging the room into darkness. He shifted his weight. He could hear Kate's clothes rustling. 'You OK?' he asked.

'Yeah. Thanks.'

Silence.

'You were pretty awesome on the track today,' said Kate.

'Thanks.' *You're pretty awesome yourself.*

'This ninja school is kind of weird, isn't it?'

'Yeah, but it's growing on me. For the first time in a long while, I feel I belong.'

'Me too,' Kate agreed.

'You miss your family?' asked Cormac.

'Yes. But I missed them long before I came here.'

Her voice wobbled and Cormac decided not to ask any more questions.

They waited in silent darkness for a long time

until they heard the sound of the metal door opening. Footsteps receded into the distance. Cormac gathered up Ghost's clothes. 'Let's go.'

They stepped back into the corridor. Cormac crept to the corner and peered around. Nobody. And the metal door was closed.

'Ghost?' he whispered.

No reply.

Kate knocked softly on the metal door and smiled when it clicked open.

'Ah, Cormac and Kate. Come in. Have a cup of tea,' said the still-invisible Ghost. They followed him inside and Ghost shut the door behind them. 'Sorry it took so long. The Jōnin guy was in here for ages.'

'The Jōnin was here?' asked Kate.

'I knew there was something important in this room,' said Cormac.

Kate looked around. 'What is this place?'

Cormac peered at the gigantic high-ceilinged room. A map of the world covered three entire walls.

'I get dressed,' said Ghost.

Cormac felt the garments being pulled from his hands, then watched them float magically towards the door.

'I'll stay on guard out here,' said Ghost. 'I'll knock if I hear people coming.'

The door clicked closed behind him. The floor-to-ceiling map was covered in little coloured pins, each labelled with a year. The pins were all connected to each other by coloured string, forming a multi-coloured web. Some of the strings led to pieces of paper – small handwritten notes and newspaper articles in many languages.

Cormac walked around the room, his eyes zooming in on the text in English.

Soldiers of Malian Empire Killed by Oriental Swordsman, Africa, 1370 . . . Attack on London Lady Foiled by Two Floating Boys' Heads, 1870 . . . Samurai Prospector Enters American Gold Rush, 1860 . . . Archaeologists report evidence of an electromagnetic disturbance in Japan in the year 1540 that warped all metals . . .

A rapid knocking made Cormac jump. He and Kate raced back to the door and pulled it open.

Ghost was now clothed and visible. 'Someone's coming,' he whispered urgently.

Pulling the door closed behind them, they hurried back to the boys' bedroom.

'Were we seen?' said Cormac once they were in.

Kate sat on the bed. 'I don't think so.'

'I don't know why they lock the door,' said Ghost. 'Who would want to steal a map?'

'I think it's more to do with what was written on the map,' said Cormac, looking at Kate. 'Could you make sense of it?'

'Not really.'

'Some of the information was weird,' Cormac said. 'Something about an electromagnetic disturbance in medieval Japan. And a samurai prospector in the American gold rush.'

'What's that got to do with the Black Lotus, and the Moon Sword?' Kate asked.

Cormac shrugged. 'Who knows?'

That map room contained something important – he knew it. Why else would the Jōnin be there alone? There was something about the Black Lotus that they weren't being told.

After a thoughtful silence, Kate stood up.

'Thanks for coming,' said Cormac.

She smiled. 'See you at breakfast.'

'Yeah, in about four hours' time.'

The next morning, the Bear took them back to the large cavern, but instead of getting them to run laps he gave them each a rope which was to be stored in a pocket in their shōzokus. For two hours they practised throwing their ropes over a pole suspended ten metres overhead, tying some complicated ninja knot, climbing to the top of the rope, sliding back down, undoing the knot and then doing it all over again.

Kate coped all right with the rope-throwing and knot-tying, but no matter how hard she tried she couldn't manage to climb more than a couple of metres off the ground. She thought the class would never end.

After breakfast, the students were divided into groups. Ami took a small group which included Cormac, Kate and Ghost. They were all yawning after their late night, but woke up when they learnt they were to go up to Niwa, the Garden.

Kate's heart did a little somersault. She missed the outdoors, the open space and fresh air – having lived on the streets for a while, she'd got used to the feeling of the sun on her face and the wind in her hair. But even more, she missed the everyday chatter of animals and birds. She hadn't heard a single one underground.

'Though it's a safe zone,' said Ami as she led them from the dining room, 'it's still visible from the air. If you hear aircraft in the sky, hide under a tree. If this is not possible, just lie on the ground and stay still. Your shōzoku will do the rest.'

'We're going outside!' whispered Kate.

'I know,' replied Ghost. 'I feel like I have been in the ground for a long time.'

Ami, clipboard in hand, led them along the West Tunnel.

'This is not the way Makoto brought us,' said Cormac.

'There must be more than one entrance,' Kate agreed.

At the end of a long flight of concrete steps, Ami punched a number into a keypad on a metal trapdoor above her head. When the lock beeped and clicked open, she pushed the trapdoor up. Sunlight streamed into the tunnel, dazzling everybody. Kate closed her eyes and felt the warmth of it on her face. A cool breeze ruffled her hair and the sweet smell of the forest filled her nostrils. She smiled. Even from here she could hear two birds arguing over a spider one of them had just found. *If there are animals here, it must mean there are no ninjas hidden in the trees.*

When everyone had climbed out of the tunnel, Ami closed the trapdoor and made sure that the creepers which had grown over the door covered every bit of metal.

Kate had no idea what time it was, but she knew it was still early because the sun was low in the sky. It pierced the overhead canopy of oaks and conifers in diagonal beams of white light, illuminating the ferns and grasses which grew between the trees. The forest was moist with dew and smelt fresh and fragrant.

Nearby, some green tape was tied from tree to tree in a long line, disappearing out of sight. Ami led them under it.

'Stealth is the shinobi's best weapon,' she said, bringing them to a stop. 'Even hundreds of years ago, they could enter guarded castles unseen, or hide for days without moving. Some say they could even become invisible. Your shōzoku will help you blend in, but you must also learn patience, how to slow down your heart, control your breathing. Much of it is psychological.

'Go and hide. Become a shadow. Blend into the forest – become a part of it – but do not go outside the green tape. Imagine your life depends on it. Shan will be seeker today.'

A small Chinese boy stepped forward.

The other students moaned. 'Not Shan,' said someone.

'Why not Shan?' Kate whispered to Chloe.

'You'll see.'

'Seeking is the second skill you must learn,' said Ami. 'At all times, a shinobi must be aware. This is called zanshin. Learn to look where no one looks. Learn to see the unseen. If you are found, you become a seeker with Shan. The game is over when everybody is found.'

Ami clicked her stopwatch. 'Go!'

The group split up, running in all directions into the forest. After a few minutes of searching, Kate found a hollow under the roots of a tree. She crawled into it, pulling loose branches on top of her. The ground was cool and damp. She listened hard. No one seemed to have followed her into this part of the woods.

She closed her eyes and breathed in the smell of the earth and trees. She wondered what was going on back home. Had America been invaded yet? And then she thought of her parents in prison, her brother in foster care. Were they OK?

She sank deeper into the leaves, trying not to think about it, letting go, relaxing, becoming a part of the forest . . .

A rustling in the leaves woke her. A few centimetres away, a small brown mouse watched her intently with dark glassy eyes. Its whiskers twitched with curiosity. Kate smiled and twitched her nose back. The mouse didn't move.

'Hi,' said Kate.

The mouse crept a little closer. 'In my house you are.'

'I'm sorry,' said Kate. 'I'm not staying.'

The mouse scampered right up to her, so close its whiskers tickled her face.

'What's your name?' asked Kate.

'A name what is?'

Of course, wild animals don't have names.

'Hungry I am. Food you have?'

Kate smiled. Wild animals were a lot like boys. Their speech was limited and they were always hungry. 'No, but I'll be getting some later.'

The mouse's ears pricked. 'Coming somebody is. With you I go?'

Kate placed him in one of the shōzoku's concealed pockets.

Minutes later, Shan uncovered her hideout. 'Organic soap?' he asked, sniffing the air.

'So unfair,' she muttered.

She followed him as he sniffed his way over to a very tall tree. Looking up, they saw Cormac hiding in the branches.

'Spotted you a mile away,' she said as he climbed down and dropped to the ground.

'Yeah, I suppose climbing a tree was a bit obvious. After all, any eejit can climb.' He laughed and Kate punched his arm – she didn't need to be reminded about her performance in the climbing class that morning.

Soon everyone had been found, except Ghost. They searched for an hour to no avail. Shan kept claiming he could smell him, but, wherever Ghost was hiding, he couldn't be found. Kate smiled to herself at the thought that he was probably standing right in front of them, stark naked.

Eventually they had to give up and Ami called for him to reveal himself. A minute later, Ghost emerged from behind a bush, adjusting his shōzoku. Even though he was shivering, he grinned cheekily.

'Well done, Ghost,' said Ami, marking her clipboard. She glanced at him, a small smile on her lips, then headed back to the trapdoor.

'I don't understand,' said Shan, frustrated. 'Why couldn't I find you?'

'A bird in the bush is worth two in the hand,' replied Ghost, running after Ami.

Shan looked at Kate. 'What is he talking about?'

She glanced at Cormac, who was smiling. 'I wouldn't worry about it, Shan.'

Kate had just slurped the last noodle from her bowl at dinner when she felt a scratching in her pocket. *The mouse!* For some reason she didn't want to tell anyone about him yet.

She wiped her mouth and stood up. 'I'm off to bed.'

'Already?' asked Chloe.

'Yeah, I'm tired.'

Chloe smiled. 'I'll try not to wake you.'

She stuffed a handful of leftover rice into a napkin and said, in answer to Chloe's questioning expression, 'You can never have enough rice.'

In her bedroom, the mouse climbed out of her pocket and Kate put him on her bed. She sprinkled some of the sticky rice in front of him. He devoured the lot, then asked for more.

'Savage,' she said, laughing. 'That's what I'll call you – Savage.'

The mouse looked up, his cheeks full of rice.

She knelt down beside the bed. 'I'm taking you back to the forest tomorrow.'

'Here nice is,' he squeaked.

She smiled at the funny way he spoke. 'That's just the rice talking.'

'No, to stay I want.'

'Fine, but don't let my room-mate see you. Not all humans like mice as much as I do.'

It's me. Miguel.

Ghost opened his eyes. He could hear Cormac breathing in the dark in the bed below him.

The scar on his chest burnt. *Miguel?*

Every night since he'd arrived at Renkondo, his little brother had spoken to him in his dreams. But it never felt like a dream – it felt real. It was as if Miguel was trying to contact him from the dead.

If only I could talk back . . .

He closed his eyes. *Miguel?*

Nothing.

He wondered if he should tell Cormac. It might help to talk to someone.

Ghost felt like he had only just fallen asleep when the Bear hammered on their door, waking them for their early-morning run.

After breakfast, the students went back to the cavern gym for more rope climbing.

'You look tired,' said Cormac, pulling his rope from his shōzoku.

Ghost yawned. 'Not much sleep.'

'More nightmares?'

Ghost hesitated. 'Just . . . thinking.'

'About what?'

Should I tell him? Surely it couldn't do any harm? He glanced around to check no one else was listening. 'Every night, I hear voi—'

Don't tell him, please . . .

Ghost staggered back. *Miguel?*

'Ghost,' said Cormac. 'Are you all right?'

Miguel, is it really you?

Yes, it's me. Do you not recognize me?

I do, but . . .

But what?

You're . . .

Dead? That's right. But it wasn't your fault.

Cormac squeezed his arm. 'Every night you hear what?'

Please don't tell him.

But he's my friend . . .

These people are not your friends. You shouldn't trust them. Trust nobody here.

'You can tell me,' said Cormac.

Ghost shook his head, though he was desperate to confide in someone.

'C'mon, what were you gonna say? Every night you hear what?'

He pulled out of Cormac's grip. He wanted to tell, but couldn't. 'Nothing,' he muttered.

He moved further up the line of kids, away from Cormac. He pulled out his rope and looked back. Kate had taken his spot and was talking to Cormac. She glanced up the line at Ghost, her face pulled into a frown.

They're talking about you.

'C'mon, Ghostbuster!' shouted the Bear. 'Wakey, wakey!'

Ghost grabbed the end of the rope in one hand and the remaining coil in the other. He looked up at the pole above his head.

Miguel?

No answer.

He threw the rope.

That night, as Ghost pulled off his shōzoku and climbed into bed, every muscle ached. But that was nothing compared to the tempest in his head. The same question had whirled around all day inside his skull. Was Miguel really talking to him from the dead? Ghost had never believed in heaven or an afterlife, but maybe . . .

Cormac came into the room, undressed and got into bed. He took a deep breath before speaking. 'Look, man. If I did something to upset you earlier, I'm sorry.'

Ghost swallowed.

'Something's wrong, isn't it?'

'I'm fine,' said Ghost.

'You know you can tell me anything.'

'Thanks.'

Cormac switched off the light. Ghost stared at the sliver of light beneath the door. More than anything, he wanted to talk to Cormac. But Miguel had said not to. All day he'd thought about it, but it was no use, he couldn't tell anyone about this.

Ghost thought back again to the fire, and afterwards – waking up in hospital, crying. He'd cried for Miguel. He'd cried for himself. He'd cried that his brother had died and that he had lived. Days had merged into nights in a feverish, never-ending nightmare. Doctors and nurses had peered at him and poked him and asked him questions, but Ghost had shut his eyes to them all. Each time he fell asleep, he hoped he'd never wake, but he always did.

Cormac looked around the classroom at the other students busily scribbling notes. Ghost sat on his own, as he'd done for the past few days. Even though they hadn't known each other long he had been Cormac's first proper friend and he missed him. But worse than that was not knowing why they'd fallen out. About a week ago Ghost had been about to say something, something about hearing a voice. And it had happened as suddenly as if a switch had been flicked – Ghost had clammed up. He hadn't really spoken to anyone since.

'You still worried about him?' whispered Kate.

Cormac nodded. 'He's still having nightmares, though he won't say what they're about.'

'Maybe he's homesick? Or wishing he hadn't joined the Black Lotus?'

The bell rang. 'Kyō no jugyō wa koko made desu,' said the Japanese teacher, bowing and leaving the classroom.

Cormac scratched his head. 'She'll eat us when the purple bird sings?'

Kate rolled her eyes. 'She'll see us tomorrow. I thought Japanese was compulsory in all Empire schools.'

'It is. But I hated it. How come you've picked it up so quickly?'

'Hello, I can understand animal languages. Human ones are easy.'

Their next class was with Ami, who seemed to have taken them under her wing. They followed her down a series of unfamiliar passageways. Walls cut from rock replaced reinforced concrete, and the air was cold and musty.

Ami stopped at a heavy wooden door. 'This room was in the original part of Renkondo. It contains all our shinobi ancestors' secret knowledge and equipment.' She glanced back at them sharply. 'So don't touch anything.'

They followed her into an ancient library lined with shelves of leather-bound books and scrolls. Cormac tried to catch Ghost's eye, but he looked away.

Ami led them to a low wooden table filled with ancient-looking artefacts. She picked up a handful of dark pointed shells. 'Shinobi didn't have the same resources as the samurai, but they knew how to make the most of their environment. Water chestnuts were used as caltrops to be thrown in the path of a pursuer to pierce his feet. Later, they made steel tetsubishi, but the principle is the same.'

Something on the wall beside Cormac caught his eye. It was a long horizontal scroll, maybe two metres in length, covered in glass and framed. More scrolls like it filled the wall.

Ami blew black powder off the palm of her hand. 'Pepper was used for blinding adversaries.'

Cormac stepped closer to the nearest scroll, a very old yellowed parchment covered in vertical Japanese writing. At the bottom of each bunch of characters was a brown smudge.

Below the scroll was another he could actually read. They weren't just words – they were years and signatures. 1736 - Takahashi Ichiro, Sasaki Kōbō. 1739 - Kikuchi Riku. Each name ended in a bloody fingerprint. This was a list of Black Lotus members, an older version of the one he had signed. He looked along the panels. Could his father's name be on one of these lists?

Ami continued with her lesson. 'Bamboo was used for breathing under water and as a blowgun.'

Cormac moved to the next panel and found names that weren't Japanese. 1753 - Oliver Crowe, Claudette Laroche, Ivan Zadornov.

He glanced back at Ami, who had slipped two metal-spiked bands over her hands. 'Togakure shinobi invented these shuko and ashiko bands for climbing and fighting.'

As his eyes moved from scroll to scroll, the parchment became paper, and the brushstrokes changed to pen. 1886 - Harry Houdini. The name rang a bell. Hadn't he been a famous magician?

Cormac looked at Kate, who was glaring at him as if to say, 'What the heck are you doing?' He raised an eyebrow and continued reading. More famous names jumped out at him. 1901 - Charlie Chaplin. 1916 - Salvador Dali.

He quickened his pace, scanning the hundreds of names. The final piece of paper was in a hinged frame. Half the paper was blank, and at the bottom of the list of names were three brown thumbprints after his, Ghost's and Kate's names. Cormac hadn't seen his father's.

'Cormac.'

He turned around. The rest of the class stared at him.

'Is my lecture boring you, Cormac?'

He swallowed. 'No.'

'Can you tell me the purpose of the shuko and ashiko bands?'

Cormac wracked his brain. Shuko and ashiko bands? 'Something to do with music?'

Kate sniggered.

'Ghost.' Ami turned to him. 'Can you tell your room-mate the correct answer?'

'They were used to climb and fight.'

'Very good, Ghost. If you hope to keep your name on that list, Cormac, I suggest you try to be more like your room-mate.'

Cormac rejoined the group, his face flushed.

Near the end of the lesson, Ami handed each of

them a tiny pair of binoculars. 'These binocs have a night-vision setting and a zoom range magnification of 300 times. They fit in a pocket on the sleeve of your shōzoku.'

While everyone experimented with the binoculars, Ami set up a display on the table using a section of a door, complete with a bolt and small padlock. She then produced what looked like a roll of sellotape.

'Our labs developed this. We call it Acid Wrap.'

She tore off a piece and wrapped it around the shackle of the padlock. Almost immediately, a tendril of smoke rose from beneath the tape.

'Upon contact with metal, the tape releases a super-corrosive acid. Watch carefully.'

A few seconds later, the piece of tape fell to the ground, leaving the area underneath almost completely eaten away. She snapped the lock in half and gave them each a roll of the tape.

'Remember, this is not a sticking plaster!'

The next day, Cormac found Kate waiting for him at the dining-room door. She nodded to where Ghost sat alone, staring at his breakfast. He looked so different from the boy who'd come with them to Renkondo.

'Let's do it now,' she said.

Cormac led the way. 'Can we sit with you?'

Ghost looked up and shrugged.

Cormac cleared his throat. 'How are you?'

'Fine.'

Kate put down her chopsticks. 'Look, Ghost. We're worried about you. We miss hanging out. Have we done something wrong?'

Ghost tilted his head as if he was trying to hear some distant sound. Then he closed his eyes and shook his head. He looked at Kate, and then Cormac, taking a deep breath before speaking. 'I am sorry for not being a good friend. But I am hearing a—'

His body suddenly stiffened, his eyes bulging in his head. For a split second he was frozen. Then his whole body bucked as if he'd been electrocuted. He fell backwards off his bench, cracking his head on the floor.

'Help!' Cormac shouted and he raced around to where Ghost lay writhing violently on the floor, teeth clamped together, fingernails clawing at his skull.

Cormac put his hands under Ghost's head, which was banging against the floor. His friend's dark skin felt cold and clammy. More students gathered around, eyes wide with worry, hands over mouths.

Cormac felt Ghost stop moving. 'Quickly!' he shouted, as a group of teachers pushed through the crowd.

'Everyone back to their seats!' barked the Bear. He lifted the inert body off the floor. Ami watched with concern.

'Take him to the sickbay,' ordered Makoto.

Ghost hung limply in the Bear's powerful arms as he ran from the dining room.

'You heard the Bear!' shouted Makoto to the lingering onlookers. 'Back to your seats!'

'What happened?' asked Ami quietly.

'It was weird,' said Cormac, trying to stand. But his legs were weak with shock, so he sat on the bench. 'He was about to tell us something. Then he just collapsed.'

'Something about what?' asked Ami.

'Don't know. But he's been acting weird. He

doesn't talk to us any more.'

Ami placed her hand on his shoulder. 'Try not to worry. He'll be given a full physical and psychiatric assessment. We'll soon find out.'

Ghost woke up in what looked very much like a regular hospital ward, except the walls were the roughly hewn rock walls of Renkondo. Medical equipment surrounded him.

His nostrils tingled with the smell of vanilla, before Ami appeared at his bedside.

'How are you feeling?' she asked, her voice soft.

'OK,' said Ghost, propping himself up on a pillow. 'What happened?'

'You blacked out.'

She sat down on the edge of the bed. Of all the teachers, she'd always been the friendliest. Maybe he could talk to her. Though Miguel had said not to trust anybody.

'I think I am crazy,' he said.

'Your friends said you'd been acting strangely.'

Ghost swallowed.

She tucked a lock of hair behind her ear. 'This school puts a lot of stress on students.'

'It's not that,' protested Ghost. He wondered again if he should tell her about the voice he'd been hearing, then closed his eyes at the memory of that pain in the dining room – when he'd been about to tell Cormac and Kate. Pain caused by Miguel? 'I don't know if I should say.'

'That's OK, Ghost.' Ami looked away, as if deep in thought.

'I hear a voice in my head,' blurted Ghost, immediately regretting his words. He braced himself for an attack of pain, but nothing happened.

Ami's dark eyes widened. 'Perhaps you have the ability of clairaudience?'

'Clair what?'

'Clairaudience. The ability to acquire information by paranormal means.'

Ghost wasn't sure he knew what that meant. 'But I already have an ability.'

'Some people have two.'

Ghost lay back on the pillow. *Another ability?* 'But what should I do? Should I listen to this voice?'

She frowned, pondering. 'Do you know the person who speaks to you?' she asked eventually.

'Yes.'

'And do you trust that person?'

'Yes.'

'Then perhaps you have your answer.' She smiled. 'You should rest, Ghost. I'll check on you later.'

She stood up and walked away, leaving Ghost alone with his thoughts. Ami had believed him, which meant he wasn't crazy, which meant the voice was real. Which meant Miguel *was* communicating with him from the dead. But why? Maybe he was trying to help Ghost. He had always been trying to help his big brother.

And what had Ghost done in return? Not

listened, not trusted. No wonder Miguel had got angry in the dining room.

If Ghost had listened to Miguel on the day of the fire, he wouldn't have gone out to play football. He'd have stayed inside with his baby brother. And Miguel wouldn't have died.

From now on, if Miguel spoke, Ghost would listen.

Ghost remained in the sickbay under observation for the next two days, but Cormac was relieved to see him enter the dining room with Makoto during lunch. Makoto called out a list of names from his clipboard, including Cormac's and Kate's.

As the class followed Makoto out of the hall, Cormac caught up with Ghost. 'Good to have you back, man.'

But Ghost just looked at him blankly, then walked ahead.

'So, he's better?' asked Kate from behind.

Cormac shook his head. 'Maybe, but he's still not talking to me.'

Makoto led them past the classrooms, and into a corridor Cormac hadn't been in before. After a short walk, they entered a dōjō – a large, wooden-floored cavern with a wall-mounted rack containing swords, sticks and other deadly-looking weapons. The students removed their boots and socks and bowed when they entered.

'Seiza,' said Makoto, and they knelt and sat back on their heels.

At the furthest wall sat Sensei Iwamoto, a small, skinny man with a bald head and a long grey goatee twisted into a braid. His eyes were closed and his body still, as if he was deep in meditation. Cormac had seen him around the school, but they hadn't yet had a class with him.

'It's time to step up your training,' said Makoto. 'This is Sensei Iwamoto.'

The sensei bowed his forehead to the ground. The students returned the bow.

The sensei allowed Makoto to blindfold him and tie his hands behind his back, then walked into the group of students. They fanned out in a circle around him.

'Imagine I am enemy,' he said. 'Attack hard, attack strong. Do not be afraid. A shinobi must live without fear.'

Cormac glanced around at the other students, who stared at the floor. Since he'd arrived at Renkondo his physical abilities had really improved. Coming top of the class in all of the Bear's physical challenges had given him a certain amount of confidence. He looked to Makoto, who nodded that he should proceed.

Cormac wasn't a fighter, but he did have the advantage of speed. He stepped quietly sideways so that he was behind the man. Then he lunged forwards at full speed, arms outstretched to the man's waist. In a blur of velocity, his blind opponent sidestepped him like a bullfighter, and Cormac crashed to the floor.

He felt the blood rush to his cheeks. Embarrassed, he pulled himself up.

Makoto held up his hand and went to the weapons rack. He tossed a two-metre wooden staff, called a bō, to Cormac.

Silently, Cormac moved around to the sensei's left side. He swung the weapon low at his opponent's feet. The sensei leapt into the air and the pole passed harmlessly beneath. But Cormac had expected that and immediately cut down with the staff, aiming for the man's head.

Again, the sensei sidestepped the blow. He moved towards Cormac, spinning 360 degrees on one foot and planting the other deep into Cormac's stomach.

Like a deflating balloon, Cormac flew back into the ring of onlookers, the pole clattering to the wooden floor.

Makoto untied the sensei's hands and removed his blindfold.

'You are brave fighter,' the sensei told Cormac. 'But ninjutsu is more than fighting. It is connection with human spirit and world around, connection so finely tuned that shinobi know what will happen before it does.'

For the rest of the lesson, the sensei showed the class how to move like a shinobi by keeping their legs far apart and their knees bent for balance. When he stepped, his back foot joined his front to protect his groin before moving forwards and out again.

'Most persons walk by moving feet like scissor-blades,' he explained. 'You must move your feet in and out like zigzag.'

For hours, they practised going up and down the dōjō until their limbs ached and their movements were barely audible.

'As defence against intruders, samurai castle had nightingale floors to squeak when person walk on them,' said Sensei Iwamoto. 'When you can cross nightingale floor without waking nightingale, you can truly walk like shinobi.'

Afterwards, they sparred. Kate was paired with Kristjan, the Ice Man. He was much bigger and stronger than Kate, but she seemed to be holding her own. Kristjan was the only student who never displayed his special ability, and this made Cormac wary of him. It still puzzled him why Kristjan had flown the helicopter that day when they were rescued from the attack on the motorway.

'Your skills, strength and fitness will improve each day,' said the sensei at the end of the lesson. 'Although weapons training does not begin until year two, I have a gift for you.'

He laid out thirteen pouches made from the same material as their suits. From his own pouch, he removed a handful of small star-shaped steel blades. From his history class, Cormac recognized them as shuriken.

Sensei Iwamoto flicked the blades at the wall. They flew through the air and struck a wooden target with five successive thunks.

'Traditionally, these were dipped in poison,' explained the sensei, 'but ours not so lethal. Your shuriken are full with powerful anaesthetic, which is released only on contact with certain tissue. They strike tree or wall, they not activate. Only human or animal tissue trigger the compressed gas, inject chemicals into bloodstream and cause unconsciousness in seconds.'

Everyone gasped.

'We use these in next lesson. They not to be used anywhere else in Renkondo.'

Cormac removed one of the shuriken and looked down at the polished metal. The idea of weapons training was fun, but the thought that he might have to use these on another human being sent a shiver through his body.

The students sat on the floor chatting as they put on their socks and boots. Cormac glanced over at Ghost, who sat on his own, his head cocked to one side, as if listening to something, his lips moving in a silent mantra.

Ghost looked up and Cormac smiled, but Ghost's eyes were full of suspicion. Then he stood and marched out of the dōjō.

What's his problem? Cormac got to his feet, wincing as his aching leg muscles screamed in protest. He ran out into the corridor. 'Ghost!'

Ghost glanced behind him, but kept walking.

When Cormac caught up, he grabbed Ghost by the arm. Ghost spun around, swinging a right hook. The fist caught Cormac on the mouth, whirling him backwards into the wall. Pain surged up the side of his jaw and a warm bitter taste coated his tongue. He spat blood on the ground.

'You ass!' said Cormac, shoving Ghost into the wall.

'Hey!' said Kate, suddenly appearing. She jumped between them and pushed them apart. 'What's going on?'

Cormac spat out more blood. 'This jerk just punched me.'

Kate looked at him, her eyes narrowing. 'What did you say to him?'

'I was trying to be friendly,' said Cormac, glaring at Ghost. 'I don't know why I bother.'

Kate raised her eyebrows. 'What's going on, Ghost?'

He stared at the ground. 'Nothing.'

'Then why are you acting like this?'

He had a wild look in his eyes. 'I don't know . . .'

His head jerked to one side as if he'd heard something. He listened intently for a few seconds before returning his gaze to Kate, his eyes now burning with intensity. 'I'm here to become a ninja. Nothing must get in the way.'

'Since when is being someone's friend getting in the way?'

'You guys do not get my message. I do not want to be a friend. Now leave me alone. For ever.'

'There's something strange going on here,' said Kate as they watched Ghost walk away from them.

Cormac grunted.

'We need to keep a closer eye on him,' said Kate.

Cormac rubbed his jaw. 'That's difficult when he keeps avoiding us.'

'Then maybe we need to get someone else to keep an eye on him.'

Time to go.

Ghost moaned and turned over in his sleep. Every night, Miguel woke him, whispering about the things they used to do together in the favela. At first, Ghost had found it comforting, but the more it had continued, the more it felt like Miguel was haunting him.

Tonight we do it.

Ghost blinked several times in the darkness. *Why won't you tell me what this task is?*

Please don't make me angry again.

Ghost remembered what had happened in the dining room. He didn't want to risk it happening again.

Under the bed sheet, he removed his underpants and climbed naked out of the bunk. The cool air chilled his sweat-coated body. He shivered and closed his eyes, trying to shut out the sound of Cormac's breathing. He concentrated, and slowly his mind emptied. When it was a blank sheet, he breathed out, purging his body of everything, including air. He didn't breathe back in.

Hurry up.

Resist! he told himself. *Resist until your body forces you to take a breath. Now!* He straightened and gasped, refilling his starving lungs with air.

Tonight—

The wave of icy coldness cut off Miguel's voice and passed through Ghost like an Arctic wind. Though he hated the way it penetrated his soul, he liked how it banished Miguel, even if it was only temporarily.

. . . to do this.

Invisible, Ghost stepped into the corridor and eyeballed the blinking camera.

He quickened his pace, his brother's voice guiding him through the corridors. Miguel had told him nothing about the task ahead. He'd said to trust him, and that once it was over he'd leave Ghost alone.

If it meant Miguel could rest in peace and stop haunting Ghost, then it would be worth it, whatever 'it' was.

A few turns later, he arrived at the glass-panelled control room. Inside, two people worked on computers.

Go in.

He pushed down on the handle and eased the door open just enough to squeeze through.

Look to your left. Behind that cardboard

box is a small bottle and a cloth.

How does he know all this?

It really freaked him out that not only could Miguel speak to him but he also seemed to be able to see through his eyes. Whatever he saw, Miguel also saw.

Clenching his teeth, Ghost moved towards the box. A couple of metres away, with her back to him, a woman keyed information into a computer from a long roll of paper. Keeping his eyes on her, he reached over and found the bottle and cloth.

Put a small amount of liquid on the cloth, but do not breathe it in. A few seconds over her mouth should be enough.

What? Please, Miguel, no . . .

Just do it!

There was something in the tone that made the voice sound different from Miguel's, but he'd promised himself that he'd never ignore Miguel again.

Ghost pushed aside his doubts, unscrewed the bottle and poured a few drops on to the cloth, the strong chemical smell making his eyes water. He placed the damp cloth in his palm and, keeping it down by his side, he crept up behind the woman, then placed it firmly over her mouth. Her hands flew to the cloth, but just as her warm fingers met Ghost's icy ones, her body went limp and her head flopped forwards.

He tried to ease her down to the desk, but lost his grip as her dead weight brought her head crashing on to the keyboard.

On the opposite side of the room, the man shouted something in Japanese. He dashed over to the inert body of his colleague and shook her. Ghost grabbed him from behind and clamped the cloth over his mouth. The man was strong and struggled to free himself from the invisible force. They crashed backwards, Ghost falling into a chair with the man sitting on his lap. Ghost pressed harder on the cloth until the energy ebbed from his captive. He wriggled from underneath, leaving the unconscious body slumped in the chair.

Good. Now put him back at his station.

Ghost wheeled the man back in front of the security-camera feeds. He let the body lie forwards on the desk so that from the outside he'd look asleep. He prayed the two controllers were OK, told himself this would soon be over and that they'd never know he'd been here.

The wall of screens showed various corridors, rooms and outside views. One showed the Moon Sword in its glass case.

Shut down the cameras.

Why?

Just do it, Ghost!

Ghost stopped. Something was definitely wrong. Miguel had never called him Ghost. Because he had only become Ghost after the fire, after Miguel died . . .

Sometimes you don't sound like my little brother.

A dart of pain stabbed at Ghost's brain, reminding him of Miguel's power.

Use the computer, Ghost . . .

Fighting the pain in his head, Ghost tapped the keys as Miguel told him, and the message 'All security cams disabled' popped up on the monitor.

Now go to the East Tunnel. Quickly!

The East Tunnel was deserted, and Ghost soon reached the huge steel security door that he'd seen on their first day on the way to the sword ceremony. This time it was open. He slipped through and walked down the concrete tunnel, lined with those deadly sensors in the walls. Disabled now. He hoped.

Where was Miguel taking him? *The only room down here is the sword room.* He stopped.

Twenty metres away was indeed the sword room, and facing him were three armed guards.

Don't make a sound. One clumsy step, and they'll shoot, even if they can't see you. All you have to do is get close. I'll tell you what to do next.

'Up wake! Up wake!'

Kate opened her eyes. Chloe's heavy breathing drifted down from the top bunk. Kate flicked on the bedside lamp to find Savage on her pillow, whiskers twitching.

She sat up. 'What's wrong?'

'Left his room did your friend.'

'Ghost?'

The mouse nodded.

Kate leapt out of bed and changed into her shōzoku. Slipping Savage into her pocket, she stepped into the dimly-lit corridor. At the end of the passageway, the red eye of a camera winked at her.

She tapped on Cormac and Ghost's door, but there was no answer. She pressed the handle down and slipped inside. Their bathroom door was open a crack, casting a sliver of light on to the bunk beds. Cormac lay curled up on the bottom, but the upper bunk was empty. She checked the bathroom. It was empty too.

'Cormac,' she whispered, shaking him awake.

'What the heck, Ghost,' he mumbled, leaning up on one elbow. 'Do we have to do this every—' His green eyes widened. 'Kate?'

'Where's Ghost?'

Cormac rubbed his eyes. 'What do you mean?'

'His bed's empty.'

He sat up, looked around the room, then frowned at Kate. 'How did you know?'

'Savage told me.'

'Savage? Who the heck is Savage?'

Kate pulled out the mouse. 'Meet Savage.'

Cormac leant closer to look at him. 'Um, hello,' he said, eyebrows arched.

'I asked Savage to keep an eye on Ghost, as he's been acting so weird. I figured there was something he wasn't telling us.' She put her hand on Cormac's arm. 'We have to find him.'

Cormac got out of bed and grabbed his shōzoku.

Kate smiled at his Superman underwear. 'Nice boxers.'

'Yeah ... I ... erm ...' stuttered Cormac as he got dressed.

Outside the bedroom door, they pulled on their cowls and followed the mouse past the security camera. Kate was surprised when no alarm sounded. *Maybe something's wrong?* She shook away the thought. The place was packed with security features – not to mention all the ninjas.

They entered the circular room and took the East Tunnel. When they passed by a second camera and still weren't apprehended, the thought that something wasn't right resurfaced in Kate's mind. As she wondered what it could be, she crashed into Sensei Iwamoto and two shinobi guards.

In an instant, Kate and Cormac were knocked to the ground and their arms tied behind their backs.

When their hoods were removed, Sensei Iwamoto looked at them with something worse than anger: disappointment. Kate wondered if it was partly because they'd allowed themselves to be captured so easily. More than two months of ninja training in the arts of zanshin and self-defence, and they'd been overpowered like mere beginners.

'I'm sorry,' Kate blurted. She felt terrible for breaking the rules and betraying the trust of the Black Lotus, after all they'd done for her. The sensei shot her a sharp glance, but said nothing.

The shinobi led Kate and Cormac back the way

they'd come – into the circular room and up the North Tunnel past the sleeping quarters. At the end of the tunnel they turned left and continued on into the map room.

Kate shot Cormac a glance. *Why are we here?*

Makoto was waiting there with the Jōnin. The guards untied Cormac and Kate and shoved them forward. They knelt and bowed as they'd been trained to do.

Makoto stared at them. 'Why were you out of your rooms?'

Kate took a deep breath. 'We were looking for Ghost. He's missing—'

Makoto raised his hand for her to be quiet. He held his finger to his earpiece and listened. After a few seconds, he looked at the Jōnin's face, framed by long silver hair. 'All security systems are down.'

The Jōnin closed his eyes.

'Sensei Iwamoto, alert the Fuyu,' commanded Makoto.

Sensei Iwamoto bowed and left with the two shinobi.

The Jōnin stared at Cormac and Kate, his blue eyes suffused with light as if a fire was glowing behind them.

'How did you know which way Ghost went?' asked Makoto.

Kate cleared her throat. 'Savage . . . that's my pet mouse. You know I can talk to animals, right?'

'Can your mouse take us to Ghost?' asked Makoto.

'If we can find him,' answered Kate. 'Your guards probably scared him off.'

She rummaged in one of her pockets and took out a piece of cookie. She broke off a few crumbs and sprinkled them on the floor.

The two men's eyes darted to the door and followed the movements of a little brown mouse scurrying across the floor. Savage got to the crumbs and started eating. Kate smiled, looking down at her friend. 'You know what they say: the way to a mouse's heart is through his stomach.'

Sensei Iwamoto had shown them how to walk like shinobi, and now Ghost put it into practice, moving carefully towards the guards. All the time, he kept his eyes on them, but they never moved a muscle – they were like statues with guns. He circled the closest guard and approached him from behind. When he dared go no closer, he crouched and waited for Miguel's instructions.

Closer.

Ghost moved closer until he could reach out and touch the guard.

On the guard's belt is a stun gun. Grab it and shoot him in the neck. Then drop the gun.

Shoot him?

If you do this quickly, the other guards won't locate you. When they surround the body, take them out too.

Cold ran through Ghost like a virus. He just wanted this to be over, one way or another.

So he inched forwards until he was by the guard's side. With his hand above the stun gun's handle, he took a silent breath and remembered his friends in the favela playing with guns, practising drawing and shooting them. He'd never taken part. 'The Ghost always disappears when the fun starts,' they used to tease. Now he wished he'd stuck around to play. He snatched the gun, springing back to avoid the slicing elbow of the guard, then pulled the trigger. A tiny dart whooshed through the air into the guard's neck. Out of the corner of his eye, he caught the movement of the other two guards. Remembering what Miguel had said, he dropped the gun. For a split second, the shot guard was frozen, his face caught in a bulging-eyed scowl, before collapsing to the ground.

His companions moved in to surround their fallen comrade. They searched for the source of the attack, their backs to Ghost. With no time to waste, he picked up the gun and pointed it into the back of one of the guards' necks, firing and then immediately aiming at the remaining guard, who spun around to face him. Ghost shot the dart at his neck. Both guards flopped to the ground, and a flood of relief washed over Ghost.

His break was short-lived.

Well done. Now you need to move fast. Become visible and put on one of the guards' uniforms.

Ghost didn't have to be told twice. He closed his

eyes and let go of the cold. As soon as he felt the flow of warmth enter his body, he began undressing one of the unconscious guards. The man was covered in weaponry: guns, grenades and even a sword on his belt like a Kat. Ghost thrust these to one side and pulled on the guard's uniform and boots, his body appearing as he dressed.

In the glass case is the sword. Tie it to your belt.

Ghost stopped, his heart dropping like a stone. *That's the task? Stealing the Moon Sword? But why?*

We don't have time for questions. Are you going to let me down again?

Ghost swallowed, as images of the fire flashed in his head.

But the Black Lotus are protecting it from falling into evil hands.

That's what they tell you.

Was Miguel right? Ghost remembered the map room, the way he, Cormac and Kate had felt the Black Lotus were keeping secrets. But still . . .

He didn't know what to believe. His hands trembled as he lifted off the glass case and reached for the Moon Sword. If Makoto had spoken the truth, this katana was all that stood between President Goda and world domination. He hesitated, his pulse racing, his eyes running along the burnished black scabbard to the gold and silver crescent moon sparkling under the lights. *Why am I doing this?* The answer came quickly.

If you don't do it, I'll hurt you again.

He removed the sword in its scabbard, and tied it to his belt.

Now take a gun and helmet and run.

Ghost obeyed, sliding the helmet's dark visor over his eyes at the sound of footsteps fast approaching.

Four guards came charging down the passageway, guns raised upon seeing Ghost, but lowered immediately as he waved them on, directing them towards the chamber. They didn't look at the sword tied to his belt.

As soon as they passed, he ran like he'd never run before, up the passageway and through the steel security door. Miguel directed him to the circular room, into the West Tunnel and up steps to the trapdoor. Ghost remembered Ami punching in a code to open it. But Ghost didn't have to, because it was already open. He stepped out into the blackness of the forest.

Cormac, Kate, Makoto and the Jōnin were about to follow Savage in search of Ghost when Makoto raised his hand for them to wait. He held his finger to his earpiece, squeezed his one eye closed and shook his head.

The Jōnin put his hand on Makoto's shoulder.

Makoto opened his eye. 'It's the sword.'

The Jōnin's face tensed.

'It's gone.'

The Jōnin met Makoto's eyes and nodded, his mouth set into a grim line.

Makoto tapped his chest and delivered the order. 'Issue code red alert.'

Cormac and Kate followed Makoto and the Jōnin through corridors crowded with shinobi, Fuyu guards, scientists and technicians, all responding to the code red alert. On the way to the sword room, Savage stopped and sniffed the air. Kate raised her hand to halt the others.

'What is it?' asked Makoto.

Kate pointed at the mouse. 'Savage has picked up Ghost's scent.'

The mouse took off, and they followed it through tunnels and up stairs. Savage was heading up, out of Renkondo.

Soon they were racing up the final flight of steps and then into the dark forest above, Savage still scampering ahead of them.

Hurry, Ghost. By now they'll be after you. The forest ahead is full of shinobi so that's what you need to become. Look to your right.

Ghost obeyed.

Under that fallen tree is a shōzoku. Change into it and hide the Fuyu uniform.

Ghost removed the bulky uniform and gladly slipped into the skin-tight shōzoku. He pushed the Fuyu gear and weapons under the tree and covered them with leaves.

The sword, Ghost.

Ghost shook his head in frustration and pulled the blade back out from under the leaves. He was so tired he didn't know what he was doing.

The end is near. Just do as I say.

Miguel guided him through the forest, Ghost

putting into practice all he had learnt about stealth and camouflage, moving from tree to tree like a shadow.

He wanted to get rid of the damn sword and get as far away from Renkondo as possible. Tears stung behind his eyes. He could never return after this betrayal – he'd never see Cormac or Kate again. He knew the entire camp would come after him, and they'd be angry. Who knew what they'd do if they caught him?

In front of you is a clearing. Bring the sword to me.

To you? Miguel? You're here? How?

Ghost stepped to the edge of the clearing. The moonlight cast a silvery outline on a figure wearing a hood. He could barely breathe.

'Miguel?' said Ghost, moving out of the darkness. 'Is that you?'

The figure turned towards him, lowering its hood.

The moon illuminated her pale skin.

'Ami?' gasped Ghost.

She stepped closer. Her lips didn't move.

Hello, Ghost.

It was still Miguel's voice, but it wasn't Miguel.

'Miguel never called me Ghost . . .'

Ami came closer, her eyes as black as the night which surrounded them.

I'm sorry, Ghost. I'm sorry I tricked you. It was the only way.

'But how . . . ?'

Everybody in this camp has special

talents, Ghost. This is mine. I am a mind dweller. If somebody has an emotional weakness, I can break into their mind. Your weakness was the guilt you felt about Miguel. Once I break into a person's mind, I can inhabit their thoughts, see through their eyes and communicate with them.

'But it's Miguel's voice . . .'

Francisco. This time, he heard his friend Squint's voice in his head. When I enter people's minds, I can access their memories and take on the voices of people they know.

Ghost felt as though Ami had put her hand down his throat and ripped out his heart. 'It was you all along?'

Ami nodded.

Ghost swallowed. So Miguel was gone. For good. 'Who are you, really?'

She spoke aloud. 'I am somebody who has spent the last eight years perfecting my plan to steal that sword. But then you came along and it was too good an opportunity to be missed.' Her gaze dropped to the blade in Ghost's hand. 'We have wasted enough time talking. Now give me the sword.'

Ghost gripped the weapon tightly. 'Why should I?'

Ami's eyes narrowed, her lips pulled back in a snarl. Suddenly she didn't look so beautiful. 'You have no other choice. If you go back to Renkondo, they'll kill you. If you don't give me the sword, *I* will.'

Ghost took a step back.

'Have you forgotten what happened the last

time you made me angry?'

He hadn't. He never would. 'What are you going to do with the sword?'

Ami opened her palm. 'Give it to me.'

A twig cracked at the other side of the clearing, and someone stepped out of the shadows.

'Do not give her the sword!'

Ghost squinted into the gloom to the source of the voice – Makoto. The clearing lit up as he was joined by the Jōnin, his long silver hair and white kimono illuminated by the light that seemed to come from inside his body.

'Come any closer and the boy dies!' shouted Ami.

Behind the Jōnin, dark shapes moved in the trees.

'That goes for the rest of you too,' Ami shouted into the night. 'One false move, and the boy becomes a ghost, for real.'

'Ghost,' said Makoto. 'Do not give her the sword. She is the enemy.'

Ami turned to Makoto. Her eyes were full of venom, and the once-beautiful face had contorted into a grimace of hate. 'Don't call me the enemy. You don't know who I am.'

'This is true,' Makoto acknowledged. 'You arrived on our mountain eight years ago. You showed us your power. We only accept children, but your skill was too valuable to refuse. We made a grave mistake.'

Give me the sword, Ghost.

'All this time,' continued Makoto, 'you were Kyatapira.'

Ami laughed. 'I'm not one of those fools. You've spent a lifetime studying this sword and its history, yet you fail to recognize me.'

Give me the sword, Ghost.

Makoto frowned.

'There's more to the Goda family than Lord Goda himself,' added Ami.

'He had a wife,' said Makoto slowly.

Ami smiled. 'And what do you know about her?'

Give me the sword, Ghost.

'There were rumours. It was said that she was a witch who could control people's thoughts. But that was hundreds of years ago.'

Ami glanced at Ghost, smiled and turned to the Jōnin. His bright eyes widened.

Ami bowed.

'Lady Kiko?' gasped Makoto.

Give me the sword, Ghost. Give me the sword, Ghost. Give me the sword, Ghost.

Ghost's head spun. How could this woman be the wife of President Goda's ancestor? It made no sense.

GIVE ME THE SWORD, GHOST! screamed the voice in his head. A bolt of pain jolted through his brain. His hands dropped the sword and flew to his head. He screamed.

Cormac couldn't believe what he was seeing. Shriek-ing with pain, Ghost fell to his knees, his head in his hands. With incredible deftness and speed, Kiko, the woman they knew as Ami, pounced on the sword, whipped off the scabbard and raised the silver blade above her head. The Jōnin took a step towards her, but stopped when Ghost screamed again and fell face down into the leaves.

'I'm serious,' warned Kiko. 'One more step, and he dies.'

She backed away, glancing behind her towards the edge of the clearing at a large rock with a crack in its centre. With careful movements, she sidestepped and walked backwards as if she was trying to find a certain spot on the ground.

The Jōnin charged forwards into the downward swing of her sword. There was a wet cutting sound followed by a dull thud. The Jōnin stumbled back, the glow from his body dimming, darkening the clearing. Makoto rushed to his side.

Then, raising the sword once again above her head, Kiko eyed an invisible target in front of her.

A blood-curdling scream pierced the night as she released her ki energy and slashed down with the sword. The air tore apart, and a blinding light burst through the gash, illuminating the forest clearing like sunlight.

Cormac fell back, shielding his eyes. He peered through his fingers and saw a shimmering mass of light, moving like liquid in mid-air. Then he saw Kiko climb into it, sword in hand. Almost immediately, the hole began to close.

Cormac saw Ghost take his head from his hands

and stumble towards the rift. Then he threw himself into it.

'Ghost!' screamed Kate, racing towards the light. She too leapt and disappeared into the brightness.

'No!' shouted Cormac, jumping to his feet and running after them.

The hole had shrunk to barely a metre wide and was closing fast. Like a dolphin through a ring, he sailed into the shrinking hole of light.

PART THREE:
YOSA CASTLE

Kate picked herself up off the ground and turned back to look for the hole she'd jumped through. A black disc shimmered and contracted before finally disappearing.

She was in a sloping forest, just like the one she'd left, except this one was bathed in sunlight.

'Over here!' shouted Cormac.

'What the heck happened?' said Kate, running over to him. She squinted up at the blue sky peeping through the overhead canopy. 'Daylight?' *How can it be light when it was dark only minutes ago?*

'Where's Ghost?' asked Cormac.

Kate looked around and saw Ghost running downhill through the trees. 'Over there!'

Cormac shot off after him. Kate searched for Ami, or Kiko as they now knew her. There was no sign of her, and Kate wasn't waiting around for her to turn up. She sprinted through the forest in pursuit of the boys, passing a patch of muddied ground covered in hoof prints, horse manure and hay. A long piece of rope, cut at one end, was tied to a tree.

She heard them arguing before she saw them.

Ghost was pulling away from Cormac's grasp. 'Let go!'

Cormac held up his hands. 'OK, but stop running for a minute.'

'No time,' said Ghost, looking behind him. 'She is on a horse, getting away.'

'She almost killed you back there. Let her get away.'

'I can't – it's all my fault,' said Ghost, turning and racing down through the trees.

Kate looked at Cormac. 'If she's on horseback, we'll never catch her.'

'I could.'

'No.' She put her hand on his arm. 'We stick together.'

They set off after Ghost, crashing through foliage and jumping over fallen trees. Kate's mind ran even faster. *What happened back there? Where are we?*

They eventually caught up with Ghost further down the slope. He'd collapsed on the ground with exhaustion.

'We have to take a break,' panted Kate.

Cormac sat down. He wasn't even sweating.

'No time,' croaked Ghost.

'Well, we can't keep running,' said Kate.

'But we must get the sword back.'

Kate shot him a look. 'Then why did you steal it?'

Ghost looked at the ground. He didn't answer – or couldn't.

'I don't know,' he replied quietly. 'But I know stealing the sword was a big mistake. I have to get it back.'

'That's not gonna be easy,' said Kate.

Cormac looked back up the hill, through the trees. 'Maybe we should go back to Renkondo for help.'

'Not me,' said Ghost. 'I'm going after the sword.'

Kate stood up. 'Let's all go. If the Black Lotus are as good as they claim, they'll have no trouble finding us.'

Deep hoof prints in the soft, sloping ground made the trail easy to follow. They walked in silence for a while until Kate felt a scratching in the pocket of her shōzoku. *Savage!* She'd forgotten all about him. And all that tumbling about couldn't have been good for him.

'Are you OK?' she asked, taking him out.

He twitched his whiskers. 'Food I need.'

'So what's new?' Kate fed him crumbs from the cookie she'd saved.

'What is this?' asked Ghost, nodding at the mouse.

'*This* is Savage.'

Ghost's nose wrinkled. 'Savage?'

'Her pet mouse,' explained Cormac.

'Ugh, I hate mouses.'

Kate glared at him. 'If it hadn't been for this mouse, you'd be dead!'

'Eh?'

'If we hadn't been there to distract her, Kiko would have killed you as soon as you handed over the sword. And we'd never have found you in the first place if it hadn't been for Savage.'

Ghost thought about it, and for a moment looked sorry, as if he was going to apologize. But then he seemed to change his mind and looked down as if he didn't know what to do. Finally, he shrugged and turned away.

Cormac grabbed him. 'We were supposed to be your friends, but all you did was ignore us!'

'Get off me!'

'You owe us an explanation!' Cormac pushed Ghost in the chest, sending him staggering backwards.

'Stop it!' shouted Kate, but no one was listening.

Ghost ran at Cormac, tackled him around the waist and pushed him into a tree. Face twisted in fury, Cormac swung a punch.

'Ow!' Ghost leapt backwards, clutching his face.

Cormac shoved him hard, and dived on him. In a flurry of limbs they rolled down a leafy incline and disappeared over a low ditch.

Kate heard a splash and ran over.

Coughing and spluttering, the two boys crawled out of a pool of muddy water, their faces marbled with dirt, their shōzokus dripping wet.

Kate put Savage into her pocket and folded her

arms. 'If you guys are finished playing, we really should get going.'

The boys scowled at each other. Ghost swallowed and stood up. He offered Cormac his hand. Cormac took it, and Ghost pulled him to his feet.

'I'm sorry,' said Ghost.

Cormac blinked. 'It's OK.'

Ghost looked at Kate. 'No, it is not OK. I was in a sad mood in the school. I was not a friend to you and Cormac.'

'We understand,' said Kate

'No, you don't understand. I must explain to you. Ami . . . Kiko, she controlled my mind. Now she has gone, the voice has gone. I hope it won't come back.'

Kate raised her eyebrows.

'It is her skill. She told me to steal the sword.'

'But why didn't you say no?' asked Kate. 'Why didn't you tell someone?'

'I didn't know it was her. I thought it was my little brother.'

'I didn't know you had a brother,' said Cormac.

'I don't. I mean, I did. Miguel is dead.'

Cormac put his hand on Ghost's shoulder. 'I'm sorry.'

Ghost looked down. 'It was my fault he died. I was supposed to look after him. Our house went on fire. Miguel died. I woke up in hospital.'

'Jeez . . .' mumbled Kate, feeling her eyes fill with tears. She put out a hand to comfort him, but Ghost brushed her away. He wasn't finished. He stared ahead, as if in a daze.

'With Miguel gone, I wanted to die. I lay in the hospital bed and closed my eyes. I let my spirit go. And it did. It left.'

Kate glanced at Cormac, who looked as concerned as she felt.

'Cold came into my body. I felt like ice. I waited for bright lights. But nothing happened. I opened my eyes, but I was still in hospital. I looked at my arms. They were gone. I looked under the blanket. My legs were gone also. But not gone – I could feel them. Invisible.'

Ghost was silent now, his gaze fixed on some distant part of the forest. Kate waited for him to continue.

'I pulled off tubes and wires and the hospital cloak. I was invisible completely. I think this is what death is – invisible spirits walking the earth. I walked down the hospital corridor past nurses and doctors. They didn't see me. Outside the sun was shining, but I was cold like snow. I walked down the street, shivering, until I could walk no more. I found an abandoned warehouse and lay down in a corner to die a second time.'

Ghost's eyes had glazed over as if he was reliving every second.

'When I woke up in the warehouse, I was alive and naked. I knew I was alive because I felt hungry and I felt my heart beating. But I felt dead. I felt empty. I had nothing: no clothes, no money, no home, no brother. All I had was this thing I could do. In the warehouse, I practised going invisible many times, watching my skin bleach, then disappear. The Bleaching. That's what I call it. I was no longer Francisco. I was Ghost. Life had stolen everything from me. I stepped out of the warehouse, ready to steal something back . . .'

Ghost fell silent again, as if he'd run out of words.

Kate wiped her eyes with her sleeve. 'Ghost, that's terrible.'

He snapped out of his daze and looked at her. 'Ami spoke to me in Miguel's voice. That's why I stole the sword.'

Kate nodded. She understood.

Cormac cleared his throat. 'I don't know what to say.'

Ghost looked at him. 'Say you'll help me fix this. Say you'll help me get the sword back.'

'Absolutely,' replied Cormac, extending his hand, palm down.

Ghost placed his hand on Cormac's.

Kate joined in too, placing her palm on top. 'We're a team,' she said. 'But we'd best get going if we're gonna catch that horse!'

Kate was glad they'd cleared the air, but their troubles were far from over. She still couldn't get her head around what had happened back there. She looked up through the trees. The sun was directly overhead, which meant it was around midday. But how was that possible when it had been night before? When they'd jumped through that hole, had they jumped forward into a new day?

Kate didn't recognize anything from their first

walk up through the forest, but that meant nothing – there must be many ways down off the mountain. As they reached the bottom, the ground became less steep, and at times they lost track of the hoof prints and worried they were going the wrong way, until they picked up the trail again. The first sign of civilization was a small shrine containing a statue with a bag around its neck. Cormac reached inside the bag and held up a handful of pebbles.

As they walked on, the mountainside changed from forest to terraced fields, all growing the same green crop. Kate didn't remember seeing these fields from the helicopter when they'd first arrived. *Perhaps we're on the other side of the mountain?*

'Paddies,' she said.

'You talking to me?' said Cormac in a funny accent.

Ghost glanced at Kate, eyebrows raised.

She shook her head. 'Paddy fields,' she explained, pointing at the terraces. 'Rice.'

At the bottom of the paddies, a narrow and dusty road snaked into the distance, but there was no sign of Kiko. The trail of hoof prints had disappeared too. As they looked around for it, Kate spotted three figures working in one of the fields. 'Let's ask them if they've seen a horse.'

'Aren't you forgetting we're dressed as ninjas,' said Cormac, 'in the heart of the Samurai Empire?'

Kate shrugged. 'I forgot.'

'We have nothing to lose,' said Ghost. 'We waste more time – Kiko goes further away.'

He strode off towards the farmers and Kate and Cormac had no option but to follow, edging along a little mud wall which divided the flooded paddies. As they got closer they could make out a man, woman and boy working in the field, pulling weeds and throwing them to one side. The man and boy wore nothing but rags around their waists. Their bodies were thin but muscular, and very tanned. The woman wore ragged clothes and a straw hat.

It was the woman who noticed the trio approaching. She let out a startled gasp, alerting the man, who looked equally frightened. The boy looked more curious than scared.

The man said something, and suddenly the three of them ran away, splashing through the water like frightened animals. When they reached the mud wall at the far side of the paddy, they raced along it as fast as they could. Once, the boy stopped and looked back, but he was soon called by the man. In minutes, they had disappeared into a clump of trees.

'The shōzokus must have frightened them,' said Cormac.

Kate thought about it. 'It might have been the suits, but I don't think they'd have recognized us as ninjas. I'm sure the Black Lotus don't parade about in public in their shōzokus.'

Ghost shrugged, turned around and retraced his steps. Cormac and Kate followed him along the narrow mud wall. As they reached the end, Ghost dashed forwards.

'Horse footprints,' he said, kneeling beside some

U-shaped indentations in the mud.

They followed the trail down the hill only to lose it again at the road.

'*Bosta!*' cursed Ghost.

The road's hard, dusty surface showed no sign of hoof prints to indicate which way Kiko had gone.

Cormac crawled around the road searching for clues, but Kate called for him to be quiet.

'What?' he asked, looking up.

Kate put her fingers to her lips and pointed to two birds warbling on a nearby branch. She cocked her head to hear what they were saying. They were arguing about the number of legs on the creature which had gone down the road.

'Four, there were definitely four, I counted four, yes, four . . .' sang one.

But the other chirped, 'Two more on top, two more on top, makes six, it does, six . . .'

Kate tuned out their chatter to think. *Four legs with two more on top? A horse and rider!*

'Which way did they go?' called Kate.

The birds fell silent and looked at Kate. The beak of one opened, but no sound came out.

'This way, this way, this way,' cheeped the other, flying off down the road.

Kate glanced at the boys. 'Follow the birds,' she said, running down the road in the direction the farm workers had gone.

But after half an hour's walking there was still no sign of people – no houses, no cars, nothing – though, judging by the reaction of the rice farmers, the locals weren't going to be of any help.

Kate started to get a bad feeling when she noticed movement in the bamboo groves that ran alongside the road. 'Don't look,' she whispered, 'but a small boy is following us.'

'Where?' said Cormac, looking around.

It was enough to frighten the boy off, and he disappeared up the hillside, leaving a path of flattened grass behind him.

'I told you not to look!' Kate scowled. 'I think it was that boy from the paddy field. He might have been useful.'

'Too late now,' said Ghost, looking up the hillside at the fleeing boy.

Cormac took off through the bamboo and up the grassy slope. In seconds, he stood holding the boy and waved back down to the road.

'Jeez, he's fast,' said Kate.

Ghost nodded. 'Like a cat out of hell.'

Kate smiled. 'I think you mean "bat".'

The boy looked petrified when Cormac grabbed him. He cowered and babbled in Japanese, and when Cormac released him he fell back into the long grass and scuttled a safe distance away.

'It's OK,' said Cormac, in a soothing voice. 'Tomodachi – friend.'

But the boy continued to talk and gesture excitedly. Cormac could only understand the odd word here and there.

'Tengu,' said the boy, pointing at Cormac.

Gasping for breath, Kate and Ghost arrived. The boy flinched when Kate flopped down beside him.

'He doesn't speak any English,' said Cormac. 'And he seemed terrified of me when I caught him. He keeps calling me "Tengu", whatever that is.'

'Well, I don't blame him,' said Kate. 'Seeing the

speed you travelled up the hill to catch him, I'd be frightened too.' She turned to the boy. 'Tengu?'

Cormac was surprised she didn't know the word. She had been one of the best in their Japanese language classes.

'Jikininki?' replied the boy.

Kate shook her head. The boy put his fingers up to his forehead like horns and growled.

Kate laughed and introduced herself, Cormac and Ghost. 'Onamae wa?'

'Yoshiro,' he answered, pointing to himself.

Kate bowed her head. 'Konnichiwa.'

Yoshiro smiled, so she asked another question. Cormac picked up the word 'ikiru' – to live.

He pointed up the hill behind him.

'Ask him if he saw a lady ride down the mountain on a horse,' Ghost suggested.

When Kate asked the question Yoshiro nodded. He pointed over the mountain and said something, and though Cormac didn't understand it, he did catch one word.

'Did he just say "Goda"?' asked Cormac.

Kate nodded. 'He said the woman is heading towards Yosa, where the shōgun, Lord Goda, lives.'

'Doesn't he mean President Goda?'

'That's what I was thinking.'

'Maybe "shōgun" is the same as "president" in Japan?' suggested Ghost.

'I don't know,' said Kate, anxiety etched on her forehead. 'We did this in history class. There hasn't been a shōgun in Japan for a long time. Who did

Makoto say Lady Kiko was?'

'Lord Goda's wife,' said Ghost.

Cormac shook his head. 'But that was five hundred years ago.'

'Exactly,' said Kate.

She was silent for a moment, her face drawn.

'I'll ask him why there are no cars on the road,' she said. But when she did ask, the boy didn't seem to understand. She made car noises and mimed steering, which made Cormac and Ghost smile, but Yoshiro just stared back at her.

Kate threw her hands up in frustration. 'It's like he doesn't know what a car is.'

Cormac stopped smiling. 'Ask him about a phone. Even if he doesn't have one, he'll know what it is.'

Kate turned back to Yoshiro. 'Denwa?'

'Denwa?' he repeated, frowning.

'You know,' said Kate, holding her thumb and little finger to the side of her head. 'Brrrring! Brrrring!'

Yoshiro looked even more confused now. He shook his head.

The three friends stared at each other.

'He doesn't know about cars or telephones?' said Cormac.

Kate spoke in hurried sentences to Yoshiro, her face growing more concerned with each of his replies. Cormac tried to keep up with what they were saying, but they spoke so quickly, he was soon lost. A bad feeling twisted in his stomach.

After a lengthy conversation, Kate turned to him

and Ghost, her face pale.

Cormac's forehead felt clammy. He knew what she was going to say. Only Ghost seemed oblivious of their predicament.

'What?' he asked defensively, as Kate and Cormac stared at him.

Kate swallowed. 'I have some bad news.'

'Bad news?' said Ghost.

'When we stepped through that hole of light, not only did we step into a new day, but also into a new century. Or rather, an old century.'

'What do you mean?'

'We've gone back in time. We are now in sixteenth-century Japan.'

Cormac watched the emotions on Ghost's face morph from puzzlement to disbelief.

'You are pulling my foot,' said Ghost.

'Leg,' corrected Cormac.

'What?'

Cormac started to explain, but Kate shook her head. 'We've gone back in time, Ghost. No cars. No phones. And a shōgun rules Japan.'

Ghost seemed to think about this for a while before nodding at Yoshiro. 'Maybe he's lying.'

'I don't think so,' said Kate. 'That hole Kiko cut in the air was some sort of door to another time. It explains the sudden change from night to day.'

'It also explains some of the things we saw in the map room at Renkondo,' said Cormac.

Kate thought for a moment, before speaking. 'So the swords are time-travelling devices?'

Ghost stood up. 'It doesn't matter. We must get the sword back.'

'Shouldn't we be more concerned about getting back home?' said Cormac, standing.

Ghost grabbed Cormac by the shoulders and looked him in the face. 'That sword is the only way to get back home!'

'He's right,' said Kate. 'We don't know how the sword's magic works, but without it we have no hope of returning to our own time. We should go.'

She bowed to Yoshiro. 'Arigatō.'

The boy asked her a question.

'Yosa,' replied Kate, pointing towards the road.

Yoshiro shook his head and spoke.

'What did he say?' asked Cormac.

'He says there's a samurai checkpoint two ri down the road.'

'And?'

'God, Cormac! Did you listen to anything they told us in class? Samurai are ruthless warriors. They don't like your bow, you're dead. You look at them funny, you're dead. Seppuku ring a bell? If a samurai screws up, they cut their own guts open with a sword. And these samurai are Lord Goda's. Yoshiro says they have no honour.'

'They're like Kats?'

'I guess. What do you think they'd do to three Black Lotus shinobi?'

Yoshiro spoke again, and Kate translated. 'He says we can cross the mountains to Yosa, though it will take longer.'

Ghost thanked him with a bow.

Cormac wasn't as enthusiastic. 'How do we know this isn't a trap? We've only just met this guy.'

'What other choice do we have?' asked Kate.

Cormac knew she was right. He nodded and bowed to Yoshiro. 'Arigatō.'

Yoshiro led the way through the long grass. At the top of the hill, the ground levelled and a little way off they saw a small village of thatched houses.

'Kini kakuretete,' ordered Yoshiro, pointing to a clump of trees, before running towards the houses.

'He said to wait here,' translated Kate.

'Where's he going?' asked Cormac.

Kate shrugged.

'He could be raising the alarm.'

Kate shook her head. 'I don't think so. From the way he spoke it seems he hates Lord Goda. The shōgun's men attacked his village recently, killing Yoshiro's grandfather.'

Cormac took out his binoculars and trained them on Yoshiro as he entered the village. Much to his relief, the boy didn't seem to be giving them away. Instead, he skulked about as if trying to avoid attention. When he disappeared into a house, Cormac scanned the rest of the village. The houses were all wooden and raised off the ground on thick posts. Smoke rose through the thatched roofs, chickens and ducks wandered between the houses, and children chased after each other over low rickety fences made from branches.

He zoomed in on a small knot of people in the

centre of the village. They were gathered around a man and woman who looked very much like the ones they had seen with Yoshiro in the paddy field. The man spoke excitedly to his neighbours. Cormac licked his lips nervously. Was he talking about them or Kiko? He focused back on the house Yoshiro had entered and watched as the boy came out and rushed towards them with a bundle of cloth in his arms.

When he reached their hiding place, he stared at the binocs.

'Binoculars,' said Cormac, handing them to him to try.

When Yoshiro first put the lenses up to his eyes, he jumped back with fright, dropping them. Cormac showed him what to do, and he gasped in wonder as he focused in on his village.

Shaking his head, he smiled and handed them three straw hats and a bundle of clothes. Kate took hers behind some trees while Cormac and Ghost changed into cotton trousers and coarse smocks made from something like hemp.

Even when Kate returned to the group dressed as a peasant, she still looked beautiful. She spun around, whipping her blonde hair over her shoulder. 'I heard hemp was hot this year.'

Cormac laughed. She smiled back and piled her hair on top of her head, hiding it beneath the straw hat.

Yoshiro gave them each a bag to carry their shōzoku and boots. He spoke to Kate, pointing to a path through the trees. Kate nodded as she listened to his directions, before bowing in thanks.

'Yes,' said Cormac, bowing. 'Arigatō gozaimasu.'

Yoshiro smiled and bowed back. 'Sayōnara,' he said, before turning towards his village.

Kate pulled her binoculars out of her bag and raced after him. She pushed them into his hand. He smiled and bowed again before continuing on his way.

Barefoot, Cormac, Ghost and Kate set off through the trees, leaving the village behind.

They trekked across grassy slopes and shady wood-land, following faint tracks through the vegetation. Rolling hills of rich green and yellow stretched towards hazy mountain peaks, in what was some of the most amazing scenery Cormac had ever seen. In the distance, they caught sight of other small villages like Yoshiro's, and once they had to leave the path and hide in the grass to avoid an approaching monk clad in white robes.

They walked for hours, mainly in silence, with Kate leading the way. The time helped Cormac sort out the mess in his head. He wouldn't have believed it if he hadn't seen it with his own two eyes, but Kiko's sword had definitely cut a hole in the night air. The blinding light that had beamed through it was daylight from another time. Another century, for God's sake. Ghost's desperate mission now became his too as he finally acknowledged the truth of what Ghost had said – that the only way they would return to Renkondo was by retrieving the sword.

They came across another shrine, and this time

Cormac recognized the statue. It was Buddha, sitting in the lotus position with his eyes closed and right palm raised. Ghost took one of the tangerines left there by visiting pilgrims. It reminded Cormac how hungry he was.

He grabbed one of the tangerines and tossed another to Kate. 'Buddha wouldn't want us to starve.'

Kate took Savage out of her bag and began to peel her fruit.

Ghost looked glum as he chewed his food.

'What's up?' asked Cormac.

'This.' He gestured at the scenery. 'This is all my fault.'

'Hey,' said Cormac. 'We're only stuck in the sixteenth century. It's no big deal!'

They laughed.

Ghost smiled. 'Thank you.'

Cormac punched him playfully on the shoulder. 'That's what friends are for. It's good to have you back.'

Kate stood up and looked across the hills at the sun sinking low in the sky. 'We'd better keep going.'

Cormac dragged his feet along the track. Technically, it was over five hundred years since he'd slept. But that wasn't right either, because the last time he'd slept was in the future, which was in five hundred years' time. His brain ached as he tried to make sense of it. He gave up and ran after Ghost and Kate, down the hillside.

As the sun dipped behind the mountains, it spilt its fire into the sky, staining it a grapefruit pink. Kate pointed out the road below them and, further along it, a town unlike anything Cormac had ever seen before. Where Ballyhook was an industrial town full of smoking factories and smog-smothered houses, Yosa had trees and winding streets, curved roofs and pointed spires. And in the centre of it all towered an imposing building, dark and hunched over like a giant cat.

'Yosa Castle,' said Kate.

'Well, the next bit should be easy,' said Cormac, looking down at the castle.

'You think?' said Kate.

'Um . . . no.'

As dusk fell, tiny lights appeared in the town. Ghost crouched with his friends behind some trees and watched the road below, where farmers pulled carts loaded with yams, greens and bamboo into Yosa. Small thatched houses lined the road, and outside them people sat at charcoal braziers, relaxing after a day's work. The place couldn't have looked more different from his favela in Rio. It sounded different too – silent, apart from the occasional muted laugh of a child or rumble of a cart. No shouting, singing, music, gunshots, screams, squealing tyres.

They followed the road, keeping well hidden behind the trees and foliage that flanked it. From a distance, their peasant attire might have fooled suspicious eyes but, up close, they were still foreigners.

At the suburbs of Yosa, they left the safety of the

trees. Using side streets to avoid contact, they followed the main road into town. The further they travelled, the busier it got. Merchants, farmers, peasants and monks hurried through the streets. Children played at the roadside, chasing fireflies and disassembling their kites after a day's play.

Ghost tipped his straw hat to hide his face, but that didn't stop a stray dog from becoming suspicious. It followed them between two houses, snarling. Kate turned around and growled, baring her teeth. The dog whimpered and scuttled off with its tail between its legs.

'Remind me never to have an argument with you,' said Cormac.

Kate laughed and continued walking.

Through open doors, they saw families on straw mats, eating with chopsticks, their sandals lined up neatly outside. Glowing paper lanterns bobbed in the evening breeze.

As they travelled deeper into the city, the surroundings became more commercial. They passed stalls selling noodles, fish and pickled vegetables. A troupe of actors performed to a spellbound audience. People queued up to visit a temple. Blue-robed monks with baskets on their heads played flutes and collected alms from passers-by.

The buildings became grander. Instead of ladders, they had stairs, and they had shuttered windows and tiled roofs, often with dolphins at their upturned ends. Behind high gates, the light from stone lanterns gave them glimpses of carp-filled ponds and manicured gardens. And all the time, Yosa Castle towered over them, a giant of stone and wood with glowing eyes.

Turning down a new street, Ghost froze, and quickly retreated. Peering around the corner, he pointed out a man wearing breeches, wooden clogs and a kimono. In his belt he carried two swords: one short and dagger-like, the other long and slightly curved. The top of his head was shaved, and the hair at the back and sides was oiled and in a knot on top. *Like a Kat!* People bowed as he marched past.

'Samurai,' whispered Kate.

There was a sudden shifting of the people's attention. Music, laughter and hawking ceased, and everybody, including the samurai, looked in the same direction. Something was approaching from the direction the friends had just come from and, as it got closer, the streets cleared and fell silent. People knelt along the roadside and bowed their heads to the ground.

From under the brim of his hat, Ghost blinked rapidly as he watched a heavily-armed cavalcade march into town. With long bows and spears, the samurai foot soldiers flanked the cavalry, who rode on stallions with bright tassels decorating their bridles. The riders wore burnished breastplates, steel arm protectors and iron helmets. Ghost noticed that the flagpoles attached to their backs bore Empire banners.

Kate pulled his sleeve. 'Get down!'

Ghost dropped to his knees, and the three

prostrated themselves before the passing samurai. Peeking out from under his hat, Ghost caught a glimpse of what the soldiers were escorting into town. The horses surrounded a palanquin carried by four men in loincloths. The curtains were open, and inside sat a man Ghost recognized from TV – President Goda.

But how can that be possible?

He wore a scarlet robe, and in his hands, openly displayed to anyone brave or foolish enough to look, was a sword. The Moon Sword!

It was only when the procession drew alongside him that Ghost saw the other passenger. Lady Kiko sat dressed in a pale green kimono, with her hair piled on top of her head and held in place using silver pins. She was more beautiful than she'd ever been as Ami. Her porcelain skin glowed in the sunlight and her eyes shone. She smiled triumphantly, scanning the crowd as she passed by.

Ghost pressed his face into the dirt. He held his breath, waiting for her voice to invade his thoughts, waiting for her to paralyze him with pain. His arms started shaking uncontrollably and he drew them into his sides, hoping his straw hat would hide them. Cold sweat oozed from every pore in his body. All he wanted to do was run, but he knew he shouldn't move, couldn't move. He stayed absolutely still until he felt someone shaking him.

'You can get up now, Ghost.' It was Cormac's voice.

Ghost lifted his head.

Cormac was crouched down beside him. 'It's OK. They're gone.'

He tried to stand, but his legs had turned to jelly. Cormac pulled him to his feet. 'It's OK.'

Ghost tried to speak, but nothing came out. *Maybe Kiko doesn't know I'm here. Maybe I'm safe*. But he couldn't be sure.

'We know how scary that must have been for you,' said Cormac. 'But we have to follow that sword.'

On wobbly legs, Ghost went with Cormac and Kate. Keeping to the alleyways, they followed the procession to Yosa Castle.

A high stone wall and deep moat protected it from intruders. Seven floors of ornate architecture reached into the sky, complete with outhouses, watchtowers and the main keep. The narrow windows twinkled, and smaller pinpricks of light moved along the walls – sentries carrying torches.

From under the cover of an overhanging roof, they watched the guarded palanquin cross a draw-bridge. A huge iron-plated door opened, and behind that a heavy portcullis rose. Ghost thought he saw a second wall and gate inside, but the door closed too fast for him to be certain.

'That was Lord Goda, right?' asked Cormac.

'Or President Goda,' said Kate. 'They're the same person.'

'But how can that be? They live five hundred years apart.'

Kate nodded. 'It's his swords – the butterfly one and the snake-eye. They were forged at the same time as the Moon Sword, so they must do the same thing.' She spoke quickly, her eyes shining. 'He obviously uses the swords to travel through time. It would explain why the ruler of the Empire has always been called Goda – and why every Goda has been really mysterious. They're all the same person!'

'And now he has all three swords,' said Ghost. It was the first time he'd spoken since seeing Kiko. Kate and Cormac stared at him.

'Are you all right?' asked Kate.

Ghost nodded. 'Remember Makoto said something about the three swords making some terrible weapon?'

'Yeah,' said Cormac. 'Goda wanted this third sword so badly he sent his own wife to the future to get it.'

Kate looked confused. 'But what sort of weapon could the three swords make? And what's he going to do with it?'

Cormac's eyes opened wide. 'Back in the map room I read something about an electromagnetic disturbance in sixteenth-century Japan which warped all metals.'

'There was loads of random stuff in the map room,' Kate pointed out.

'But this stuck out,' Cormac insisted. 'It happened so soon after the swords were forged. Maybe that was the last time they were all together, before the Black Lotus stole the Moon Sword. Maybe that's what they can do when they're combined.'

Kate thought for a moment. 'But that's not such

a terrible weapon, is it?' she asked. 'I mean, what's the big deal if a few bits of metal get warped?'

'No big deal in the sixteenth century because there was very little metal. But imagine what it could do to a modern city. Most buildings are built with metal frames. Vehicles are metal. Electronics are metal. Our army's defences are metal.'

Kate gasped. 'The Empire is about to attack America! New York is a metal city!'

'Another reason to get that sword back,' said Ghost.

The three of them looked up at the castle.

'Well, we know where it is,' said Cormac.

Kate nodded. 'All we have to do is get it back.'

Keeping to the shadows, they circled the castle. There was no way in.

'Could you just run up those walls or something?' asked Kate.

Cormac shook his head. 'Not with that moat in front.'

Ghost examined the castle wall through his binoculars. 'Get your binocs, Cormac.'

Cormac rummaged in his bag till he found the binoculars in his shōzoku.

'Follow the samurai along the moat,' said Ghost.

Using night vision, Cormac moved the binocs along the wall until he found a samurai patrolling the outside edge of the moat. The samurai crossed a narrow bridge over the water to a small service gate in the wall, then spoke briefly with the guards, before being admitted inside.

'I can get in there,' said Ghost.

Kate shook her head. 'You're not going in alone.'

'I got us into this mess. I will get—'

'I don't care. You're not going in alone.'

'Yeah,' said Cormac. 'We're a team.'

Ghost held his hands up. 'OK. So I go inside and throw a rope over the wall for you guys.'

'Sounds like a plan,' said Cormac.

The three friends hid in a lean-to full of firewood until the town fell quiet. When they finally left their hiding place, the sky was full of stars, the streets were empty and the lamps in most of the houses were out.

'Watch the flag on the wall,' said Ghost. 'I will use it to signal I am ready.'

He stepped behind a water barrel and undressed. He closed his eyes, cleared his mind and let himself drift until he felt the freezing wave wash through him. When he was sure he could no longer be seen, he stepped out from behind the barrel and tiptoed over to Cormac and Kate. 'Boo!' he said, causing them to stumble backwards in fright. It felt good to laugh.

'Very funny!' said Kate.

'You must change too,' said Ghost. 'Into your shōzoku, and don't forget the night mode.'

'Listen, Ghost,' said Cormac. 'I just wanted to say . . .'

Ghost smiled and headed off towards the castle, not waiting to hear Cormac's goodbye speech. They'd soon realize he wasn't there.

He crossed the bridge and approached the wooden gate. Two fat samurai guarded the entrance. Their hairstyles reminded him of Kats'. One held a long pike, and the other, a bow. A quiver of arrows hung on the second samurai's back.

Ghost squatted on the ground. *This had better not take long.* He was already exhausted and the invisibility was quickly draining his energy reserves. He looked back towards Cormac and Kate, but couldn't see them.

The guards moved at the sound of the gate being opened from the inside. Ghost sprang to his feet and crept forwards. He edged behind one of the guards and waited. The gate opened and a samurai emerged, greeting the guards with a bow.

Ghost quickly slipped through the gate and into a large yard with some trees in one corner. Outside a nearby stable, two samurai cursed and whipped their horses into a stall.

As Ghost had suspected, he wasn't inside the main building yet. A tall stone wall stood between him and the castle, and along the top of it ran buildings with tiled roofs. He didn't want to think about how they'd cross it. One wall at a time.

He made his way along the inside of the outer wall to the flagpole. Using the pole and wall, he climbed to the tiles on top. He stood up and peered out into the shadowy streets of Yosa. It was time to give Cormac and Kate the signal. He couldn't see them and they wouldn't be able to see him. All they needed to see was the flag.

While Kate dressed behind the same water barrel Ghost had used, Cormac pulled on his own shōzoku and boots. It felt good to be wearing them again. He found the button inside his sleeve and activated the night mode. Immediately, the magnetized balls on his suit turned inwards to reveal their non-reflective black sides. He was now a shadow.

He picked up the binoculars. With night vision, Yosa Castle glowed a phosphorescent green and white. Scanning along the moat wall, he found the Empire flag fluttering in the breeze.

'I'll bring Ghost's bag,' whispered Kate from behind the barrel.

Cormac glanced behind him. 'It might give us away. Just take out his shōzoku – maybe tie it around your waist?'

When he looked back through his binocs, he noticed the flag had changed. Instead of fluttering in the wind, it was rolled tightly around the pole. Ghost!

'Time to go,' he whispered, returning the binoculars to his sleeve pocket and removing his rope.

A samurai guard passed by.

'When the guard is gone, we move.' Cormac pulled his cowl on, then fixed his face mask, sealing it at the edges.

He watched Kate do the same. If anything went wrong, this could be the last time he'd see her. He felt like he should say something, but Kate was pointing towards the castle. The guard was gone. There was no time for words. They looked at each other for a brief moment, and then ran towards the castle.

Teenagers moments before, they now became the ninjas of legend, moving like shadows in the night. Cormac's heart pounded as he waited for the cry of alarm or the arrow that would end their run across the open space to the moat. But neither came, and they reached the water safely.

Cormac looked up to where Ghost should be standing. He took the coil of rope in his right hand, holding on to the end with his left. There would only be time for one shot at this before the patrolling guard returned. He flung the rope towards the flagpole. It sailed across the moat in a perfect arc and would have continued over the wall if it hadn't been plucked out of the air by invisible hands.

'Carry a rock,' whispered Cormac, pulling one from the bank. 'It'll keep you under water.'

Kate did the same and Cormac passed her the rope. Together, they slid into the moat.

The cold hit Cormac as soon as he entered, but his shōzoku acted like a wetsuit, keeping his body warm. The rocks kept them at the bottom, and the shōzoku supplied a steady flow of oxygen to their masks. It was pitch dark, but following the rope they made it to the stone wall at the other side. As soon as they reached it, there was a tug on the rope – a signal it was safe to go. Kate dropped her rock and began to climb.

After a few seconds had passed, Cormac let go of his rock and floated upwards. When his head broke the surface, he looked up and saw Kate climbing on to the top of the wall.

He placed his feet on the wall and pulled himself up the rope. The rubber toes of his boots clung to the stone, and in seconds he lay beside Kate on the capping tiles. She pulled off her face mask and frowned.

Instead of being inside the castle, they were in an outer courtyard. The fortress lay behind another wall. The buildings on top made it twice as high as the moat wall. Four samurai guarded a closed wooden door.

'We do the same again for the next wall?' said the voice of Ghost.

Cormac turned his binocs back to the inner wall. 'No, I have a better idea.'

Kate watched Cormac slide down the flagpole into the yard and follow the inside of the moat wall towards the castle. The guards were too busy talking to notice the figure in black running straight up the wall and on to the rooftops.

'You go first,' said the invisible Ghost.

Kate slid down the pole. Hugging the wall for cover, she traced Cormac's route. She heard the guards talking, but also animal voices. As she crept forwards, the animals' conversation got louder and louder until they were right beside her. In a stable, two horses complained about the way their masters treated them. Kate's heart ached. It took a lot to make horses complain.

She soothed them with gentle whispers through the stable door. The animals immediately relaxed, and one of them poked his head out to investigate. Kate stroked his muzzle, and the horse snorted with pleasure.

'What are you doing?' murmured Ghost.

Automatically, Kate turned around, but of course Ghost wasn't visible. He nudged her, urging her forward. She continued along the wall, only glancing behind once to see that she was still being closely observed by the two horses.

They were almost at the far wall when a noise that sounded like Ghost stumbling came from behind her. She froze, as did the guards' conversation. They looked in the direction of the sound, hands on sword hilts.

Heart pounding, she remained absolutely motionless, as she'd been trained to do. To her horror, she saw two of the gate guards begin to walk in her direction. She knew Ghost was behind her, invisible, but she was trapped, with nowhere to hide and nowhere to run.

The guards kept coming, their faces pale and alert in the moonlight. They couldn't see her yet, but in seconds they'd be beside her. Even her shōzoku wouldn't save her. They kept coming, and just as they were upon her, a raucous clamour arose from the stables. The horses neighed wildly and kicked the doors. The guards cursed and headed towards the crazed animals, away from Kate.

She closed her eyes and released her breath.

The guards shouted. Kate looked over her shoulder and stiffened at the sight of the horses being beaten with sticks. Tears filled her eyes, but she had to make the most of the diversion. She hurried towards the wall, where Cormac had secured a rope for them to climb.

She grabbed the rope and, using her rubber boots to grip the wall, climbed up past a window protected by iron bars. Below her, the noise from the stables faded away. She clambered on to the roof tiles and crawled to the ridge, to where Cormac was waiting. Panting, she lay on her back and looked up at the sky. Thousands of stars pinpricked the night. Under different circumstances, she would have thought them pretty.

Puffing and panting, the invisible Ghost joined them. Kate gazed down into the main castle courtyard, which was lit by torches and patrolled by samurai guards. All around its edge, buildings were linked together by paths, streams, walls, arches and opulent gardens, but it was to the castle keep, or donjon, that her eyes were irresistibly drawn.

Sitting on a sloping foundation of stone, seven stories of plastered walls and curving roofs rose into the sky. Lights burnt in its narrow windows, and silhouetted sentinels kept watch. The main entrance lay below – a large wooden door reinforced with iron and guarded by samurai.

'The royal rooms will be in the highest part of the tower,' said Kate. 'But how will we get up there?'

'The roof is guarded, but I think I've found a weak spot,' said Cormac from behind his binocs. 'If we continue along this roof, we'll reach the foundations of the keep. From there, I can scale the walls to the first-floor roof and lower a rope for you guys to follow.'

Kate nodded.

Like cats, they padded along the roof tiles, silent and black, conscious that one wrong move could alert the guards below. The three ninjas reached the castle keep unnoticed. They lay face down on the tiles, watching the patrolling guards below.

When the coast was clear, Cormac sprang to his feet and ran towards the keep. When he reached the stone foundations he kept running vertically like a two-legged spider. With amazing agility, he grabbed the protruding roof edge while letting his feet drop from the wall. His body swung outwards, threatening his tentative hold.

Kate gasped, but Cormac's grip didn't falter. For a moment he hung there, swinging like a black rag in the breeze, and then, using the strength of his arms alone, he pulled himself up on to the roof of the keep.

Kate watched in terror and awe, as Cormac crawled up the steeply inclining roof to a dark window in the wall. He tied his rope to one of the window bars, slid back down the roof and dangled the other end over the edge.

'Ladies first,' whispered Ghost.

Kate crawled along the ridge tiles to the rope. She couldn't use the wall for assistance now and was glad of all the hours they had practised going up and down ropes. Cormac pulled her on to the roof and they lay on their stomachs, waiting for Ghost.

She saw the rope moving as Ghost made his way

to the top. But it took him so long, Kate worried he might not make it. She guessed that staying invisible must be draining, because in training he had always been one of the first to the top. Panting heavily, he eventually joined them.

'Maybe you should change back to visible again?' suggested Kate.

'I'm fine,' gasped Ghost.

They crawled up the roof to where Cormac had fixed the rope. He untied it and replaced it in his shōzoku.

'All the windows are barred,' he whispered, 'but we may have something to help.'

He removed his roll of Acid Wrap and tore off two pieces, which he wrapped around the top and bottom of the middle bar. The wrap fizzled at the edges, the chemical reaction producing a toxic smell, with tendrils of smoke curling into the night air. A few seconds later, the wraps dropped off, revealing eroded rings of metal.

Cormac yanked the bar and it snapped clean off. 'Are we ready?'

'No,' said Ghost.

'What?'

'I go alone.'

'No,' protested Cormac and Kate.

'The place will be full of samurai. Only I can move totally unseen.'

'What about Kiko?' asked Cormac.

'She does not know I am here,' replied Ghost.

Kate shook her head. 'It's too dangerous.'

'Who would you say has the best chance?' asked Ghost. 'Three people or one invisible person?'

Kate shrugged in reluctant agreement. 'But are you up to it?'

'Yes.'

'And how will you get the sword out?' asked Kate. 'Don't you think the guards will notice a sword floating past them?'

'I have a plan.'

'And are you gonna tell us what it is?'

'There is no time – I must go.'

They listened to Ghost's grunts as he squeezed in through the gap in the bars.

'Stay here,' were his final words. 'If I do not return in one hour, you leave.'

The reason Ghost didn't tell Kate his plan for getting the sword out of the castle was that he didn't have one. He wished Cormac hadn't mentioned Kiko. He'd managed not to think about her until then. But here he was, in *her* castle, ready to steal *her* beloved sword. He shuddered to think of what she'd do if she found him.

He shivered and looked around the room, trying to ignore the icy cramps gripping his body. Moonlight from the window revealed a large rectangular room with high ceilings of polished wood, a floor covered in straw mats and sliding walls made of paper and wood. Shōji. He remembered the word from his classes in Renkondo.

Ghost stiffened at the sound of footsteps. The profile of a man moved across one of the paper walls. There was the unmistakable silhouette of two swords in the man's belt. As his footsteps disappeared into the night, Ghost slid open the shōji and looked out into a corridor lit by a glowing torch on a stone wall.

Apart from a servant boy carrying a stinking bucket, the corridor was empty. Soon, Ghost came to a steep flight of wooden steps. Kate had said the top of the keep would be most secure and thus the most likely place to find the sword, but he heard voices and footsteps below. The commotion could be about the sword. He had to investigate.

With legs like concrete, he hobbled down the stairs as quietly as possible. The next floor was patrolled by a samurai, his face drawn and nervous-looking.

Looks like I'm going the right way.

He slipped past the man and continued along a passageway until he came to another staircase leading down. And this one was guarded.

Que bom! He smiled, listening to the sound of many footsteps on the floor below.

Carefully, he stepped between the two samurai, remembering what Sensei Iwamoto had said about nightingale floors in Japanese castles. To prevent the steps from squeaking, he stood on the edge of the treads where they were attached to the wall. Though slow and awkward, it worked, and he made it noiselessly to the bottom.

The sword had to be on this floor, because there were guards everywhere. They watched every window, their hands resting on the hilts of their swords, unaware of the boy creeping past them. In the most heavily guarded corridor, Ghost found two sentries guarding a closed shōji.

Ghost continued down the corridor and around the corner to where more guards protected a door into the same room.

Guarded on all sides? This had to be it – but how would he get in?

He was exhausted. The temptation to rest was almost overwhelming, but he couldn't stop now. All he needed was a few seconds to slide the shōji open and slip inside. But first he needed a distraction.

In a nearby alcove sat a small flower arrangement. Ghost put his hand into the vase, took out a pebble and made his way to the least guarded shōji in the corridor. Although the stone was small, he couldn't simply carry it because to the guards it would appear to be floating towards them in mid-air. Instead, he carried it along the floor and against the wall, bending over as he walked, but all the time watching the two samurai. He had used this trick plenty of times before while stealing wallets or jewellery from occupied bedrooms.

It worked, and the pebble slid unnoticed right up to one of the guards' feet. Ghost placed it behind the samurai, and then crept around the other side of him so that he was now standing at the shōji and in between the two guards. He picked up the pebble. The next bit would be tricky. He needed to throw the stone down the corridor without the guards seeing the direction it had come from.

He held the stone behind the samurai's head. He

was so close to the man that he could smell the perfume in his hair. If the guard tilted his head back, he would feel Ghost's hand behind him. Ghost held his breath and waited.

When the samurai twisted his head to look down the corridor, Ghost flicked the pebble the opposite way. It clattered on to the wooden floor, causing both guards to spring into fighting stance, each partially drawing his sword. They took a few tentative steps towards the source of the noise, and Ghost put his hand on the shōji. One of them stooped down to pick up the pebble, and that's when Ghost eased open the screen, just enough to slip inside. Quickly he closed it again and waited. A memory of holding his breath in the apartment in Copacabana flashed into his mind, but was quickly banished by the sight before him.

Row upon row of samurai knelt with their backs to him in one of the largest and most ornate halls Ghost had ever seen. All around, the paper walls were painted gold and adorned with pine trees, hawks and tigers. The pillars which held up the red-and-gold panelled ceiling were carved with animals and horned monsters.

There must have been at least a hundred samurai, and each carried a sword. Every soldier wore shining red armour and some carried the Empire's all-too-familiar banner with the image of the two crossed swords. Separated by a metre-wide aisle of tatami mats, the samurai were split into two groups facing a raised platform at the top of the hall. In the centre of the stage sat a cushion and a small wooden chest.

An air of silent anticipation hung in the hall. Everybody remained motionless, including Ghost. Or at least he tried to, but his shivering was becoming uncontrollable. He needed to move. Before he could, a voice from the top of the hall called out something in Japanese. The only word Ghost picked up was 'Goda'.

Like a wave, the kneeling samurai bowed to the ground. Goda entered, dressed in a red kimono and wearing two swords.

Ghost's heart skipped a beat as the leader of the Samurai Empire – the president he knew from TV – stepped on to the stage, faced his audience and bowed. The samurai straightened up from the floor.

Goda began addressing his army. Ghost couldn't understand what he was saying. He looked around for Kiko, but she was nowhere to be seen. Was one of the blades in Goda's sash the Moon Sword? He needed to get closer to be sure.

Though worried about his fatigue, Ghost carefully walked up the aisle between the kneeling samurai. He held his breath, but none of them blinked or looked sideways as he passed – their attention was on the stage.

Goda had stopped talking and had removed one of his swords. He carefully laid it across the raised cushion.

Heart pounding in his chest, and terrified that he'd stumble or cough, Ghost stepped closer to the stage. One of the corners of Goda's mouth curled upwards in a faint smile and his eyes burnt bright as he stared at the sword on the cushion.

Ghost leant closer. The sword's scabbard was black and shiny, exactly like that of the Moon Sword, except it was decorated with a gold and silver eye instead of a moon.

Now, Goda removed his second katana, marked with a gold butterfly. He placed it across the other sword to form an X. He began to speak once more, pointing at the swords, his voice ringing out over the hall. Ghost listened in, recognizing a few of the words – 'Oosutoria, Firipin, Shingapooru, Indo, Furansu, Suēden, Indoneshia.' *Countries!* All part of the future Samurai Empire.

Goda opened the wooden chest and removed a red piece of cloth – the Empire flag.

He placed the flag with the crossed swords on the wall, above the crossed swords on the cushion, and then raised his hand and beckoned someone through the doorway Ghost had just used.

Ghost's legs almost gave way when he saw who entered. Lady Kiko carried a black sword in outstretched arms and pattered down the aisle towards him in tiny steps. Her face was powdered white, her blood-red lips painted into a smile, and her eyes dark and menacing. Terror rather than cold froze Ghost solidly to the floor as she headed for him. She was going to crash straight into him if he didn't move. But he couldn't. His legs were paralysed by fear.

He closed his eyes as she approached, already foreseeing what would happen in a fast-forwarded movie reel inside his head. She'd bump into him, real-ize who it was, enter his brain, flood it with agonizing pain and, if he was lucky, finish him off with the sword.

But when nothing happened, he opened his eyes to see that Kiko had passed by him and joined Goda on the stage. She placed her sword across the other two on the cushion, to form an asterisk. It was the Moon Sword. This was it. This was what he had come here for. And though it was within arm's reach, he couldn't take it. You couldn't just float a sword out past a hundred samurai.

Ghost's attention shifted to Goda, who was opening the wooden chest. He removed a small pot and a paintbrush. Dipping the brush into the pot, he painted a crude third sword on the Empire flag, to mirror the three swords on the cushion.

Goda returned to the chest and removed a large roll of paper and a carved box. Kneeling, Kiko helped him unroll the scroll on the floor while Goda held the curling corners down with four polished stones.

Ghost stepped closer. The scroll was a map of New York City. Goda reached into the wooden box and began placing red plastic models of samurai soldiers in the centre of the map. He spoke excitedly to Kiko as he moved the models around the map. The words 'Nyūyōku' and 'Amerika' were repeated again and again. Goda was planning an attack on New York City.

Ghost turned back to where the three katana lay on the cushion. The Swords of Sarumara. Makoto had talked about them on their first day at Renkondo. The Black Lotus had spent hundreds of years protecting one, and here they were, all three together.

Ghost turned and glanced around the hall, wondering what his chances of escape would be if he just grabbed them and ran. But a hundred pairs of warrior eyes stared up at him from the back of the hall. He might make it out of there before they realized what was happening, but three floating swords would immediately alert Kiko to his presence. She wouldn't even have to stand up to strike him down dead.

Suddenly the red samurai in the hall stood, in perfect unison. Ghost staggered backwards with fright. Goda beckoned one of them forward and gave him the Moon Sword. He then gave the man lengthy orders in Japanese. The samurai blinked and then bowed, before marching down the aisle between the two groups of warriors. Half of the soldiers followed him in single file.

Ghost watched his prize disappear out of the hall. *Bosta!* He glanced back at the remaining swords, but Goda was replacing them in his sash. With his wife at his side, Goda headed for the door through which he had entered.

Ghost glanced between the two exits in panic. *Which way should I go?* Moments before, he could have taken the three swords. Now they were leaving the hall in different directions.

Ghost ran after the Moon Sword, stumbling past the samurai filing out of the hall. He followed the marching soldiers along corridors and up wooden stairs, racing past them whenever he got a chance. Though he had to be careful about not bumping into them, he didn't have to worry about being quiet. The castle donjon was filled with the sound of fifty pairs of feet marching along wooden passageways and stairs.

Higher and higher they went into the keep, Ghost still overtaking samurai when he could, in a desperate attempt to get to the sword before it was locked away out of reach. Panting for breath, he caught up with the leading samurai just as he stepped into a room, carrying the sword with him.

Ghost followed him into a bedroom with walls of stone instead of paper. The man placed the blade on a wooden stand beside a low futon. He then poured a clear liquid from a ceramic jug into a cup on a low polished table. Ghost's nostrils tingled at the smell of alcohol.

The samurai ran his hand along the Moon Sword before leaving the room and closing the heavy wooden double doors. Ghost heard him bark orders, and saw his red armour through the gap between the doors.

Ghost hugged himself. His body was like a block of ice, screaming at him to lie down. But he couldn't. Not until his job was done.

He'd found the sword, but how would he get it out? He looked around the room. It was large and dimly lit by an oil lamp in one corner. A single narrow window looked out on to the night sky. Already there were traces of pink on the horizon. The window was guarded by iron bars. But even if he could remove them, the opening was too narrow to climb through. The ceiling was supported by thick beams of wood which sat on red pillars with gold carvings of foxes and deer. Somebody important used this room, and would be coming to bed soon . . .

His gaze fell on the black scabbard inlaid with a gold and silver moon. The sword looked more beautiful than dangerous, yet it had caused so much trouble for hundreds of years.

He stepped carefully across the floor, keeping his eyes fixed on the closed wooden doors. He held his breath and bent down to take the blade. It felt heavier than he remembered. How the hell was he going to get it out past fifty guards?

The answer came in the most unexpected manner. First, he heard a tiny scurrying noise, and then he noticed movement along one of the ceiling beams. A mouse ran down one of the red pillars towards him. As it got closer he realized it was carrying something in its mouth, something that looked like a piece of black plastic. *Savage!* It looked around the room, then sniffed its way right up to him and dropped the object at his feet.

Ghost put down the sword and picked up the object – two pieces of black plastic joined by a thin wire. The comm from his shōzoku! He inserted the earpiece and listened. At first there was nothing, and then came Kate's voice.

'Ghost, can you hear me?'

'Yes,' he whispered, glancing back at the door.

'I hope you'll treat Savage with a little more respect from now on,' she said.

'Yes.' He nodded, looking down at the little mouse who was sitting up on his back legs, waiting.

'Is everything OK?'

'Yes.'

'Any sign of the sword?'

'I have it, but I don't know how to get it out.'

He described the situation as quickly and quietly as he could.

Cormac's voice came through the comm. 'How many floors did you go up?'

Ghost tallied up the number of staircases he'd climbed. 'Four, I think.'

'Is there a window in the room?'

'Yes, but it is too small to climb through. And it has bars.'

'Look out and tell me what you see.'

Outside, the stars were almost all gone, and crimson streaked the morning sky. Below, the town of Yosa slept. Sticking up above all the buildings was one which looked like a miniature version of the castle he was in.

'I think I see a temple.'

'Describe it.'

'It's white with four curved roofs . . .'

'Does it have a spike on top and a large gate in front of it?'

'Yes.'

'Got it. Now tie the sword outside the window. I'll climb up and get it.'

'And me?'

There was a brief silence before Kate spoke. 'If Savage distracts the guards outside, you can open the door and leave.'

Ghost's teeth chattered with the cold. 'Um, OK. And how do I tell Savage the plan?'

'Hold the comm to his ear.'

Ghost did as she requested.

When Savage ran away, he asked, 'What will I do with the comm?'

'Leave it,' said Kate. 'Now hurry!'

Ghost hid the comm behind the oil lamp in the corner. Using the scabbard's belt cords, he tied the sword to a window bar so that it hung on the outside of the castle wall. It would be impossible to see from the ground, and the only thing visible from inside was a leather string.

Ghost crept to the door and listened. All was quiet. He waited, his hand on the door.

Suddenly the guard outside said something, then stepped away from the door. Ghost guessed he'd spotted Savage. He eased the door open a fraction to look out. The guard had taken a step forward to watch the mouse. Savage ran in circles, chasing his tail, then stood up on his back legs and fell over.

Ghost pushed open the door and slipped out, closing it again just before the guard looked behind him. Seeing nobody, he shook his head and turned his attention back to the mouse. The show was over, however, and Savage scuttled off down the corridor. The puzzled guards returned to their posts, and without a sound Ghost stepped past them.

The adrenaline that had carried Ghost in and out of the room had dissipated. His head drooped, his arms hung limp by his sides and every step was like walking knee-deep in mud.

On the stairs, he couldn't take the care that he'd taken on the way up, and a loose tread squeaked when he stepped on it. The samurai at the bottom spun around, hands automatically dropping to their swords, but there was nothing to see. Ghost continued past them recklessly. Further down the corridor, he brushed into a passing guard, who also drew his sword, but Ghost trudged onwards, barely noticing.

At the next staircase, Savage waited for him.

Ghost smiled weakly at the mouse before stumbling down after him. As if in a dream, he followed the mouse down two more flights of stairs, clinging to the walls for support. When he stepped into the corridor, his legs buckled beneath him, and he crashed on to the floor. His mind screeched at him to move, but his body had given up. He lay there disabled by cold and exhaustion.

He knew he wouldn't make it. Even if he did, he'd only ruin Kate's and Cormac's chances of escape. Better to end it here. He had retrieved the sword. He had put things right. He could die with honour.

He crawled to the nearest shōji. Careless of who might be behind it, he slid the door open and dragged himself in. He tried to close it again, but his body went limp. Sleep draped itself over him like a heavy blanket.

23

Sitting on the roof, Kate looked out over Yosa towards the mountainous horizon. The sun was almost up. She still hadn't heard from Cormac.

A scrabbling noise on the windowsill diverted her attention. It was Savage. In a flurry of squeaks, he told her what had happened. She quickly updated Cormac via her comm.

'I'm going in to get him,' she said.

'Be careful.'

'Have you reached the sword yet?'

'Who do you think I am, Superman?'

'Well, you do have Superman underpants.'

Cormac laughed.

'I gotta go,' said Kate. 'Be careful, Superman.'

'You too, Ninja Girl.'

Thinking about going into the castle made Kate

nervous. Even with her shōzoku and training, she wasn't Ninja Girl, or any other superhero. But her friend was in there, and he needed help.

She tightened Ghost's shōzoku around her waist, slid between the same gap in the iron bars that Ghost had used to enter, and dropped to the floor inside. At the corridor, she slid the shōji open just enough for Savage to dart out to check for samurai. When she heard his squeak, she followed the mouse down the passageway. They raced up the stairs and along another corridor until they came to the partially-closed shōji.

Inside, Ghost lay on the floor. Her legs felt suddenly weak, and she held on to the shōji for support. *What if he's dead?*

Averting her eyes from his naked body, she closed the shōji and grabbed a rolled-up quilt from against the wall. She placed it over him and knelt beside him. Relieved to hear him breathing, she was about to contact Cormac when she heard footsteps marching down the corridor. They stopped outside the room. The shōji slid open and three samurai warriors stepped inside.

In a race against the rising sun, Cormac ran vertically up the central keep of Yosa Castle. He launched himself at a large bronze tiger-headed fish which hung out over the corner of the roof. He swung up on to the roof of the third floor. Crouching like a cat on the fish's back, he surveyed Yosa. The wind tugged at his shōzoku. Through the slit in his cowl, Cormac tried to locate the temple again.

He caught sight of the spire, rising above its surroundings. With superhuman speed, he sprinted across the tiles to the other side of the castle keep. In a split second, he crossed the sloping roof to a stone wall. His momentum took him obliquely over the face of it, skipping narrow windows on his way to the over-hanging roof. He dived forwards, twisting his body 180 degrees in mid-air so that he faced the wall he had jumped from. Once he gripped the roof, he propelled himself up on to it.

He landed in a crouch and scanned the wall of the fifth floor until he saw what looked like a black stick hanging from the middle window – the Moon Sword.

In his cowl, he was more like Spiderman than Superman as he crawled up the sloping tiles of the roof, wary now of archers. The sword's scabbard banged against the wall as the wind pulled at it. Creeping forwards, he reached up and silenced it with both hands. It was truly a thing of beauty, the gold inlay of the moon catching the first rays of morning light.

Cormac stood up to untie the sword and came face to face with Lord Goda on the other side of the window.

The three samurai reached for their swords. Kate dipped into her shuriken purse, pulled out the bundle of blades, and released them at her opponents. They zipped through the air, hitting one samurai in the neck and another in the arm. Before they could draw their swords, the tranquillizer entered their bloodstreams. They wobbled drunkenly before slumping to the floor, unconscious.

The third samurai drew his katana. He flew at Kate with the blade raised. She rolled aside before the weapon sliced down and struck the floor where she'd been kneeling. Still crouching, she drove the sole of her foot into his exposed ribs, pivoting on her supporting heel at the last moment to deliver full force. The samurai fell sideways, but quickly rolled upright again.

Kate knew she was no match for him. She staggered back as he approached, a venomous sneer on his face. He swung his sword. Kate stepped back, narrowly avoiding the tip of his katana. She stumbled over one of the unconscious samurai and fell on her back. Her attacker laughed and raised his sword for the death blow, but something small raced up the man's body and on to his face. The samurai screamed in pain and dropped his sword, swiping wildly at the mouse clinging to his nose.

Kate seized the opportunity and retrieved a stray shuriken embedded in a wooden post. The samurai flung Savage across the room. With a bloody bite-mark on his nose, he reached for his sword, but the spinning shuriken bit into his leg. He gasped and then fell silent. His face contorted into grotesque grimaces before he collapsed to the floor.

Savage raced over to Kate. She picked him up and wiped the samurai blood from his face. 'You really will eat anything.'

'Rice I prefer,' he squeaked.

Kate kissed him, and placed him in her pocket.

She looked at the four unconscious bodies. How was she going to get Ghost out of there?

Lord Goda's bloodshot eyes met Cormac's. For a second, neither moved, and then the shōgun's face became a mask of anger. He roared and grabbed for the sword.

Cormac cried out with terror, and pulled back, but Goda had a hold of the leather cord. He yanked it, but Cormac held tight. In a desperate tug of war, Cormac jerked the scabbard, whipping the leather cord from the man's hands, sending himself and the sword falling backwards down the roof. He tumbled downwards, the scabbard smashing tiles as he dug it into them to slow his descent. It was working, but not fast enough. He tumbled over the roof's edge.

In mid-air, he righted himself and prepared to land on the next roof. The tiles rushed towards him, and his feet smashed into them in an explosion of splinters, but his bent knees absorbed most of the impact. He rolled forwards and on to his feet, the sword still firmly in his hand. His momentum, however, carried him perilously forwards, down the roof.

Cormac knew he couldn't stop, but perhaps he could control his route. He veered sideways towards the corner of the roof and a large bronze dolphin statue which overlooked the town of Yosa far below. He grabbed its tail, but his body kept moving. His legs shot out over the edge and his arm was jerked into a painful stretch. He flopped on to the dolphin's back, glad now of all the years he'd spent running over the rooftops of Ballyhook. He checked for the sword and scabbard, and then smiled.

The smile vanished when he heard a clarion call from the top of the keep. The noise was so loud it could only be one thing: an alarm.

Ghost too heard the horn. He stirred, looked up at Kate leaning over him and then underneath the quilt. 'You looking at my ass again?' he said groggily.

'More like *saving* your ass.' Kate stood up and tapped the comm on her shōzoku. 'Cormac, can you hear me?'

There was no reply.

She knelt beside one of the unconscious samurai. 'That sounded like an alarm. They must have spotted Cormac.'

'Bosta!' gasped Ghost, sitting up and staring at the inert bodies strewn around the room. 'Are they dead?'

'No,' said Kate. 'They're just unconscious, but for

how long I don't know.' She untied Ghost's shōzoku from around her waist and threw it over to him.

'No peeping,' said Ghost.

'Shut up and get dressed.' She turned her back on him and tapped the comm on her shōzoku. 'Cormac, are you OK?'

'Yes,' he panted. 'But they've spotted me. We need to get out now.'

As if to prove his point, footsteps rushed down the corridor. Kate quickly closed the shōji just before a troop of samurai ran by.

Ghost zipped up his shōzoku. 'How do we get out?'

Cormac jumped down to the next roof and immediately came under fire. From the keep's narrow windows, archers loosed arrows upon him like rain. He sprinted on as several whistled past his head. He dropped on to the next roof, only to come under attack again. Below in the courtyard, samurai streamed out of buildings and into battle formation. Rows of archers lined up, waiting for him to come into range.

He continued his downward run at superhuman speed, swinging from one roof to the next until he landed back where he'd started, above the first floor.

'I have to leave without you,' he shouted into his comm as he leapt from the central keep. He dropped thirty metres on to the wall below and landed in an explosion of roof tiles.

As he rolled out, he felt a bolt of pain race up his arm, from where his wrist had smashed into the tiles. Switching the sword to his other hand, he raced along the top of the inner wall. A hail of arrows darkened the sky, but Cormac had already disappeared into the outer yard.

He came up running in the direction of the final wall. Samurai warriors had formed a defensive line across the outer yard and now came charging at him, their swords raised and their battle cries filling the air. Cormac sped headlong into the approaching line of blades, which closed in on him from all sides.

They met halfway across the yard, and a dozen samurai swung their katanas just as Cormac launched himself into the air. He heard their blades ring off each other as he sailed cleanly over their heads, ran straight up the outer wall and disappeared over the top.

Kate took off one of the unconscious samurai's clothes and put them on over her shōzoku. She looked at Ghost, who had done the same. 'You look cool.'

'I don't like cool.' He rubbed his arms. 'Warm is better.'

Kate smiled. 'Ready?'

'What about our faces? Samurai aren't black or female.'

Kate pointed at three suits of leather armour on stands. She guessed they were why the men had come into the room. The helmets wouldn't completely hide their faces, but they would certainly help.

Outside, the corridor was filled with samurai, all running in the same direction. Kate tightened her helmet, shoved open the shōji and ran after them. Ghost followed her along the corridor and down a set of stairs.

They joined the troop of men hurrying out of the keep, and followed them across a courtyard, through a narrow gate and into the inner yard of the castle. They continued through the wooden door which they'd seen earlier. The outer yard was filled with soldiers, many of whom were pointing at the top of the exterior wall or gesturing towards the castle keep. The iron portcullis was being raised and orderly divisions were preparing to leave.

'He escaped,' whispered Ghost.

Kate nodded. 'Cormac may have escaped, but he isn't safe yet and neither are we.'

In the stables beside them, servants hurriedly saddled horses and led them outside to be collected. Kate recognized the two horses that had saved her earlier. They were tied to an iron ring set into the wall. Their ears pricked as she approached.

'I saw how your masters treat you,' she whispered. 'Do you want to get out of here?'

Both horses whickered softly in agreement.

'Help us escape, and I promise you'll never have to come back here.'

She led the two horses towards Ghost.

'Do you know how to ride?' she whispered, climbing into the saddle.

'It's like a motorbike?' he asked, copying the way she'd stepped into the stirrups.

She shook her head. 'Just hold on. The horse knows what to do.'

Kate's horse cantered towards the main gate. Glancing back, she saw the other horse following, with Ghost holding on for dear life.

Cormac placed the sword on the bank and crawled out of the moat, flinching as pain shot through his wrist. Behind him, the castle erupted with noise as troops mobilized to pursue him. He had only minutes before thousands of samurai poured into Yosa, combing through every square inch of the city. There was no place to hide. He had to make a run for it.

He raced across the open ground surrounding the castle and into a side street. At the water barrel where he'd stashed the clothes Yoshiro had given him, he considered changing to disguise himself, but then he heard the tramp of feet. He peered around the corner of the building to see a large group of samurai coming his way.

There was no time to change, so he sprinted forwards, racing down laneways and weaving a zigzag path through the town. In his wake, the streets filled with samurai, rousing sleeping dogs into a cacophony of noise.

'Where are you?' panted Kate in his earpiece.

'Somewhere in Yosa, being chased by samurai!'

'Have you got the sword?'

'Yes.'

'Get to the main road.'

'Why?'

'Just do it!'

Cormac turned left, startling a sleepy-eyed woman on her veranda. Her mouth fell open as the ninja raced past, sword in hand. When he arrived on the main street, he looked back towards the castle. Two samurai on horseback approached at full gallop. He sprinted away from them, wondering why Kate had directed him into danger.

'Stop running!' she shouted in his earpiece.

'I'm being chased!'

'It's us, you moron!'

'What?'

'The two horses, behind you – it's us!'

Cormac slowed and turned around. As the riders got closer, he recognized Ghost and Kate under their helmets. Not far behind them were more samurai – real ones.

'Ride with Ghost!' shouted Kate. 'Sit in front of him so you won't be seen from behind.'

Cormac climbed up into the saddle in front of Ghost. He was no sooner on than the horse took off at lightning speed.

Kate's horse, Areno, was lathered in sweat and foaming at the mouth, but didn't slow.

'Keep going,' urged Kate into the horse's ear. 'This is as much your escape as mine.'

Areno snorted in reply and pushed forwards.

They left Yosa behind and raced through the countryside on the same road they'd followed into the town. The sun was now up, and they met the first of the pedlars pushing their carts towards the town. The locals all knelt and bowed to them as they passed.

After half an hour's ride, they lost sight of the samurai behind them and Kate began to think that perhaps they hadn't even been chasing them. After all, nobody seemed to have noticed them as they left the castle. Perhaps nobody had seen them pick up Cormac either. From behind, they had probably just looked like two samurai in search of the thief. She slowed Areno to a trot, to allow him to recuperate. Cormac and Ghost rode up beside her on their horse, Sora.

'You OK, Kate?' Cormac asked, smiling.

'Yeah, you?'

'Fine.'

'Anybody want to ask me?' asked Ghost.

'Sorry, Ghost.' Cormac laughed, turning in his saddle. 'How are you?'

'Not good. I am a pain in the ass.'

Cormac and Kate laughed loudly.

'What?' protested Ghost. 'It is really painful!'

Kate's laugh stuck in her throat when she saw what lay ahead of them. Two large gates stretched across the road, with buildings blocking the way on either side. Banners flew from their rooftops, and even from a distance she could tell they were Goda's. Now she remembered why they'd avoided the road the previous day. This was a samurai checkpoint.

Kate looked up at the forested slopes on either side of the road. The horses would never make it through the dense foliage. If they abandoned the animals, they could make their way into the hills and avoid the checkpoint, but that would mean breaking her promise to the horses.

Her mind was made up for her when she heard galloping hooves behind them. Goda's men were charging towards them on horseback. They were trapped!

Kate quickly relayed instructions to the horses. Areno snorted, and both animals took off towards the checkpoint, away from one enemy and towards another.

As she got closer to the checkpoint, Kate saw that the gates were now open and a farmer was passing through, pushing a cart of vegetables. A guard stepped on to the road and held up his hand. When he realized they weren't slowing, he gave orders for the gates to be closed, but the cart was in the way. Areno and Sora picked up speed, and Kate knew they were pushing themselves to their limits.

Two samurai shoved the farmer and his cart out of the way. The gates began to close. The horses pressed forwards at breakneck speed. They couldn't have stopped now even if they'd wanted to. The gap between the gates narrowed. They were either going to make this or die trying. Just before the two wooden gates met, Areno and Kate burst through, with Sora, Cormac and Ghost on their tail.

The crossed swords on the checkpoint's banners fluttered as the two horses thundered past. Looking behind her, Kate saw the gates finally close, blocking Goda's soldiers. That might just give them the time they needed to get away. They urged their horses on. It was clear now that Goda's men knew they had the sword and were after them.

Kate studied the passing scenery for a landmark, something that would lead her to the mountain trail. As she rounded a bend, she recognized the paddy fields they'd come through the previous day, so she guided Areno off the road. She dismounted and led him up the steep hill. Cormac and Ghost followed suit, and together they ran up the terraced slopes, constantly checking the road behind them for Goda's samurai.

When they reached a small row of trees, they led the horses into shelter. Kate instructed the animals to lie down. She lay across Areno, the thunderous drum-beat of his pounding heart echoing in her ears. The horses' muscular bodies were slippery with sweat. Whispering praise, she patted their necks, knowing they wouldn't have made it much further.

Using Cormac's binocs, she looked out through the branches at the road below. A boy had appeared out of nowhere and was strolling along the road. Kate zoomed in and realized it was Yoshiro. Seconds later, Goda's samurai galloped around the bend, scanning the hills for their prey.

Yoshiro immediately prostrated himself at the side of the road. The samurai stopped, and the lead rider addressed him. The boy pointed down the road, and the horses raced off in that direction. Kate watched them disappear, and then returned her focus to Yoshiro. He waved, looking at her through an identical pair of binocs. She waved back, before getting the horses to their feet again and continuing up the mountain.

Cormac led the way upwards, out of the paddy fields, picking up their trail from the previous day. He couldn't believe that had been only yesterday. It felt like a life-time ago. He massaged his injured wrist as his horse walked past the shrine and into the forest.

In her saddle, Kate was undoing her samurai armour and discarding it along the way. She also pulled off the samurai clothes underneath and hurled them into the bushes. 'They stink!'

Ghost did the same.

'I'm guessing the plan is to use the sword to reopen that hole thingy to get back to our own time?' said Cormac.

Kate nodded.

Miraculously, they'd made it this far, but it would all have been for nothing if the next step didn't work.

Everything rested on the logic that the sword that had got them into this mess would also get them out of it.

They eventually arrived at the piece of muddy ground where Kiko's horse had been tethered, and continued on to a familiar-looking clearing.

Cormac took the black scabbard and drew out the glinting blade. He felt a strange power thrumming from the katana, the moon emblem glowing softly. He took a deep breath, but Ghost raised his hand.

'I need to do this,' he said, taking the blade from Cormac.

Kate and Cormac watched intently as he raised the katana above his head. Dispelling the air from his lungs in one sharp burst, Ghost sliced downwards with the sword. It made a whistling noise but did nothing else. Cormac swallowed, his worst fear now becoming a reality.

Ghost tried again and again, but nothing happened.

'Let me try,' said Kate.

She sliced the air in every direction, but without success. She threw the sword down and collapsed to the ground. 'We're stuck here!'

'Maybe it needs to be done a special way,' said Ghost, panic in his eyes.

Kate's voice cracked when she spoke – she sounded on the edge of tears. 'Or maybe only special people like Kiko can use it.'

Anger swirled inside Cormac like a hurricane gaining momentum. Everything he'd been through over the last few months – his recruitment by the

Black Lotus, the attack on the motorway, his shinobi training, the theft of the Moon Sword – had led to this point. And now it seemed it had all been for nothing!

He grabbed the katana, ignoring his sore wrist, and held it overhead. Screaming with fury he brought the blade down.

The air ripped, and an explosion of brightness lit up the clearing. Cormac shielded his eyes. When he looked back, Ghost was grinning widely as he stood beside a shifting pool of light. When he stepped inside, the edges of the hole shimmered and Cormac knew they had to be quick. He grabbed Kate's arm and hauled her to her feet.

'The horses!' she shouted, pulling away from him to get the animals that were standing nervously nearby. As she led them towards the portal, cajoling them with soft whispers, Ghost re-emerged from it, a look of terror on his face.

'Get back!' he shouted.

Cormac pointed the sword towards the window of light.

A small reptilian creature about the size of a hen jumped out of the portal into the clearing. It stood on two hind legs and had a long tail covered in greenish scales. Its arms were tiny and its head moved from side to side in quick jerky movements, sizing up the humans with large yellow eyes.

Cormac raised the sword, and the creature snarled at him, baring rows of sharp, pointy teeth. It retreated towards the shrinking hole of light and jumped back into it before the hole closed and disappeared.

'What the heck happened?' asked Cormac.

'I was in the jungle, and then around me came the little . . .'

'Dinosaurs?'

'Yes, the wrong place, definitely.'

'Do you remember when Kiko opened the portal to this place?' said Kate. 'She put a lot of care into standing in the correct spot. Perhaps you need to cut in exactly the same place that we entered this world.'

Cormac nodded and looked around him, trying to remember where that had been. It was only then that he spotted a large round shape at the edge of the clearing. He hadn't seen it earlier because it was covered in ivy. He ran over to it and began pulling off the vines.

'Help me!' he called to the others.

They ripped off the ivy to reveal a large boulder with a crack down the centre of it. Cormac remembered Kiko standing beside it, back in the twenty-first century, when she had swung her sword.

'Stand back,' he said, raising the katana again.

With a shriek, he slashed down with the blade, opening up another pool of light. Through it, they heard a girl scream and the clip-clop of horseshoes on hard ground.

This time, Ghost didn't step into the light, but stuck his head in. Cormac joined him. On the other side was a city with tall houses and cobbled streets. Horse-drawn carriages trundled by noisily. A man wearing a scruffy long-tailed coat and a tall hat stood on a pavement in front of them. He held a knife to the throat of a petrified girl in a hoop skirt. They stared wide-eyed at the two boys' heads floating in the air before them.

'Unhand that girl or I will rain fire down upon you!' boomed Cormac in a deep voice.

The man dropped the knife, and the girl ran off down the street. Cormac smiled at the man before withdrawing.

Ghost winked at Cormac. 'The ladies' man.'

Cormac waited for the portal to close before taking a step sideways. He made two more cuts with the sword, but didn't step blindly into any of the portals, which was just as well because one opened out on to the ocean and the other looked down on a polar landscape sixty metres below. After each incision he adjusted his position, and on his fifth cut, instead of opening up a fissure of light, he opened up one of darkness. How strange it looked in the soft morning light, an aperture of velvety blackness gently contracting and contorting.

Gingerly, Cormac put his head inside. In front of him was a moonlit clearing in a forest, very like the one they were standing in. It was only when Makoto stepped out of the shadows that Cormac was certain it was the right place.

He pulled back and called to Ghost and Kate. 'This is it! Hurry up!'

Kate quickly led the horses towards the black hole. Ghost stood aside to let the animals through. The horses tossed their heads and snorted nervously, but Kate comforted them with whispers. They sniffed the edges of the portal, but wouldn't enter. Kate whispered something into Areno's ear, and stepped into the pool of darkness. Areno followed, crossing over the threshold like a dressage competitor. Scared of being left behind, Sora leapt into the hole, which was already starting to contract.

Cormac grabbed the scabbard off the ground, sheathed the sword and followed, his heart quickening at the sight of their welcoming party – the Jōnin and Makoto.

The Jōnin smiled at him, his face glowing gently in the darkness. Cormac nodded back, thinking what a sight they must look – him in his ninja's black shōzoku, the Moon Sword in hand, and Kate dressed the same way and accompanied by two warhorses prancing nervously on either side of her.

He turned to watch Ghost's dramatic entry.

The gash of sunlight wavered before beginning to close in upon itself.

'Where's Ghost?' asked Makoto.

'He was right behind me,' said Cormac.

All eyes watched the wobbling pool of light as it continued to shrink.

Ghost . . .?

The portal got smaller and smaller.

Kate grabbed Cormac's arm.

'Ghost!' he shouted.

There was no reply.

The portal was shrinking fast. The forest darkened as the light disappeared.

Cormac knew he should do something, but he

was frozen to the spot, his heart pounding in his chest. A figure in white raced past him towards the portal. The Jōnin thrust his arm into the pool of light to prevent it from closing. Only the stump of his other arm could be seen through his kimono. Cormac remembered the Jōnin's attempt to retrieve the sword from Kiko. He remembered how his body's glow had been quenched when he stumbled away from her. She had cut off his arm!

With his remaining arm, he wrestled the shimmering fissure of light. When he had stretched it wide enough, he placed his head then his upper body inside. For a few seconds, he remained there, half in and half out of their world. Then his body suddenly stiffened, and he fell backwards into the twenty-first century. The hole of light snapped shut, swamping them in darkness.

Cormac dashed to the Jōnin's side. He lay on his back, an arrow with a red feather fletching protruding from his chest. A black stain of blood spread across his kimono like the map of some malevolent empire. His glassy eyes stared straight ahead, the brightness fading.

Makoto felt for a pulse, then shook his head.

He was gone. And so was Ghost.

PART FOUR:
NEW YORK CITY

'Cormac, we have to get Ghost,' said Kate.

He didn't answer, just stared at the lifeless body of the Jōnin.

'Cormac!' shouted Kate.

He snapped out of his daze and looked at her.

'We have to get Ghost. Open the portal.'

He nodded and lifted his sword.

But before he could strike, an explosion shook the forest. Kate's ears rang and she felt a painful pressure inside them. As if in slow motion, Areno and Sora, the samurai warhorses, reared up on their hind legs before bolting from the clearing. Kate saw Makoto running towards her, shouting, but couldn't hear what he was saying. Her legs wobbled. Bright flashes erupted in the darkness and all around her branches splintered, leaves fell and the forest floor seemed alive, spitting pine needles into the air.

Makoto pulled her to the ground. He was still shouting at her, but she heard nothing. Makoto motioned for her to follow him. Copying the way he slid along on his belly, forearm over forearm, she followed him to the large cracked boulder at the edge of the clearing. As the ringing in her head faded, her hearing returned. The sounds were muted at first, but quickly increased in volume, until her head was filled with a noise she recognized from the motorway attack: gunshots.

Cormac joined them at the rock.

'Are you OK?' shouted Makoto, his voice barely audible above the gunfire.

Cormac nodded.

Makoto pressed his comm to his ear, his eyebrows bunching together with the strain of trying to hear whoever was communicating with him.

'Renkondo is under attack!' he shouted to Cormac. 'Kyatapira. You have to escape with the sword.'

'Where to?' yelled Cormac.

Makoto whipped his head around. A Kat had burst through the foliage into the clearing, and was scanning the darkness down the barrel of his gun. Makoto leapt up and raced at the man, who swung around with his weapon in time to see the heel of Makoto's hand drive into his throat. The blow lifted the Kat clean into the air, sending him crashing into the bushes.

'GO!' shouted Makoto, before turning back to deal with the Kat, who was already reaching for the gun he'd dropped.

Cormac pulled Kate to her feet. 'Come on!'

She followed him out of the clearing and into the pitch-dark forest. Together, they ran through the trees, the steeply inclining ground propelling them danger-ously downhill. Branches lashed her face as she ran blindly through a forest alive with bright flashes and the rat-a-tat-tat of automatic gunfire. When her foot caught on a fallen bough, she screamed and fell forwards on to her shoulder. She tumbled head over heels, hitting something hard on the way down. She rolled downwards and ploughed into something soft, which ended her descent.

A low groaning noise told her it was Cormac she had collided with. Kate untangled her legs from his, and groped about in the darkness until she found his chest. Her hands travelled up the beaded surface of his shōzoku to find his face. She leant forwards and whispered, 'Cormac, are you OK?'

At first he didn't move and Kate's heart fluttered in fear. But then she heard a moan and felt him shift beneath her.

'Are you OK?' she repeated.

'Yes,' he croaked.

It was so dark she could barely see him. Leaves brushed her face as she looked around. They seemed to have fallen into a clump of bushes on the edge of a moonlit path. 'What'll we do?' she asked.

'Shh!'

Kate listened. Distant gunshots could be heard higher up in the forest, but the nearby firing had stopped.

Cormac grabbed her arm. She heard what he'd obviously heard too: the cracking of twigs as footsteps drew closer.

Kate's blood froze when a red dot of light appeared on the path beside her. It danced across the leafy ground and was followed by a shiny gun barrel mounted with a laser sight. Then a pair of legs came into view. Kate recognized the wide black trousers. Kyatapira.

She heard the crackle of a walkie-talkie and then a coarse voice like pieces of sandpaper rubbing together. 'Ta-tashikani yatsura wo mitazo.'

Kate did a quick translation. *I think I saw them.*

She held her breath and stayed absolutely still, her eyes fixed on the legs of the Kat. If she had reached out, she could have touched them.

A branch cracked, and the Kat reacted instantly. His body rotated as if he was scanning the forest for the source of the noise. But Kate knew the sound had come from high up in the canopy. Slowly, she tilted her head back and peered up into the trees. All she could see were black branches and black leaves against a slightly less black sky. Then one of the branches seemed to grow legs and arms, mutating into human form and crawling across the boughs above their heads. Black as a shadow and silent as a breeze, it moved along the overhead tangle of branches until it was directly above the Kat. It sat crouched on the edge of a branch for a brief moment, before dropping down.

The ninja fell to the ground like a stone, and a

grunt from the Kat told Kate that the ninja had found his target. Kate peered out on to the path to see the Kat lying on the ground, having dropped his gun. It lay within arm's reach of her. Nearby, a Black Lotus shinobi got to his feet, and so did the Kat.

The shinobi lunged at his opponent, sending him staggering backwards, but he recovered quickly. Now that they were side by side, Kate could see that the police officer had the advantage of size. When the shinobi swung a roundhouse kick, he easily blocked it and counter-attacked with a punch to the stomach. The shinobi doubled over and the Kat followed up with a two-handed hammer blow to the back of the neck. The shinobi collapsed, and the Kat pinned him to the ground by kneeling on his neck.

When the Kat pulled off the shinobi's mask Kate had to stifle a cry. It was Kristjan!

The Kat stood up and laughed. Kate heard the brush of steel as he drew his sword. Then she saw him raise it above his head. On the ground, Kristjan pulled himself up on to his knees.

Kate reacted without thinking. She reached forwards and grabbed the gun, pointing it towards the Kat. When the red dot of the laser landed on his thigh, she squeezed the trigger. A burst of automatic fire exploded from the weapon, its recoil twisting her wrist painfully.

The Kat fell to the ground, and Kate dropped the gun and dashed out of the bushes, her ears still buzzing from the gunfire. When the buzzing faded, she heard the agonized cries of the police officer as he squirmed on the ground, grasping his leg. She pulled Kristjan to his feet. He seemed as surprised to see her as she had been to see him.

'Are you all right?' asked Cormac, scrambling to his feet beside her.

Kristjan nodded and pointed at the sword in Cormac's hand. 'Is that . . . ?'

'Yes.' Cormac glanced at the Kat, who was scrabbling about in the leaves for his fallen sword. Cormac kicked the blade out of reach and said, 'Let's get out of here.'

Kate and Kristjan followed him downhill, going slower now so as not to fall. Behind them, the gunfight still raged, but the way ahead was quiet. That didn't mean there wouldn't be a Kyatapira ambush lying in wait. And Kate regretted not taking the Kat's walkie-talkie. It would only be a matter of minutes before Empire reinforcements were on their tail.

'Wait!' said Kristjan.

Kate and Cormac stopped running and looked at the boy.

He pointed into the trees. 'This way.'

Kate and Cormac followed him through the black trees, wondering where he was taking them. After a few minutes walking he stopped and glanced around as if he was lost. Then he seemed to spot something on the ground and dashed forwards. He lifted up some sort of net, covered in leaves. The moon glistened on a metal trapdoor like the one they had used to exit Renkondo for forest training.

Ghost watched Cormac, Kate and the horses disappear through the floating black portal. One more step, and this would all be o—

In Japan, we have a proverb — After victory, tighten your helmet cord.

He spun around. Kiko stood before him in her flowing green kimono. Her hair fanned out around her, and her eyes looked black against her pale face. In her hand she held a longbow, and a quiver of red-feathered arrows was slung across her back. An arrow was notched in her bow and pointing straight at him.

As Ghost turned to jump through the shrinking portal, a paralyzing pain raced through his body and into his head. He tried to scream, but his jaws were locked tight.

He collapsed to the ground, teeth clenched,

body convulsing with agony. He heard what sounded like an arrow whistling through the air, followed by a strangled gasp. His brain was about to shut down, when suddenly the pain eased. It ebbed away, but left something in its place – something that kept its finger hovering over the pain switch.

He opened his eyes. The forest blurred and he tasted blood in his mouth. He ran his tongue over a loose flap of skin inside his cheek. The trees came into focus, and with them Kiko, her bow now arrowless. He looked behind him, but the portal was gone. He searched his body for an arrow, but found none. His eyes met Kiko's, now burning with rage.

The presence that lurked in his brain flicked the switch. Ghost was thrown backwards as if he'd been electrocuted. Every nerve in his body screamed in agony. He dug his fingernails into his skull, trying to gouge out the piercing torture stabbing his brain.

The pain faded, leaving him exhausted, his body an empty husk. He lifted his head out of the dirt and spat out a mouthful of blood, then struggled to his knees.

I tried my best to spare you.

She approached. The polished steel of a dagger glinted in her hand.

But you give me no option.

He felt the blade at his throat.

Unless . . .

He closed his eyes.

Perhaps I can find a use for you . . .

He opened his eyes.

I give you a choice: die now, or join us in carving out a new world.

He swallowed, feeling the sharp edge of the knife dig into his skin.

Do you want to die?

No.

Good. Then I will control your mind.

Ghost felt tears pool behind his eyes.

Do not resist.

She removed the dagger and brought her face down in front of his. Her dark eyes closed and Ghost felt a rush of cold air inside his head. This was different. Before, he had heard her voice in his mind; now he felt her consciousness fully inhabit his own. It was a living presence, like an insect, settling and pulsing inside his skull.

Kiko opened her eyes. The insect wriggled its legs when she spoke.

Can you feel me inside your head?

Ghost flinched at the sensation, but nodded.

Good. Step out of line once more, and . . . Well, I think you know what will happen.

Ghost nodded again. A single tear ran down his nose. It clung to his nostril before dropping to the ground.

The insect squirmed. *Follow me.*

Kiko turned and walked down through the trees. Ghost stood up and followed. He couldn't think straight. His thoughts were jumbled like in a dream. *Better not to think at all. Just do what you're told . . .* Easy.

He walked behind her through trees and paddy fields to a road where men waited with horses. When she told him to get on a horse, he did. When she told him to ride, he did.

They passed through a gated checkpoint and continued onwards. The place seemed familiar, yet he couldn't quite remember why. He felt empty inside, broken even. He wiped tears from his cheeks, not knowing why he cried.

As they reached a town, they were met by more men, soldiers with spears and banners, who escorted them the rest of the way. The morning sun felt warm on his back, but inside he was a frozen wasteland.

The people in the town bowed.

A large castle stood before him. He recognized it as if from a dream.

Hundreds of soldiers in red armour waited outside the castle walls in orderly lines. They carried banners displaying two crossed swords. And like a tsunami of metal and lacquer, they bowed when Ghost and Kiko passed. Inside the castle wall, more lines of men waited – hundreds, maybe thousands.

Ghost followed Kiko's horse through a large door in the inner castle wall, and into a smaller yard. When she told him to get off the horse, he did. She walked away and left him standing, only to return and place her hand on his shoulder.

Insectoid legs wriggled in his brain. *Wherever I go, you follow.*

He followed.

In the castle gardens, she was greeted by a man

in a red kimono carrying two swords in black scabbards. Ghost recognized him but couldn't remember his name. When they'd finished speaking, the man raised his hand to a soldier waiting at the door they'd just passed through. Moments later, the army from the outer courtyard marched towards them in single file.
Follow.

Ghost followed Kiko and the man. The army followed Ghost. But they weren't heading for the castle. They took a path that led to a small house in the gardens. A whole wall had been removed from the building, and Ghost saw into the empty interior. It was big enough to hold a handful of people. He glanced behind. The army approached.

Kiko and the man entered the house. Ghost followed. A cherry tree was painted on one of the paper walls. The room was empty except for an object in the centre which looked totally out of place. It was a small black shiny box with three tall thin legs. A green light flashed on top. It was only when Ghost got closer that he recognized what it was: a camera.

Kristjan put his palm on the keypad beside the door. He closed his eyes and concentrated. The keypad beeped and the trapdoor popped open.

Cormac held the Moon Sword to his chest and followed Kate inside. Kristjan pulled down the netting before closing the door. He flicked a switch, and the darkness was banished by overhead lights.

'How did you do that?' Cormac asked.

Kristjan squeezed past him on the narrow stairs. 'What?'

'How did you open that door?'

'My skill,' he said. 'Like you run and she talk to animals.'

Your skill is opening doors? Cormac wanted to ask, but the boy had pushed past Kate too and was already descending the stone steps.

'How did you know about that door?' asked Kate.

'I use it before.'

'Does it lead to Renkondo?' asked Cormac.

'No. Renkondo is gone.'

'What about the other students and teachers?'

'No time for questions,' said Kristjan, turning around on the stairs to face them. 'We must hurry.'

Cormac nodded and followed Kate and Kristjan. At the bottom of the steps, Kristjan used his skill to manipulate another keypad and open a metal door.

'What the heck . . .?' said Cormac, gaping at what lay on the other side.

They stood in an enormous cavern about the same size as the one in which they'd trained with the Bear. Giant floodlights hung from the rock ceiling, illuminating a concrete runway which led to a gigantic hangar door.

Cormac and Kate ran to catch up with Kristjan, who marched towards the end of the runway. They passed a line of helicopters tucked away securely at the edge of the airstrip.

'Look,' said Kate, pointing at the Kyatapira chopper.

'Is that the helicopter you rescued us in?' asked Cormac.

Kristjan nodded, but didn't stop walking.

At the far end of the runway, the air seemed to warp and shimmer, like a mirage in the desert. Cormac squinted. *What is that?* As he got closer, a shape materialized. A plane of some sort. A fighter jet!

Its sleek wings and pointed nose gave it the appearance of a bird ready for flight. Under its belly it carried four transparent capsules, like missiles.

'Wow!' He ran his fingers along its beaded surface. 'Is this made from the same material as our suits?'

Kristjan shrugged and hit a button on the wall. At the opposite end of the runway, the huge hangar door growled to life, opening on to the side of the mountain to reveal the night sky. Outside, they heard the faint popping of machine-gun fire.

'Are you gonna fly this thing?' asked Kate.

Kristjan nodded and climbed up on to the wing of the plane. He extended a hand to pull up Cormac.

Cormac looked at Kate. 'What about Ghost? We can't just leave him.'

'I know,' said Kate.

'Ghost can turn invisible,' said Kristjan. 'If anyone can survive, it will be Ghost. You go back out there, you will die.'

Kate thought about this for a moment, before speaking. 'You know, Ghost is probably in the safest possible place right now.'

She was right. He was almost half a millennium away. 'We'll return for him when it's safe.'

'We must hurry,' said Kristjan, reaching down towards Kate.

She took his hand and he pulled her up on to the wing.

Cormac handed Kristjan the sword and climbed up. 'Have you flown this before?'

'Not on my own,' said Kristjan, staring at the sword, before returning it to Cormac.

'So how come they let *you* fly these things while *we* play with ropes?'

'My skill – I told you.' Kristjan opened a hatch into the body of the plane.

'What exactly is your skill?'

'Mastery of machines. I can control any machine or technology.'

'How?'

'Just can. Now, hurry, please.' Kristjan motioned for them to climb in.

Kate swung her legs through the hatch. 'Where are we going?'

'Out of danger,' replied Kristjan.

'Where do I sit?' she asked from inside the aircraft.

'You don't sit. You lie in pod.'

Cormac stepped through the hatch. 'What sort of plane is this?'

'BX-12 Kestrel,' said Kristjan. 'Sixth-generation air-superiority prototype.'

When Cormac climbed in, he realized he was standing in one of the transparent capsules he'd seen from outside.

'Lie on your stomachs,' said Kristjan, before closing the hatch.

Kate and Cormac lay in the two capsules below the centre of the plane. Despite the cramped space, the capsules were quite comfortable, and because they were transparent, Cormac and Kate could see each other, and the runway beneath them.

At the front of the plane, they heard another hatch close and saw Kristjan strap himself into the cockpit and put on headphones. A whirring noise made Cormac twist his head. Above him, a Perspex cover slid into place, sealing him into the capsule.

'Cormac,' said Kate through a tiny speaker in the pod.

He looked to his left to see Kate staring at him anxiously.

'What about the rest of the students and teachers?' she asked.

'We had to get out of there,' replied Cormac.

'But—'

Kate's words were drowned out by the roar of an engine. She gripped the foam cushion under her chin as the plane vibrated.

Cormac looked ahead through the front of the capsule to the open door at the end of the runway. 'Is there a chance we'll be attacked?'

'No,' said Kristjan. 'Kestrel's stealth technology is best in world.'

With a blast, the jet shot off along the short runway at incredible speed and out into the night sky. A wave of nausea hit Cormac, but once they were airborne he relaxed. He looked out of the window beneath him, but saw only a black mountain. Here and there, flashes of light illuminated the trees down below where the fighting still raged.

But it felt like they were dropping instead of climbing.

'Shouldn't we be going up?'

'We fly under radar,' said Kristjan.

Cormac moved his arms under his head and rested his face on the backs of his hands. Looking out at the blackness, he felt his eyes droop. He was so tired.

But then he shook himself awake. How could he think about sleeping when Renkondo was under attack? His home . . . And the people there – the teachers, the other students. His friends.

'I think you must look at this,' said Kristjan.

Cormac glanced around, but all he saw was darkness. 'What?'

'Lie on your back.'

Cormac moved the sword at his side, and rolled over on to his back, resting his head on the foam cushion. Now looking up at the underside of the capsule lid, he saw that it was fitted with a screen which was flickering to life.

He looked over at Kate, who was doing the same in her pod.

'TV channels all over America show this,' said Kristjan.

A female newsreader appeared on screen in front of a large picture of President Goda's face. A ribbon of text appeared at the bottom of the screen: EMPIRE ISSUES ULTIMATUM.

'Let's take another look at the message which has shaken America,' said the newsreader.

The screen flicked to amateur footage of President Goda, not dressed in the white suit he normally wore for his rare television appearances, but in the kimono Cormac had seen him wear in the procession through Yosa. Nor was the footage shot in his usual presidential office. A painted cherry tree decorated the wall behind him, rather than the two crossed swords of the Empire. Goda's face was not as composed and confident as it usually was when he appeared in the media. His long hair was spilling untidily from his topknot and his eyes blazed with a wild intensity.

He spoke a single sentence in Japanese, and paused as his words were translated by a woman off-screen. The voice sounded like Ami's – Kiko's. 'This is a message to the people who have what belongs to me.'

Cormac gripped the Moon Sword and glanced at Kate, who stared at him in horror through her Perspex pod.

Goda spoke again, his words immediately translated by his wife. 'Unless I get it back, you will never see your friend again.'

The camera zoomed out, showing the interior of a small room with paper walls. The lens panned to the right and stopped on a boy in a shōzoku. Ghost! He had often looked detatched in Renkondo, but now he looked lifeless. His head slumped forwards, and his eyes were blank, possessed almost.

The image returned to Goda, zooming in on his face until it filled the frame. Again he spoke in Japanese, his piercing gaze threatening to crack the camera lens.

Kiko spoke again: 'You have until sunrise to

return what is mine. I'll be waiting at my favourite place in all of America.'

The programme returned to the studio, where a panel of experts began to discuss the meaning and implications of the recording. They wondered who the message was for? And what was the possession that Goda wanted back so desperately? And where was Goda's favourite place in America? Nobody seemed to think President Goda had ever *been* to America.

'Turn it off,' said Cormac.

Kristjan shut off the footage. Cormac turned over on to his stomach and looked at Kate. She stared back at him, her face pale, dark rings around her eyes.

'What'll we do?' she said.

Cormac shook his head.

'You made promise to protect sword,' said Kristjan.

'Our friend is more important than a promise!' spat Cormac angrily.

Kristjan paused before speaking again. 'You need to think. Will you risk losing sword to save friend?'

'Yes!' shouted Kate. She was leaning up on her elbows, eyes wide and bright. 'Back in the forest just now, we could have stayed hidden in those bushes with the sword. If we risked losing the sword to save you, we'll risk losing it to save Ghost.'

Nobody spoke. Cormac looked out into the blackness, but there was nothing to see.

After a while, Kristjan spoke again. 'I'm sorry. You are correct. I owe you my life. Whatever you do, I help.'

'Even if we wanted to do something,' said Cormac, 'how are we supposed to know Goda's favourite place in America?'

There was silence in the plane for a few moments. Then Kate spoke. 'Maybe we do know.'

Cormac frowned at her.

'Maybe it's not President Goda's favourite place but Kiko's – she was the one speaking, after all. Remember the first day we met Ami? She told me it was Times Square in New York City.'

Cormac nodded. 'I remember.'

'So although that message was broadcast to the world, only we know where that place is.'

Cormac sighed. 'Clever. But we'll never make it there before sunrise.'

'Kestrel can accelerate to Mach 3.3,' said Kristjan. 'That is more than three times speed of sound. We can be there in less than three hours.'

'And what about fuel?' asked Cormac. 'Surely this little thing can't carry enough to take us to America?'

'It is powered by NASA nuclear energy.'

Cormac looked at Kate, who for the first time in ages was smiling. She nodded at him.

'Let's do it, Kristjan!' shouted Cormac.

'You guys sleep. I wake you before we arrive.'

Kate lay back and shut her eyes, sighing. But Cormac looked out at the night sky, catching sight of the moon passing behind a cloud. They could do this. They'd stolen a sword from a heavily-guarded medieval fortress, so surely they could rescue their friend.

He looked through the side of his capsule to see Kate now fast asleep. Her chest rose and fell with her breathing. She looked so calm.

Overwhelmed with tiredness, Cormac lay back on the cushion and closed his eyes.

Kate awoke to the sound of the TV blaring over her head. 'The US army have formed a defensive perimeter around most American tourist attractions. Much of New York City has been evacuated and a curfew is in place for all residents. We now go live—'

The TV muted and Kristjan's voice came through the speaker. 'Awake now?'

In his capsule beside her, Cormac yawned and smiled. Kate looked through the floor of her pod and was amazed to see land beneath them. Tiny lights burnt in houses, and traffic headlights moved through the pre-dawn streets.

'Where are we?'

'Over Philadelphia,' said Kristjan. 'ETA five minutes.'

'Five minutes!'

'Why didn't you wa—?'

Cormac was cut off by Kristjan. 'No time for questions. Listen to me carefully. This is no-fly zone so we go in and out quick – no landing. I drop you in river.'

'What do you mean, drop us?' asked Kate.

'Pods are designed to drop in water. They travel under water using sonar to avoid obstacles. Then they rise to surface. Red button above your head will open pod. You can swim, yes?'

Kate and Cormac looked at each other anxiously, and both answered, 'Yes.'

'OK. You swim to riverbank.'

Through the pod, the New York City horizon approached rapidly.

Kate felt a scratching in her pocket. *Savage!* She took him out and placed him on the cushion.

His whiskers tickled her nose. 'Hungry I am.'

Kate smiled nervously. 'How did I know you were going to say that?'

Savage joined her in gazing through the floor of the capsule at the New York City rooftops sailing by. She glanced at Cormac. He winked, but his eyes showed he was just as apprehensive as her. The aircraft dived down, until the dark waters of the Hudson River were all that could be seen through the base of the pod.

'Where will you go, Kristjan?' asked Kate.

'I don't know. But I will be OK. Good luck.'

Kate gripped the foam cushion beneath her chin. She heard a click and suddenly she was in the sky, her stomach lurching with the drop. A surge of panic raced through her body. *Please God, don't let me die.*

Kate crashed forwards as the pod hit the water, cracking her head against the front of the capsule. She pushed her face away from the Perspex, sliding back along her cushion. Savage squeaked in terror as the pod sank into darkness. Bubbles and little bits of debris raced past the nose of the pod. A whirring noise alerted her to some mechanical device in the rear of the craft. The pod veered sharply to one side, narrowly missing an algae-encrusted shopping cart.

She blinked a drop of perspiration from her eye. The tiny pill-shaped container started to decelerate and rise in the water, heading for the surface. Steadily it climbed towards the greenish light, finally breaking the surface.

The sky was still dark, but a muted cerise along the Manhattan skyline announced the approaching sunrise. She hit the red button above her head and, with a hydraulic hiss, the roof slid back. Cold water lapped over the side, spurring her into action. She scooped up Savage and knelt in the tiny boat, feeling the cool breeze on her face.

'You need to go inside my mask so you won't drown,' Kate said to Savage.

Fumbling with her hood, she pulled out the mask. She dropped Savage into it before sealing it around her face. Nearby, Cormac's pod pitched and bobbed in the waves of the river. More water spilt into the pod. Worried that she'd get caught in the sinking shell, Kate stood. She listened for the reassuring fizz of oxygen in her mask before diving into the river.

She swam for the riverbank with Savage clinging to her nose. At the water's edge she dragged herself out of the river and pulled off her mask and hood. Savage crawled out on to her chest. She lay on her back and gasped for breath.

Savage sniffed the air. 'Happened what?'

Kate managed a smile. 'Good question.'

She heard splashing nearby.

Cormac clambered out of the water, pulled off his mask and rolled down his hood. 'You OK?'

Kate nodded, but she didn't feel it. She wondered why she wasn't excited about being back home. Maybe it was because of the task that lay ahead of them. Or maybe it was because this wasn't really her home any more – Renkondo was.

Cormac looked at the sky, which was already brightening. The pink line on the horizon had soaked up into the sky, silhouetting the New York City skyline. 'How long until sunrise?'

Kate pocketed the mouse and stood. 'I don't know, but not long.'

'Lead the way, New Yorker.'

Kate smiled and nodded, and together they ran through the ornamental gardens by the river, then followed a path to stone steps leading up to the highway. On her way up, she heard something she'd never heard in New York City before: silence.

At the top of the steps, the highway, which normally buzzed with traffic, day and night, was empty and silent. A few cars lay abandoned in the middle of the road. The hazard lights flashed on one and a radio blared through its open door.

She looked at Cormac, who just shook his head.

Spurred on by a new sense of urgency, she crossed the highway, heading for the office blocks in the distance. In the gardens across the road, they raced along paths, past empty benches and silent playgrounds.

On West 66th Street, she expected some life, but there was nothing. All stores and businesses had their shutters down, windows were blacked out and the street was empty. She stopped in the middle and scanned her surroundings. Somewhere a dog barked, but otherwise there was only eerie silence. At a fourth-floor window she saw a curtain twitch, and a tiny face appeared at the glass. The child smiled and waved down at Kate, before being pulled away.

When they turned on to Broadway, they heard the rumble of a truck.

'Get down!' said Cormac, crouching behind a subway entrance.

Kate hunkered down beside him. 'What is it?'

He pointed at a khaki-coloured armoured car rolling by on the opposite side of the road. An armed soldier stood in the roof hatch of the vehicle, surveying the streets.

'We'll be arrested if we're seen,' said Cormac.

'Or shot,' added Kate.

She glanced at the sky again before continuing down Broadway. She ran side by side with Cormac down the vacant street, glad now of all the training she'd done with the Bear. It seemed like a lifetime ago. It was hard to imagine Renkondo gone, and perhaps the Bear too, and who knew how many others – Makoto, Chloe, Shan . . . She forced the thoughts from her mind. She could do nothing to help those people. But she could help Ghost.

They passed the corner of Central Park and crossed over the roundabout, continuing down Broadway past towering skyscrapers whose glass facades reflected an orange glow in the sky. It was weird seeing one of the busiest streets in the city deserted.

She thought she saw movement ahead, and stopped running.

'What is it?' asked Cormac.

'Give me your binocs.'

Cormac fished them out of his shōzoku and handed them over.

Through the zoomed lens she saw that the street ahead was completely blocked with tanks, jeeps and armoured cars. US soldiers manned the barricade, their weapons all pointing in her direction.

She handed the binocs to Cormac. 'Take a look. On the news they said parts of the city had been completely evacuated. Nobody's getting in!'

'Let's try another street.'

Kate nodded and they turned off Broadway and ran to 7th Avenue.

Cormac peered through the binocs again. 'It's blocked too.'

Kate looked up at the sky. 'It's nearly time,

Cormac. What'll we do?'

Cormac scanned the soaring towers of glass and steel. 'I could get in.'

Kate didn't want him to go alone, but what choice did they have? There was no time to do anything else. She nodded.

'Get off the streets,' said Cormac, detaching the comm from his hood and fixing it to his ear. 'Find somewhere to hide. I'll keep in touch.'

Again, she nodded.

Cormac looked at her and smiled. 'Go!' he said, using the sword to point down the street.

There was nothing else she could do. Kate turned and jogged away from Times Square. She stopped after a few steps and looked back to say goodbye, but Cormac was already gone.

She continued up 7th Avenue, trying not to think about the momentous task that lay ahead of Cormac. He was putting his own life in extreme danger to rescue their friend, and even if he did manage to trade the sword for Ghost, who knew what terrible deeds Goda would do with his new weapon? Were they saving one friend at the cost of thousands of lives? Millions, even?

She stopped running and jumped behind a parked van. Up ahead, another armoured car crossed in front of her. She knew the army were there to protect the city, but this didn't make her feel safe. As she wondered what to do, she heard a whisper nearby.

'Psst!'

From the doorway of the hotel beside her, a lady

with a bandana tied around her head looked out. 'Get off the street, girl.'

Kate ran over to her. 'Where's a good place to hide?'

The woman eyed Kate from head to toe and laughed. 'What are you, a ninja?'

Kate smiled. 'Yeah, something like that.'

The woman looked up and down the street before opening the door wide. 'Come in.'

Cormac crept down a side street and peered around the corner at the army barricade. Between trucks and armoured cars, the soldiers stood on high alert, their backs to Times Square, guns pointing in his direction.

He pulled his head back in and gazed up at the glass-fronted tower block beside him. If he could reach the top, perhaps he could find a way down to the other side. He'd scaled many tall buildings in Ballyhook, but never anything like this. As his eye travelled up the sheer glass face of the skyscraper he noticed how bright the sky had become. There was no time to think about it.

He darted down an alleyway opposite the building, then turned and faced the challenge that would really put his ability to the test. Taking a deep breath, he ran as fast as he could, praying that his momentum would take him to the top. Pushing himself harder than he'd ever done before, he hurtled dangerously towards the ground-floor windows. He shot up the glass wall, passing the first, second, third and fourth floors with ease. After that, he felt his speed decreasing and he glanced up at the summit. But it was too far away – he wasn't going to make it. Normally, his momentum was enough to take him to the roof, but now, for the first time, he needed to accelerate while sky-running.

He forced power into his thighs and, though his muscles screamed in protest, his speed increased, taking him higher and higher up the office block facade. Halfway up, he faced a new problem.

Wind whipped between the buildings, threatening to send him off course. He needed to maintain a straight line, because if he veered toward the corner of the building he was in serious trouble. He couldn't change course mid-run, and with nothing to grab on to, any deviation from his intended route could mean a hundred-and-twenty-metre plummet to certain death.

Leaning into the howling wind to compensate for how it pushed him off course, he summoned more power to his legs, bursting forwards, higher and higher into the sky. His arms pumped like pistons, the weight of the sword slowing him down. His accelerations, however, became less and less effective as the roof got closer and his body drained of energy.

He screamed into the wind and willed his legs to push him across the last stretch of glass. Stepping up on to the roof, he balanced on the edge for a moment, before flopping forwards.

He didn't know how long he would have lain there if he hadn't heard Kate in his comm. 'Cormac?'

He opened his eyes. 'I'm fine.'

The sky was so bright he was sure he'd missed the sunrise, but when he stood he saw the radiance of the sun just below the horizon.

There was still time.

'Where are you?' asked Kate.

'On top of the skyscraper.'

He ran to the opposite side of the roof and gazed down. He'd never been in New York City before, but he imagined Times Square was never as empty as it was now. Not a single thing moved. There weren't even soldiers down there.

The sound of a passing aircraft shifted his attention to the sky, but there was no sign of anything. Looking around, he saw a doorway off the roof and dashed over to it. The door was locked, but when he ran at it with his shoulder, it burst open. After racing down three flights of stairs he found a lift. It pinged open when he pressed the button.

Inside, he watched the floor numbers count down, hoping he wouldn't be too late. He still didn't know what he was looking for or where to find it, but he did know he only had minutes before the sun was up.

On the ground floor, he found that all the doors and windows out on to Times Square were locked, but a fire exit gave him access to a narrow side street. He rushed down it and out into the middle of the square just as the first rays of the morning sun lanced across the rooftops.

In panic, he looked around the square, but there was nobody to be seen. The first rays of the sunrise warmed his face and cast his shadow, long and narrow, across the ground. Was he too late?

'Come away from the windows,' said the woman in the bandana. 'We're not supposed to be in here.'

She led Kate across the empty hotel foyer and down a long corridor. As they walked, Kate heard noise – the murmur and hum of a large crowd. When the woman opened double doors into a conference room, Kate was faced with a huge gathering of people. They talked excitedly to each other, voices raised, faces angry. Many carried weapons: guns, knives, baseball bats.

'What *is* this?' asked Kate.

The woman picked up an iron bar which had tape wrapped around one end to form a club. 'This is New Yorkers getting ready to protect their city. If those Empire Kats show up, we'll chase 'em back out again.'

She left Kate and joined a woman and two men who were studying a large map spread out on a table. Kate grabbed a bread roll from a tray of food, took a bite and found a quiet corner to feed Savage. As the little mouse devoured the bread, Kate put the comm in her ear. 'Cormac?'

There was a moment of silence before Cormac answered, 'I'm fine.'

'Where are you?'

'On top of the skyscraper.'

Cormac's panic turned his legs to liquid and his skin cold and clammy. He looked around again. And that's when he saw the undulating black orb floating in mid-air. It was exactly like the portal he'd opened in medieval Japan.

The US army had obviously cordoned off Times Square as a potential target, but they were expecting visitors from the outside, not from within!

Cormac dashed towards a parked taxi and scrambled behind it. Peeping over the bonnet, he watched the orb increase in size as if it was being stretched from the other side.

Even on the flight here, he hadn't thought about how he was going to do this. He'd presumed he would have Kate with him to help figure it out. But now he was alone and needed to think fast. This could go one of three ways. One – he'd escape, with Ghost and the sword. Two – he'd escape, with just Ghost. Or three – they wouldn't escape, and all three Swords of Sarumara would be in enemy hands.

The pool of black had grown to the size of a man. Kiko stepped through, face painted white, dressed in green. She turned towards the gateway of darkness from which she'd emerged, grasped a hand and pulled it. Still in his shōzoku, Ghost allowed himself to be led through by Kiko. Cormac was so overcome with relief at seeing his friend still alive that he had to force himself not to run out and give him a hug. But Ghost now seemed to be a shadow of his former self, as if something had sucked the life out of him. His body was limp, his eyes dead. What had they done to him?

The portal wavered and began to shrink, but not before another face that Cormac recognized emerged from it. It was the face that had peered down at him every night from its frame on the wall of the Hinin House dormitory. It was the face he had met at the window on the top of Yosa Castle. It was Goda. Dressed in a red kimono and wearing two swords, he turned and watched the portal contract and disappear.

Cormac ducked down behind the taxi. How was he going to do this? If he revealed himself with the sword, Kiko and Goda could overpower him and take his one and only bargaining chip by force. He needed to hide the katana. Holding his breath, he pulled the taxi's passenger door handle. Luckily, it wasn't locked and popped open easily. To Cormac's ears, the noise it made sounded like a gunshot and he froze with the door half open. He peeped through the glass, but nobody looked his way.

He stashed the Moon Sword under the seat and eased the door shut. Perhaps now they wouldn't harm him, for fear that they'd never find their precious sword. They weren't to know it was only a few metres away.

Instinctively, he reached for his crucifix and found it wasn't there. *Mum, Dad, wherever you are, help me make it out of this alive.*

Cormac stepped out of hiding.

Kiko was the first to spot him. She pushed Ghost into Goda's arms and stepped towards Cormac.

He raised his hand. 'Stay where you are!' he shouted.

She kept walking. 'Or what?'

'Or I'm out of here before you can blink twice.'

She stopped walking and looked around. 'Who is with you?'

'Nobody.'

She stared at him. 'Where is the sword?'

'Hidden.'

'No sword, no Ghost.' Behind her, Goda held his katana under Ghost's throat.

Cormac's heart beat so wildly in his chest he could barely speak. 'No Ghost, no sword!'

Kiko smiled. 'So I will bring Ghost and you will bring the sword. That is honest.'

'You're kidding! There's nothing honest about you, *Ami*.' Cormac was surprised by his own courage, but then, if you couldn't be brave when everything was on the line, when could you? The sight of Kiko also fuelled his rage. She had betrayed him and the Black Lotus. She was the enemy.

Kiko nodded, as if impressed by his guts. 'What do you suggest?'

'Send Ghost over, and when he's a safe distance away from you, I'll give you the sword.'

'Why should I trust you?'

'You shouldn't. But you and I both know that if I don't give you the sword, you'll come after me and kill me.'

'That's true,' said Kiko. 'But we'd make you watch Kate and Ghost die first.'

Cormac swallowed. That was no idle threat.

The sunrise filled the sky with glorious oranges and flaming pinks. Its rays speared through the gaps between the skyscrapers, banishing the pre-dawn gloom. A gentle breeze ruffled Kiko's kimono and blew a strand of hair over her face. She moved it aside and nodded to Goda, who released his captive.

Hesitantly, Ghost walked towards him with laboured steps. Cormac was tempted to run out and meet him, but he wanted to maintain a safe distance from Kiko. And so he waited.

Ghost's face was pale and his eyes blank.

'Are you OK?' asked Cormac.

Ghost nodded.

Cormac glanced over his friend's shoulder to where Kiko and Goda stood side by side, watching closely. 'I want you to run as fast as you can up the street. Don't stop until you reach the soldiers. They'll protect you.'

Ghost nodded. 'What about you?'

'I'm going to run the opposite way with the sword.'

Ghost looked him up and down. 'Where is it?'

'In the taxi.'

Ghost thought for a second, then nodded. 'Good

to see you, man.' He held his arms out for a hug.

Cormac frowned, wondering what his friend was playing at, but moving into the embrace all the same. And that's when Ghost's head shot forwards, smashing into Cormac's nose.

He staggered backwards, feeling blood pump out of his nostrils. Ghost followed up with a kick to the groin which doubled Cormac over in excruciating pain. A knee in the face finished him off. His world spun, then dimmed. Then darkened completely.

Ghost stepped over the boy and pulled open the taxi door. After hunting around, he removed the sword from under the seat and held it up to show Kiko, who, along with the man in red, was running towards him.

She took the Moon Sword, gently separating the hilt from the scabbard to check the blade within.

Well done, Ghost. He felt the insect in his brain squirm and twist. *You have proved your worth.*

He watched her tie the scabbard to her waist before unsheathing the blade again. She stepped towards the boy and raised the katana in the air. Something in Ghost snapped.

Wait!

What? The voice in his head sounded surprised.

Don't kill him.

Why not?

Ghost looked down at the bloody-nosed boy. He was sure he recognized that face, but couldn't think who it was. He was beginning to feel stronger, his own voice louder inside his head. *Let him go. He can't harm us now.*

Kiko looked at Ghost, her dark pupils probing him for something: a reason – a reason to kill the boy, a reason not to? He could feel the insect wriggling in his brain, as if reaching for something. Perhaps Kiko looked a little nervous, as if she didn't want to do anything to upset Ghost . . . *I'll do this for you, Ghost*, she said, eventually, lowering the sword.

The boy was conscious again and trying to stand. Ghost helped him to his feet. 'Run.'

The boy wiped his bloody mouth and glanced at the three adults, before returning his gaze to Ghost. 'What have you done?'

'Go!' shouted Ghost, pushing him away.

The boy stumbled away from them, stopping once to look back, before disappearing down the street.

Let's go.

He followed the adults to an empty part of the square. Kiko and the man looked at each other, and nodded.

It is time. Take this.

Kiko handed Ghost the Moon Sword. He felt its weight in his palm, its energy against his skin. The two adults unsheathed the other blades. The man barked a command.

On three, we cut.

Something in Ghost rebelled, but Kiko's mind grasped at his own, stopped him from thinking.

The man waited with his Butterfly Sword raised. Now Kiko spoke aloud, a faint tremble in her voice. 'One. Two. Three!'

The man screamed and together they cut into the air with the three swords.

Ghost was aware of a blinding white light and the sensation of flying through the air.

Cormac opened his eyes. He lay face-down on the hard ground. A throbbing pain pounded in his head. He peeled himself off the street. Something wet ran down his neck. He put his hand to the back of his head. Blood. An armoured car lay upturned beside him, completely mangled, as if it had been chewed by some great beast then spat out. Holding on to the vehicle's crumpled frame, he pulled himself upright.

Somewhere, bending metal groaned. Nearby, glass shattered, shards tinkling on the ground. A distant rumbling was followed by a muted explosion. Around him, human groans filled the air.

Cormac hobbled through the mess, kicking aside a rifle, now corkscrewed into a piece of modern art. As he picked his way through the debris, he remembered what had happened.

Ghost had saved his life and sent him running. Cormac had raced towards the army barricade at the edge of Times Square, shouting for help. The soldiers had spun around to face him, a dozen guns pointing straight at him. Then there had been a giant flash of light from behind him and his body had lifted into the air . . .

He staggered up the street. Cars lay overturned or on their sides, crushed by some invisible force. Signs, traffic lights and lamp posts, everything made of metal was twisted and bent. The once sleek and shiny skyscrapers leant drunkenly in the sky. Windows which normally reflected the sun had been replaced by thousands of dark holes. A pillar of smoke rose from one of the crumbling office blocks.

Glass crunched beneath his feet as he turned into a side street. He almost tripped over the body of a dead soldier. The man lay crushed beneath an over-turned car, his face the same colour as the sidewalk, a pool of dark blood around his head. Cormac turned away from the horror, overcome with nausea, and leant against a misshapen trash can. He retched. But nothing came out, just a loud bark and the bitter taste of bile.

Kate!

Feeling dizzy, he tapped his chest and spoke into his comm, but received no reply. He pulled the device from his ear to check it. The plastic casing had ruptured and its internal organs were a fried mess of melted wires and transistor chips. Flinging it aside, he teetered up the street. He had to find her.

Some buildings had collapsed entirely, spilling rubble on to the streets, and everywhere crooked vehicles littered the road as if they'd been dropped from the sky. As he passed the smouldering remains of a burnt-out car, his legs gave way and he fell to his knees. Blood loss, fatigue and shock brought his body to a standstill. He would have flopped forwards on to his face if a pair of strong arms hadn't caught him.

Ghost sat up and wiped a thick layer of dust off his face. He looked around him at a scene of utter destruction.

He had seen Times Square on TV many times. But now it was barely recognizable. The skyscrapers, normally radiant with flashing lights and neon advertising, hunched over like old men, grey and lifeless. Their windows were empty eyes, staring out at a city covered in broken glass. And all around, paper and dust fell like snow.

A noise diverted his attention. A man in a red kimono knelt on his hands and knees, coughing and spitting.

I know him. Goda. President of the Samurai Empire.

When Goda had cleared his lungs, he looked about frantically, reached under the wreckage of a car and pulled out a gleaming sword. He struggled to his feet, put the blade in a dark scabbard and rushed over to an inert body lying under a pile of green silk. From beneath the silk, he pulled out another sword and sheathed it, before lifting the person up and pulling dark tresses from a pale face. Kiko.

The memory of what had just happened came surging back.

Ghost glanced around at the carnage. They had done this. With their swords. The Empire was taking America.

But that was as far back as his memory reached. How he had got here was still—

Ghost.

His body froze, as if turned to stone. She stared at him, her black gaze penetrating his mind, becoming a poisonous serum coursing through his body, ready to attack. He remembered that insectoid presence she'd planted in his head, the one that gave her full control over him. But now he couldn't feel the wiggle of its legs or the squirming of its scaly body. It seemed to be gone. Perhaps the explosion had got rid of it? Her voice was still in his mind, but Ghost could think, remember and move on his own. Though Kiko didn't seem to know this – and Ghost wasn't about to tell her.

Come here. Bring the Moon Sword.

He looked around and found the blade nearby. When he brought it to her, she sheathed it in the scabbard at her waist.

The force unleashed by the three swords had blown everything into heaped piles at the edge of Times Square. Contorted cars and crushed concrete surrounded them in a ring of disaster.

Goda looked around the square as if getting his bearings. He took a step forwards, then adjusted his position by shuffling sideways on his feet. He kept glancing around as if searching for something. When finally satisfied with where he stood, he swept away the glass on the ground with his foot.

He drew one of his swords, held it above his head and smiled at his wife. She smiled back. Goda's scream echoed around the square, bouncing off the shattered skyscrapers. He cut down with the blade, slicing another dark hole in the air. It contorted and contracted, its edges wobbling like jelly.

Kiko moved to the hole and pulled at its edge, stretching the opening.

Grab the other side.

Ghost obeyed, curling his fingers around the gelatinous rim.

Wider.

The opening wanted to close, but Ghost pulled harder until it was wide enough for two men to pass through.

And that's what happened.

Two medieval samurai, dressed in red armour, stepped out of the black hole. They bore Empire banners and carried extra armour in each of their hands. They bowed to Lord Goda and began dressing him in leather and iron. More followed, carrying a helmet and other paraphernalia. Soon Goda was dressed for war. He ordered two samurai to replace Ghost and Kiko at the portal.

Warriors continued to stream through the hole, two carrying green armour for Lady Kiko. As she dressed for battle, samurai formed a protective ring around Times Square, spears and swords pointing outwards towards the ruined skyscrapers.

Ghost looked to see who was coming through next, then jumped out of the way.

A horse galloped through, covered in chain mail and leather. The rider had swords on his hip and a banner on his back. His horse vaulted over a smashed taxi and disappeared behind the rubble. Then another came, and another, as a stream of riders emerged from the portal to form regiments across the square and in the surrounding streets. Times Square was soon filled with the sound of iron-shod hooves on stone and the snorting of warhorses.

The cavalry was followed by archers, two at a time, jumping through the opening and running off in orderly lines. Ghost was dizzy watching the torrent of men pouring into the city. Soldier after soldier emerged, clad in iron, armed to the teeth, all marked with the Empire's insignia.

When the last soldier had stepped through, the samurai released their hold on the portal and it snapped shut. Goda surveyed his troops. The square and countless streets around it were filled with samurai in their divisions. Their bright banners, glinting steel spearheads and quivers full of red-feathered arrows brought colour to an otherwise bleak scene.

Kiko asked her husband a question in Japanese. Ghost didn't understand, but for some reason he understood Goda's reply: 'Ichimannin'. He had a vague memory of learning Japanese numbers in a classroom.

'Ichiman' meant ten thousand.

'Come with me.'

Cormac looked up at the man who was helping him to his feet. 'Makoto! How did you get here?'

Makoto smiled. 'Same way as you.'

Cormac remembered hearing a plane in the sky when he was on top of the skyscraper. 'You followed us? But how?'

'Your shōzoku contains a tracking device.'

'What about Renkondo?'

'It's gone.' He bowed his head, but quickly he pulled himself together, his face grim. 'Most of us escaped, but there were casualties.'

'Who?'

'You can't stay here,' said Makoto, ignoring the question. 'It's too dangerous. Come with me.'

Makoto put Cormac's arm over his shoulder and

led him down streets strewn with wreckage. A woman holding her bloodied arm emerged from a doorway. Her face was pale and her eyes desperate. She started to hobble towards them, but Makoto drew Cormac away. They walked on through the chaos. It was as if someone had picked up the city, shaken it and then dropped it on its head.

They eventually stopped in a doorway to rest. Cormac sat on a crate.

'Are you OK?' asked Makoto.

Cormac nodded. But he was far from OK.

Makoto put his hand on his shoulder. 'Tell me what happened.'

Cormac gave Makoto a quick summary of events, telling him how Goda, Kiko and Ghost had entered through a portal in Times Square and how Ghost had taken the Moon Sword. 'The last thing I remember was the explosion. What *was* that?'

'Goda combined the power of the three swords to produce an electromagnetic pulse which affects anything electrical or metal.'

'He's invading the USA,' Cormac said. 'It's really happening.' He looked up at Makoto. 'But America has a massive army, right?'

'You saw what the pulse did to their weapons and tanks,' Makoto replied. 'Without them, and without aircraft and communications, they're powerless.'

Cormac had a sudden thought. 'Have you found Kate?'

Makoto shook his head. 'We were tracking her shōzoku, but the pulse disabled all our equipment.'

'We? Who else is here?'

'Come, and I'll show you.'

Makoto led him around the corner to a large paved square surrounded on all sides by dark and lifeless tower blocks. Words full of irony looked down at them from above the doorway of the GE Building: 'Wisdom and knowledge shall be the stability of thy times.'

But the place was empty.

And then something by one wall caught Cormac's eye. A figure emerged from the stone – a shōzoku-clad shinobi, only visible because of his movement. Others appeared from hiding, rolling out from under tables, dropping down from trees, slinking out of the shadows. They approached Makoto, bowed and stood before him in neat rows. Two of them stepped forward and pulled down their hoods.

'Bear!' exclaimed Cormac. 'Sensei Iwamoto!'

The two men bowed.

Cormac looked past his teachers to what must have been two hundred shinobi. 'You brought an army?'

Makoto shook his head. 'Once the Renkondo students had been taken to safety, myself, the Bear and Sensei Iwamoto flew here. We have Black Lotus agents all over the world. This is the New York division.'

'More are on the way,' said the Bear. 'With all communications down, it's been difficult to rally the troops.'

'Situation report?' ordered Makoto.

'Goda's forces have entered Times Square

through a portal. We estimate their numbers to be in the region of ten thousand.'

Makoto was silent for a moment, his face drawn.

'After Goda's video message, the US army stationed troops at all well-known national landmarks. They've spread themselves thin.'

'And rest of troops are at border,' added Sensei Iwamoto. 'They expect external attack, not attack from interior.'

'It's up to us then,' said Makoto. 'What sort of weapons have we got?'

'We have over two hundred firearms,' said the Bear, 'as well as swords, knives and spears for another three hundred.'

Makoto turned to Cormac. 'The guns are all plastic or ceramic so they haven't been affected.'

'You knew this electromagnetic thing would happen?' asked Cormac.

'We had to be prepared for the possibility that it could happen again.'

'Again?'

'It happened once before, in sixteenth-century Japan.' He looked at Cormac severely. 'As you know from your trip to the map room.'

Cormac winced. There'd been no secrets at Renkondo after all.

Makoto faced the troop of shinobi. 'Agents of the Black Lotus, we face grave danger. Goda has led an army ten thousand strong into Times Square via a sword portal. He plans to take control of the city to allow an Empire invasion. He wants to turn the world into medieval Japan.

'If we can defeat this army, the city has a chance to defend itself against an invasion. We have firearms, but we lack personnel. Seek out the people of New York City, convince them to join us and meet me at Times Square. You've spent your lives in a country free from the shackles of the Empire. You've been our dormant force of resistance in the free world. But now the time has come to wake, to defend your homeland.' He clenched his fists, his single eye burning. 'The time has come to show Lord Goda that he cannot win.'

Cormac crawled across the office floor, which was strewn with paper and shattered furniture.

'Stay low,' said Makoto, removing a weapon from his rucksack.

Using his boot, Cormac swept away the broken glass from beneath the window and listened. Silence. He peered out from the fourth-floor window on to Times Square. An army of medieval samurai stood below in neat, motionless rows. The sun glinted off the polished steel of swords and spears. Empire flags and banners fluttered gently in the morning breeze.

Blocks of archers pointed their bows down the streets leading into the square. On the periphery, the cavalry waited, in horned helmets and masks, in orange-and-red plate armour. Their horses pranced uneasily under chain mail, metal blinkers and scarlet tassels.

Makoto sat beside Cormac under the sill. Using a small handle he twisted a ratchet on the plastic gun in his lap. The mechanism clicked as the chamber pulled back.

'It's like a crossbow,' explained Makoto, flipping open the chamber lid.

He reached into the rucksack and removed a glass ball that was divided into two halves, each filled with liquid – one transparent, the other yellow. 'Glass bombs.'

He dropped the sphere into the empty chamber and closed the lid. Pointing to the trigger, he said, 'Aim and fire.'

Cormac took the gun apprehensively. 'What do they do?'

'Upon contact with air, one liquid turns to smoke, reducing the enemy's visibility and hopefully causing confusion. The other liquid turns into a tear gas, which will cause temporary blindness. When you see a flare in the sky, launch as many of these as you can into the centre of the square.'

Cormac nodded.

'Then you stay here until this is over. Do you understand?'

Cormac nodded again.

Makoto clapped Cormac on the shoulder and crawled back to the doorway.

And then he was gone.

Cormac knelt and placed the barrel of his gun on the window. He looked into the square for Ghost, but there was no sign of him. Had his friend really betrayed him and joined forces with Goda? Or was his mind being controlled by Kiko? And where was Kate? He'd told her to find somewhere to hide. What if she was trapped inside some collapsed building? Or worse?

He noticed movement to his left. A samurai dressed in ornate red armour rode a white horse through the soldiers into the centre of the square. He shouted in Japanese. Goda!

Cormac felt for the trigger on his gun without taking his eyes off Goda. The man drew his sword from his scabbard, thrust it in the air and screamed.

At the same time, a bright flare soared across the sky.

My signal! Cormac squinted down the barrel of his gun, pointing it into the middle of the square. He pulled the trigger, but the sudden release of the chamber kicked the weapon back into his shoulder, launching the missile high into the sky, rather than down below. It arced through the air in silent slow motion, before landing amongst a regiment of samurai infantry. A bulbous cloud of white smoke engulfed the immediate area. Soldiers emerged from it, rubbing their eyes, crying in pain and falling blindly over one other.

He reloaded the gun, but this time sat the butt into his shoulder and rested the barrel on the windowsill. He took aim and fired, bracing himself against the weapon's recoil. The missile shot straight into the centre of the square, bursting into a puff of thick smoke and blinding gas.

He fired missile after missile into Times Square until he had only one left. The area below was cloaked in dense smoke. He loaded the final sphere and stood to get a better view of the terrain below. Spotting a smokeless corner, he launched his final bomb.

No sooner had he pulled the trigger than a swarm of dark arrows emerged from the smoke. He tried to duck, but was too late. He felt a sharp pain in his chest, which sent him stumbling backwards into the office, as more arrows poured in through the windows. He tripped over a fallen computer and crashed on to his back, a black arrow protruding from his chest.

He stared at where the shaft had entered his shōzoku, waiting for a darkening bloodstain. But none came. And the pain subsided. He grasped the arrow and pulled it free from his beaded suit, overwhelmed with relief as he saw the blood-free arrowhead. Rubbing his chest, he threw the arrow aside and crawled to a different window to look out.

The smoke had dissipated, revealing coughing, retching samurai, many of whom had whipped off their helmets and were on their knees, rubbing their eyes.

But his bombs had only made a small dent in the army. The unaffected remainder headed for the melee which had spilt into all sides of the square. Scanning the perimeter, Cormac saw a battle raging between Black Lotus warriors and Goda's army. Wearing face masks, the shinobi somersaulted and cartwheeled into battle, swinging ceramic swords and firing plastic guns. Up close, they used nimble ninjutsu kicks, punches and throws to disarm the samurai, clumsy in their cumbersome armour.

On the other side of the square, civilians armed with homemade weapons battled against samurai swords and halberds. Petrol bombs arced into the square, bursting into angry infernos. Horses reared. Arrows flew and bodies fell: samurai, shinobi and civilian.

A bright light diverted Cormac's attention. A woman with long black hair, dressed in green lacquered armour, swung a mighty katana. Kiko! Each time she swung, her sword left a glowing trail of white light in the air – mini-portals – which dissolved seconds later. And each time she swung, a New York City civilian fell. She forged her way through the mob, cutting them down like bamboo, leaving a trail of death in her wake.

A ninja followed her, as if in a trance. *Ghost!* He seemed oblivious to the battle around him and it was a miracle he hadn't been injured or killed. But now Cormac was sure. This was not a soldier who'd changed allegiance. This was an innocent boy, brainwashed by an evil woman.

Cormac ran to the door. He had to get his friend out of there.

Cormac pushed at the exit door, but it wouldn't budge. He shoved harder, and it opened enough for him to see that a large wheelie bin had been wedged up against it. Makoto's handiwork. Perhaps an attempt to keep Cormac safe from passing samurai.

He took a step back from the door and kicked it. The bin screeched as it was rammed aside, leaving an opening wide enough to squeeze through.

A fire blazed to his right, and through the smoke two figures fought with swords. But it was in the other direction, towards the square, that he needed to go. An acidic tang scratched his nostrils – the remnants of his smoke bombs.

Cormac put his head down and ran headlong into the battle, knowing he could outrun any crazed samurai, but not a bullet or arrow.

Times Square looked like an apocalyptic scene from some video game. But this was no game. A horse reared, throwing off its armoured rider. A samurai swung his sword, cleaving in half the rumpled metal dustbin lid a woman had been using as a shield. A shinobi fought two soldiers with lightning kicks and punches. A guy in a tracksuit fell to the ground clutching an arrow in his neck. Petrol bombs curved through the air, bursting into fountains of flame. Volleys of arrows rained down on the mob of New Yorkers who invaded the square waving crooked crowbars and firing stones. The air churned with smoke and screams and gunfire. And the dead carpeted the ground in a bloody tangle of limbs, some wearing armour, some jeans and some shōzoku.

'Shinobi!' screamed a man behind him.

Cormac whirled around to see a horse with a metal mask charging towards him. On its back was a samurai in a horned helmet. Cormac turned and fled, leaping over a crumpled taxi, and hitting the ground running on the far side. Glancing back, he saw the horse vault over the vehicle in pursuit. Cormac picked up speed, weaving through the war-torn square. Swords swung at him, but by the time they'd executed their strike, he was long gone. He slid between the caved-in carcasses of two vehicles and looked behind him. The samurai who'd been following pulled up his horse and searched the battlefield. Failing to find what he was looking for, he galloped off in search of new prey.

Cormac scanned the square where he'd last

seen Ghost, but there was no sign of him. *Where is he?*
Cormac left the safety of the vehicles and ran for a
closer look, his eyes skimming over the bodies of the
fallen, looking for a shōzoku. But there was no sign of
him. Ahead, he saw that the fighting had moved out of
the square. A line of samurai warriors, led by Kiko in
her green armour, pushed a mob of New Yorkers up
the street, leaving a trail of bloodshed. A single ninja
followed them with slow, weary steps. *Ghost.*

Cormac dashed forwards, pressing himself into a
doorway when he came alongside his friend. 'Ghost!'

Ghost stared straight ahead, his eyes sunken, his
face vacant.

'Ghost!'

This time Ghost stopped. He looked at Cormac
blankly, seeming not to recognize him.

Cormac ran up to him and grabbed his shoulders.
'Ghost, it's me, Cormac.'

Ghost frowned.

'Don't you remember me?'

'I remember you,' said a voice in his ear.

Cormac spun around.

Kiko smiled, and swung her sword.

Ghost gasped when Kiko hit the boy with the hilt of
her sword. A spurt of blood arced through the air. The
boy fell. Cormac. He knew that name. He knew that
boy.

Cormac looked up as Kiko approached. 'Help

me, Gho—'

Kiko drove her foot into the boy's chest, pushing him into a wall. He slumped to the ground. Cormac. From the school. Renkondo. His room-mate. His friend.

Kiko raised her sword.

'No!' shouted Ghost.

She looked at him. *What?*

He stepped towards her. 'Don't kill him.'

Stay out of this.

He moved closer. 'He's my friend.'

Stay where you are.

Kiko lowered the sword and approached him, her eyes burning with black rage. *You are on my side now.*

'I was never on your side! I was under your *control*!' he shouted. As if a gate had opened, the memories flooded back – the school, the training, Cormac and Kate. Miguel. Ami.

But her voice in his head reminded him of the power she still held, the pain she could still inflict. *You've had enough chances.*

She'd tricked him . . .

It's time to do what I should've done ages ago . . .

But then he remembered something else. That time when he'd been turning invisible, when he'd banished her voice. She could control his mind when he was visible and when he was invisible, but not when he was changing from one state to the other.

He closed his eyes and pushed everything out of his mind. Kiko's presence pushed back, but Ghost fought it.

Goodbye, Gho—

Just like it had done in Renkondo, the icy wave washed over his body, cutting off Kiko's voice and presence and turning him invisible. He had only seconds of an advantage.

He jumped back as the sword came crashing down, then leapt at her, punching her hard in the face. She stumbled, but held on to the blade. Although his shōzoku meant he was still visible, she was no longer in his head and that gave him a chance. He ran at her, but she was on her feet, her mouth and nose a bloody mess, her brow creased in concentration.

She pushed into his mind. *Nice try, Gh—* but her words were cut off as Ghost crashed into her. The two of them tumbled over a dead body and landed hard on the ground.

Ghost jumped up and scrambled to safety at the other side of the street. Kiko stared at him. He felt her hovering at the fringes of his mind and knew he couldn't keep her out much longer. He ran at her again. Kiko raised the sword and swung down, but Ghost slid under its arc. He felt the rush of air on his face and heard a tearing noise as the weapon scored a gash in the air.

He skidded into Kiko's legs, and she toppled forwards. Ghost rolled over to face her. She stood up, but she'd lost the sword. Behind her, light spilt from the wound she'd sliced into the air. A salty breeze ruffled her jet-black hair as she searched for the weapon.

Ghost tackled her around the waist, and they both fell through the open portal into a world of blue.

'No!' she screamed.

Ghost lost his grip and tumbled down a hill, grabbing at vegetation to slow down. He plunged into a thorny bush, ending his descent. Pulling the branches away from his face, he crawled out of the tangle and dragged himself to his feet.

They were on a high cliff. The wind howled and waves crashed on to rocks below. A long, narrow wooden boat floated on the sea. It had a square red-and-white striped sail, and its prow was carved into a serpent's head. The sides of the ship were lined with colourful circular shields, behind which men moved on board.

Kiko lay at the cliff's edge, her head resting on a rock, blood oozing from beneath it.

At the top of the hill, a grey hole shimmered in the sky. Inside it lay New York City. Ghost turned and ran, summoning the dregs of his reserves to battle the steep slope and the powerful wind.

The grey hole contracted even further.

I'm not going to make it.

He raced forwards, but by the time he reached the summit, the hole had shrunk to the size of a football. It wobbled precariously, about to snap shut.

He lunged at the hole, his fingers finding its empty centre just before it sealed up. He pushed his fist into it, feeling its liquid perimeter tighten around his arm, desperately trying to close. Prising it apart with his fingers, he managed to get his second hand inside. With the last of his strength, he roared into the wind and wrenched his arms apart.

Pain coursed through his shoulders, but it worked. The gap widened enough for him to put his head through. He craned his neck into the opening, twisting his arms through at the same time, as if trying to get into a sweater ten sizes too small.

He could feel the rim of the portal squeezing his body. He kept squirming, and had dragged himself through as far as his waist when he felt a cold hand grip his ankle.

His heart froze before anger consumed him. Screaming, he raised his other foot and drove his heel backwards, feeling the sickening crunch of bone as it connected with Kiko's face.

'Give me your arms!' It was Cormac.

Ghost stretched out his arms and Cormac pulled. Kiko lost her grip, and Ghost fell to the pavement. The hole snapped shut, locking the cliff, the sea, the wind, and Lady Kiko, into the past for ever.

35

'Ghost,' said Cormac, to the headless figure, slumped on the ground. 'Are you hurt?'

'Just let me change . . .' said Ghost.

Cormac watched as his friend's head materialized between the shoulders of his shōzoku.

When his hands had reappeared, Ghost stood and looked at Cormac. 'Your face . . .'

'This?' Cormac pointed to his own face. 'This is nothing. You should see the other guy.'

Ghost smiled weakly. 'I think I am the other guy. I'm sorry.'

'Forget it. I know it wasn't really you who hit me. It was that witch. Where is she?'

He shrugged. 'Gone.'

'And we have the Moon Sword,' said Cormac, holding it up.

Ghost ran his finger along the moon and flames engraving. 'I don't know how you got here. But thank you.'

Cormac slapped his friend on the back before glancing around. The battle had moved on, but the sound of fighting wasn't far away.

'Kate is missing,' said Cormac. 'We have to find her. Are you OK to run?'

Ghost nodded, and they took off down the street, following the sounds of battle. They soon caught sight of it.

Cormac took out his binocs 'Samurai. We need to get to the other side.'

They turned off 7th Avenue and ran down smaller streets untouched by fighting, but still affected by the electromagnetic blast. They weaved between the crumpled cars and jumped over manholes whose metal covers had popped off.

The sounds of battle were now closer, and the boys turned back towards 7th Avenue, hoping to arrive behind their own army. As soon as they reached the avenue, they saw shinobi and New Yorkers. But they seemed to be retreating.

Makoto emerged from the mob, his face etched with concern. 'I'm glad you're both OK.'

'What's happening?' asked Cormac.

Makoto glanced behind him. 'They're just too strong.'

'You mean we can't beat them?'

Makoto nodded.

'We must do *something*,' said Ghost.

Cormac agreed. 'All of this can't have been for nothing.'

'We can do no more. We're out of ammunition and people.'

They watched the remnants of the Black Lotus and New York City army retreat towards them. At the far side of the melee, swords clashed and the wounded cried. A distant figure in armour, riding a white horse, pushed the assault from behind. Goda.

Suddenly they heard a strange sound from behind them – a distant roar. Cormac squinted down 7th Avenue, away from the battle, unable to quite believe what he was seeing. Cars were being pushed aside by an elephant. And on the back of it, a person waved. A girl in a shōzoku!

Behind her marched an army of exotic animals: rhinos, gorillas, hippos, lions, tigers, panthers, cheetahs and wolves. Hordes of monkeys swung from the crooked lamp posts and clambered over the piled-up vehicles. The sky above them was filled with large birds of prey: eagles, hawks and vultures.

They were let loose from the zoo when the metal warped, Cormac realized. All their cages must've broken!

The sounds of the battle were soon drowned out by the most extraordinary clamour of animal roars, screeches, growls, howls, barks and hisses.

'It's Kate,' said Cormac to Makoto. 'Tell your army to fall back. Tell them to keep tight to the sides of the street. They can regroup behind the animals.'

Makoto dashed into the middle of his army,

relaying the order, and soon shinobi and New Yorkers alike raced back towards the approaching zoo, fanning out to both sides of the street to allow Kate's animals through.

Cormac slipped into the stream of people racing towards the animals. He made eye contact with Kate as she charged past on her elephant. He could have sworn he saw her wink.

Kate raised the hockey stick above her head and screamed encouragement to the horde of animals behind her. From her vantage point, she saw Goda's samurai give chase as the Black Lotus shinobi and New Yorkers fled to safety behind her. When they saw the approaching beasts, however, the samurai ground to a sudden halt, frozen in stunned disbelief.

The cats attacked first. Led by Zula, the lioness, tigers, panthers and cheetahs broke free from the pack and pounced on the samurai soldiers. The men's armour did little to protect them from the dagger-like teeth and claws.

The next row of samurai formed a defensive wall of swords and spears. Kate called two rhinos, who charged through the barricade, scattering the warriors like bowling pins. They were followed by a silverback gorilla, who entered the fray and flung samurai about like rag dolls, throwing them through shop windows and into walls. The birds attacked next, swooping down with razor-sharp talons. Eagles, hawks, falcons and vultures clung to the faces of their enemy, stabbing at their eyes with pointed beaks. A pack of wolves scrambled over the hood of a taxi. Goda's army retreated, but the wolves hunted them down.

Kate saw the samurai on the white horse – Goda. He wheeled his steed around and galloped back towards Times Square.

'Follow the horse!' ordered Kate.

Goliath, the elephant, took off through the street of warring humans and animals. As they passed a side street, Kate saw what she hoped was the arrival of her second wave of attack. The ground seemed to ripple and move, as if a black magic carpet was racing towards her. It was only as they got closer that this apparent mirage materialized into thousands of small creatures: mice, rats, dogs and cats. New York's finest pets, strays and sewer dwellers had answered her call and were united in defence of their city. They swarmed into the fight, running up armoured bodies to faces where flesh was exposed. Their sheer numbers were enough to terrify the enemy.

Kate's elephant charged through the samurai army unchallenged. Most jumped aside to allow them through and stared wide-eyed as if they'd never seen such a sight. As she reached the end of Goda's army lines, her heart burst with joy at the sight of a US army battalion approaching to trap the samurai warriors in a pincer movement. Their tanks and helmets were obsolete, but their crooked rifles and bent machine guns had been reinvented as bats and clubs.

Kate wanted to turn around and join them as they closed in on the medieval army, but she continued towards Times Square. She couldn't let Goda escape.

On her journey to and from the Bronx Zoo, she'd seen the damage to New York City. But she was shocked to see Times Square, normally so bright and shiny, now completely obliterated, the ground paved with the dead and injured.

In the centre, Goda dismounted, drew his sword and swung it, creating an arc of white light in the air. He put his head into the light, immediately removed it and swung his blade again, opening another portal.

'Faster!' said Kate to Goliath. 'We can't let him get away.'

Goda checked the new portal before disappearing inside.

'Let me down,' said Kate.

Goliath stopped running and knelt. Kate slid off his back and, armed with her hockey stick, ran forwards. But it was too late – the portal had closed.

Kate stood for a moment, the sour taste of defeat in her mouth. But then human cries and animal roars filled the square as the remnants of Goda's army arrived, fleeing from the animals of the Bronx Zoo. The samurai huddled in the centre of the square as a hundred species of animals closed in on them. A circle of foaming mouths, raised hackles and bared canines tightened around the medieval warriors.

'Call off the animals,' Kate ordered Goliath.

The elephant raised his trunk and trumpeted into the air – a high-pitched penetrating call which echoed off the crumbling skyscrapers. The ring of animals froze, growls died down and birds alighted on flattened vehicles. The square was silent by the time the US soldiers and shōzoku-clad shinobi arrived with what was left of the ragtag army of New Yorkers.

Kate wondered where the shinobi had come from, but in a square full of zoo animals and medieval samurai, anything was possible. They marched up to the ring of animals, and one of them stepped through and called out something in Japanese. Kate picked up the word 'weapons'.

Without hesitation, Goda's army laid down their spears and swords.

Cormac and Ghost came running towards Kate.

'You sure know how to make an entrance,' said Cormac.

She tossed her hair. 'It's a New York thing.' Ghost laughed and she hugged him tightly. 'I'm so glad to see you.'

She kissed Cormac on the cheek, turning his face bright red. 'You did it.' The joy of victory was instantly extinguished by roaring sounds from above. She looked up to see helicopters and jets approaching. Her heart clenched with fear. The Empire! Shadows fell across the ruined city as they approached.

As they flew closer, Kate bit back a shout of frustration. Would everything they'd fought for be lost so quickly? But as the aircraft passed overhead, she broke into a broad smile. Stars and stripes. It was the US Army! They were safe. The city was safe.

While the New Yorkers were busy tying up the samurai army, a troop of shinobi approached, led by Makoto. Kate wondered how he'd got here.

He smiled at her. 'Good work, Kate.'

She bowed.

Makoto then turned to Cormac and pointed at the sword he was still holding. 'I think I'd better take that off your hands.'

'Please do,' replied Cormac, giving him the blade. It sparkled in the early-morning sunshine and Kate recognized the moon-and-flames engraving near the hilt. The Moon Sword.

'Kiko still has the scabbard,' said Ghost. 'But I guess that doesn't matter.'

Makoto shook his head. He seemed relieved, but worry still lingered in his eye. 'What about the other two Swords of Sarumara?'

'Goda escaped with them through a portal,' said Kate, pointing at where he'd disappeared.

'He's gone back to medieval Japan,' said Ghost. 'We should go after him.'

'Not now,' said Makoto. 'Enough blood has been spilt.'

He turned to the Bear and said, 'Have the army place round-the-clock guards here in case he returns.

We need to get the Moon Sword to safety.'

'Back to Renkondo?' asked Ghost.

'It's gone, but we have a backup safe house.'

'Renkondo is gone?' gasped Kate. 'What about . . . Oh, God, Chloe!'

'Chloe is fine,' said Makoto, 'as are most of the students.'

'And what about us?' asked Cormac. 'What do we do?'

'Lie low for a while. We can't take you with us just yet, but I'm not worried – you can clearly fend for yourselves.' He smiled and pulled a wad of dollars from his pocket. 'There'll be no hotels or restaurants open in the city centre, but this should help you find somewhere nearby. The place will be swarming with cops and soldiers for some time, but when things die down, we'll be in touch.'

'How will you find us?' asked Cormac.

Makoto smiled. 'We'll find you.'

37

A noise woke Kate. She opened her eyes in panic, but relaxed when she saw the heavy drapes at the hotel window. *That was the best night's sleep of my life!* She lay back on the soft pillow and thought back to the events of the day before.

After leading the animals back to the zoo, Kate, Cormac and Ghost spent the entire previous day patching up the animals' cages and homes. It was only when the zookeepers arrived in the evening that they felt it was OK to leave, by which time the police and army were restoring law and order to the city, helping the injured and clearing the streets.

The three teenagers found an abandoned department store and changed out of their shōzokus and into brand-new clothes. Kate insisted that they leave some cash on the till.

'I agree,' said Ghost. 'My stealing days are over!'

Then they crept into a vacant hotel, afraid of being arrested for breaking the curfew.

Kate's thoughts were brought sharply back to the present by a knock on her door, followed by Cormac's voice. 'Room service!'

She hopped out of bed, pulled on a fluffy bathrobe and crawled back under the duvet.

'Come in!' she called.

Cormac entered wearing a chef's hat and carrying a large tray. Ghost, in a red-and-gold bellboy's hat, carried another.

Kate laughed out loud, but stopped as soon as she saw what was on the trays: plates piled high with fruit, bread and pastries, and tall glasses of orange juice.

Savage joined them on the bed and they devoured the lot, not speaking until their bellies were full.

Kate wiped her mouth with a napkin. 'You'd think I hadn't eaten in years.'

'Well, I think the last thing I ate was that tangerine,' said Cormac. 'So technically, that was five hundred years ago.'

Kate smiled. Again, she heard the same noise that had woken her, and glanced towards the window.

Cormac peeped through the curtains.

'What is it?' asked Ghost.

'Army, and what looks like a construction crew.'

Kate moved the tray off her lap. 'We'd better get out of here.'

'But where will we go?' asked Ghost.

Cormac pulled the wad of dollars from his jeans. 'We have money, but nowhere to spend it.'

Kate got out of bed. While attending to the animals the previous day, she'd had a lot of time to think. 'My house is empty.'

'But you said you were homeless?' said Cormac.

Kate gathered up her clothes and sneakers and headed for the bathroom to get dressed. 'I was, but I think it's time to go home.'

It was almost dark by the time they reached Elmsford.

'I'm cat tired,' moaned Ghost.

'We're almost there,' said Kate. 'Just around this corner.'

They stopped in front of a tall wooden house. Kate was relieved to see it still standing. On the seven-hour walk here, they'd witnessed the colossal damage caused by Goda's electromagnetic pulse. The worst-affected buildings were the more modern high-rise towers constructed with a steel framework. The older stone buildings, and wooden houses like the ones in this neighbourhood, remained relatively unscathed.

'I don't have a key,' said Kate.

Cormac pointed at the front door, which hung lopsided on one hinge. 'I don't think you'll need one.'

She was overcome with emotion as she climbed the steps to the front door. It had been almost a year since she'd been in this house. She wasn't the same girl any more. And the house wouldn't be the same without her parents and Jamie. Her mind flooded with memories of the last time she'd seen them, at the airport as they departed for war-torn Norway as aid workers. Then the news that they'd been thrown into an Empire prison. Then the social workers taking her and Jamie away. Then her escape from the orphanage to live on the streets . . .

Her hand shook as she pulled open the creaking door. She'd only opened it a crack when she spotted a candle burning inside.

She scrambled back down the steps, her heart pounding.

'What's wrong?' asked Cormac, alarmed.

'Somebody's in there.'

'Squatters,' he replied, picking up a length of wood as a weapon.

Kate slipped behind Cormac and watched as a figure appeared from inside the house. A man pushed open the front door and stepped out on to the porch. Her racing heart froze. Her eyes filled with tears.

'Dad!' she shouted and raced up the steps.

Her dad opened his arms in time for Kate's embrace. She held him close, breathing in his smell and warmth. Her mind spun, she could barely think. She'd never felt so happy.

'Baby,' he muttered, stroking her hair.

'Who is it?' said a voice behind him. *Mom!*

Kate disentagled herself from her dad's arms and watched her mother's mouth drop open as she recognized her daughter. She tried to speak, but nothing came out.

Kate felt tears roll down her cheeks.

Her mom rushed out, arms stretched wide. She wrapped her daughter in a tight embrace and Kate sobbed loudly into her mother's shoulder, releasing almost a year's worth of loneliness. Small hurried footsteps arrived on the porch.

Kate looked down. 'Jamie!'

'Kate!' shouted her little brother.

She lifted him up and hugged him tightly.

'They released you?' asked Kate, turning to her dad.

'Not exactly . . . We had some help to escape.'

'Welcome home, Kate,' said her mom, kissing her wet face.

Kate put Jamie down on the porch and he ran back into the house. Her mother took Kate's face in her hands and looked her in the eye. 'I'm sorry things turned out the way they did. We'd always intended for you to join us in Norway, but when the resistance failed . . .' She wiped her cheeks. 'I feel like we abandoned you.'

Kate hugged her again. 'You didn't abandon us. You were fighting for freedom. Now I am too.'

Her mom held her at arm's length. 'What do you mean?'

'It's a long story,' said Kate, looking down at the two boys at the bottom of the porch steps. 'These are my two best friends, Cormac and Ghost. Is it OK if they stay?'

'Absolutely,' said her dad, coming forward to greet the boys with an extended hand. 'Any friend of Kate's is a friend of ours.'

'And Savage too?' She pulled out the mouse, who sat on her palm and looked up at them all. Kate glanced at her parents. 'I have a lot to tell you.'

'No kidding!' laughed her mom.

'So, boys, how long will you be staying?' asked her dad, putting his arm around Kate's shoulders as they all went into the house.

Cormac looked at Ghost, and then Kate. 'We're not sure,' he said, smiling. 'We're waiting on a call.'

GLOSSARY

akero	– open the door
arigatō	– thank you
bō	– a long Japanese fighting staff
bushidō	– the samurai way of life – it literally means 'the way of the warrior'
dōjō	– a training place for Japanese martial arts – it literally means 'place of the way'
Fuyu	– elite Black Lotus ninja guards – it literally means 'winter'
genpuku	– a historical Japanese coming-of-age ceremony
hinin	– society outcasts – it literally means 'non-human'
Hinin Houses	– workhouses in the Samurai Empire for society outcasts such as the homeless, disabled, addicts and orphans.
Jikininki	– human-eating ghosts
Jōnin	– the leader of a ninja clan
katana	– Japanese sword used by the samurai
keibiin	– security guard
ki	– a spiritual energy/force within the human body
kimono	– traditional Japanese full-length robe
Kittens	– nickname for Kyatapira Youth
konnichiwa	– hello
Kyatapira	– military police of the Samurai Empire
Kyatapira Youth	– military police trainees
ninjutsu	– martial art practised by ninjas

Niwa	– meaning 'garden', it is the forest and mountainside surrounding the Black Lotus headquarters
Renkondo	– the underground headquarters of the Black Lotus
ri	– a unit of measurement in medieval Japan equivalent in use to mile or kilometre
samurai	– knights of medieval Japan
sayōnara	– goodbye
seiza	– Japanese term for the traditional formal way of sitting – literally means 'proper sitting'
sensei	– teacher – literally means 'person born before another'
seppuku	– samurai ritual suicide
shinobi	– ninja
shinobi shōzoku	– outfit worn by ninjas
shinshoku	– priest in the Shintō religion of Japan
shōgun	– military governor of medieval Japan
shōji	– traditional Japanese sliding door or room divider
shuko and **ashiko**	– ninja hand and feet claws used for climbing and fighting
shuriken	– ninja throwing stars used as weapons – literally means 'sword hidden in user's hand'
tengu	– legendary Japanese demon
tetsubishi	– a ninja weapon made of sharp iron spikes designed to injure the foot when stepped upon
zanshin	– a state of total awareness

ACKNOWLEDGEMENTS

Before I set out on this extraordinary journey seven years ago, I thought novel writing was a solitary endeavour. And for the most part, it is. But like every great journey it is punctuated by people who help the traveller on his way.

I credit my parents, Mary and Jim, for starting the whole thing – indulging an awkward child and providing a childhood which is still my main source of inspiration.

Massive thank you to all the critters from CC, especially Suja, Eamon Ó Cléirigh (Cheeno), Blandcorp and Chelly Wood. You taught me so many things and were with me every step of the way. There are little pieces of each of you in my book.

To Kathryn, a brilliant writer, and my number one crit buddy. Your advice and support played a huge part in getting this novel published, and for that I will always be grateful. There is a LARGE part of you in this book.

Thank you to all the members (past and present) of the Scribblers Writing Group. You guys rock!

Conor Kostick's writing course was also really helpful. I recommend it to all aspiring authors.

To all the writers, teachers, lecturers, editors, publishers and agents I encountered over the years – thank you for inspiring me.

To my wonderful agent, Sallyanne Sweeney, thank you for your dedication, professionalism and enthusiasm. But most of all, thank you for believing in me, and being in my corner.

A huge debt of gratitude is owed to Barry Cunningham of Chicken House, who spotted the potential in my wart-infested manuscript. Thank you for giving me and so many other debut authors a chance.

Thank you to my amazing editor, Rachel Leyshon, for killing off the warts in my manuscript and working your magic on it. You helped me write the book I always wished I'd written.

I am deeply appreciative of the efforts of everyone at Chicken House – Jazz Bartlett, Laura Myers, Elinor Bagenal, Rachel Hickman, Esther Waller, Sarah Wilson and especially Kesia Lupo for your keen editorial eyes.

Thank you to the wonderful freelancers who worked on my book: to Claire Skuse for her work in the early stages, to Sarah Levison for the structural edit, to Miranda Baker for a brilliant copy-edit, to Helen Jennings for the proofread, to Steve Wells for my cool cover, and to Laura Smythe for publicity.

Thanks to Ai Kiminomori for helping with the Japanese (at the last minute!).

The children's literature community in Ireland is an amazing group of people. There are too many of you to mention, but you know who you are. Thank you for doing what you do.

Cheers to all my students, friends and family for taking an interest in what I do.

If what they say is true – behind every great man is a great woman – then I must be truly great, because

I have three! To Emma and Lara, thank you for NEVER disturbing me while I was on the computer, for never distracting me with puppet shows, dance routines or teddy bear birthday parties! And most importantly, Carol – thank you for your constant support and encouragement and for making the time for me to write. I couldn't have done this without you.